I0550501

DEAD

ON

COORDINATES

A Wright Series

Book 2

Linda McKown

DEAD ON COORDINATES
ISBN-13: 978-0-9997357-1-8

Author:
LindaMcKownAuthor LLC
11574 E Running Deer Trail
Scottsdale, AZ 85262
http://www.lindamckown.com

Any names of people and entities are fictitious in this story having been created by the author's imagination.

Front Cover Photo of the book is copyright through Shutterstock. Book title manipulation was done by Joseph McKown

Dedicated to my amazing family who helped create a beautiful video on LindaMcKown.com.

Their first names are there.

Contents

1   Jess and Derek's Decision 1

2   Louisa's Story...12

3   Butler's Son...25

4   Planning the Search 32

5   Diamond Smuggler.......................................44

6   Stew Avery and Ship's Telescope 49

7   Stew Meets Chesin 57

8   Miami Wife Tami 63

9   Toy Company 67

10 Head Out to First Coordinates 71

11 Sub at First Coordinates...............................78

12 Santan Chesin's Party 83

13 Second Set of Coordinates............................92

14 The Dolphins and a Deal 107

15 Louisa's Chest and the Rest.........................115

16 Sunken Items and Rendezvous 122

17 Nuit Vaisseau (Night Ship)..........................133

18 Return of Necklace to Louisa 139

19 African Diamond Heist.................................144

20 Arrival in Curacao 149

21 Unloading the Boats 156

22 Plans for Masquerade Party 163

23 Smuggler and Red Tribe Plans 168

24 Stew Hiding in Curacao................................174

25 Guinea-Bissau Friend Arrest 177
26 The Three Parties Began............................183
27 Almost Demise of the Red Tribe 194
28 Fireworks Party End 199
29 Diamond Smuggler....................................204
30 Book Signings..217
31 Chesin's Hired Set Up 223
32 Last Book Signing 227
33 Louisa's Dream of a Killer 233
34 Stace, Friend or Foe..................................236
35 The Mask 241
36 Friends of Friends......................................249
37 Maggie Keats...254
38 Sphinx Overthrow......................................258
39 The Congo 265
40 Robots and Things that Move.....................271
41 Louisa's Notebook.....................................275
42 Underworld and Two Objects.....................282
43 Miami Dead Girl...286
44 Objects from Auction House 290
45 Miami Party Plans......................................294
46 Golden Obsession 298

1   Jess and Derek's Decision

DEREK WRIGHT WATCHED as his wife, Jess, entered their elaborate hotel bedroom suite. Her white sundress accentuated her blonde hair and tanned skin. She smiled at him and slowly sank into one of the elegant gold brocade chairs.

The children were brought along, because the vacation to Rome, Italy, was truly for relaxation and play. After touring the ancient churches, statues, wonderful art museums, and eating pasta with coffee at the outside cafes, the Wrights had driven to Louisa Renaliere's apartment in the city. The fact-finding mission was arranged, and they met her yesterday.

Louisa shared her library the previous day with their children who were now in the next room immersed in a pirate book. Their son, Justin, was reading to their daughter, Sami. Derek wondered how much his son was embellishing the story. Their children would be occupied for a while. It was a good time to discuss important facts.

He notified his security people that his family was staying in their room until this evening, giving his team personal time off to sightsee.

Jess watched her husband as he slowly approached the small desk where the telescope stood.

She knew to be quiet. Taking a break from his job as investigator in Los Angeles, they knew this visit could change things.

"Are you ready?"

"Yes," she responded.

Jess and Derek received enough information from Louisa Renaliere to plan their next year's vacation. The information divulged was churning in both their minds. It was hidden within the Renaliere family for at least two centuries or so. Louisa miraculously shared the same information with Dean Crain when he was alive. Only she hadn't shared the telescope.

"I believe her story."

Derek nodded. "I do, too. She said there was a small paper inside the lens. If so, the cargo could definitely be that *something* word."

The Wrights' special language to each other revolved around this word in the past. It's meaning was a multitude of things, such as a dead body, a crime, or anything dangerous. It could mean the opposite such as something above everyone's expectations. It also stood for more, a grand scale, or magnificent object. Something meant way beyond the norm. It was an item that should be explored. Usually, the timeframe was as soon as possible.

In his job, he met all kinds of people, and Louisa Renaliere was the genuine article. He looked at the mahogany and brass ship's scope, touching the smooth surface of the wood and noticed a small dent in the brass. He knew other men handled the telescope long ago. The oil from their hands darkened the wood in spots. How many revolutions occurred during the telescope's earthly existence? The history of those years added up to a floodgate of tremendous knowledge. It was amazing the object survived. It was more startling that Louisa would part with a treasured family item. She, evidently, loved the piece and locked it away all these years.

The question arose in a person's mind of why it was locked away. Obviously, the scope held importance with the Renaliere family's own history. Was it to hide knowledge from tyrants? There was a whole conversation that could exist about those facts. It was a mystery to be explored. Derek knew his wife was a keen investigator and explorer. She would have been on the first boat to somewhere else. At times, he believed that he married an explorer or gypsy. But then, he was a wanderer, too. They would have started their own revolution together. He laughed. He could see Jess with a sword. She would have been proficient at the skill.

He looked at the scope. He was intrigued. It represented an earlier time of cunning and danger. No one was safe from deceit. Even nations had their problems like the current politics. Everyone had an opinion and then some. Knowledge was for sale everywhere. The tricksters were messing with the news and every aspect of the flow of information in today's events. He was brought back into the room. There was only the telescope waiting for him. He tried to see inside the scope. This piece looked just fine, except it belonged in a museum.

Also, little did Derek know, there was private information passed to his wife by the old woman during their visit. Jess was always good at secrets and hiding things. Derek was glad his wife was relaxed today and in good spirits. He thought that he had seen a flicker of her disappointment in him yesterday. He worried about what was bothering her. He sighed. He knew to wait for her to talk to him about any bothersome feelings. He blew out a full breath of air.

Jess, indeed, was a good actress. Remembering the strength of the old woman and her young daughter, the bond was there. It was a bond fueled by real strong energy. There was more than one secret revealed. Louisa provided Jess with a piece of news that was of utmost importance.

When the time came, Jess gladly left Louisa's apartment. Jess learned something about her husband that she didn't know. Louisa gave her the names of some gang Derek caught earlier in his career. Louisa thought those two people would bring the Wrights trouble in the future. Jess would need to be prepared for danger and protect her family. Louisa hadn't wanted any harm to come to them. Derek never told her about this case. There must be a good reason for this fact. Jess needed to be in the moment in their hotel room. Resigning herself to forget about the information for now. When they returned home, she would read the newspaper article about Amy and Minnow Surf and a foiled bank robbery.

It was not the correct time to talk with her husband about that story. There was another story with more important revelations. The object sitting on the desk shone when the morning light filtered in the window. The brass was a pinpoint of light where the sun's rays hit it in one spot. Jess remembered her dear friend, Dean Crain, and wished he was here. Dean gave Jess and Derek his friendship, love, and introduced them to a mixture of his old crony friends. He helped steer the two of them together in what seemed like another lifetime. He was a great poker player who loved adventure. The bad guys were just con artists or other dirt bags to be collected in the garbage. He was always ready to enter the chase to catch them.

When their friend, Dean, passed away he left them his motorboat, helicopter, and moneyed holdings. But he also left them an auction brochure which showed a large diamond and emerald necklace that originally was owned by the Renaliere family. In his note, he told them that it, too, had been stolen and was still missing. He bought a sub, and his intent was to search for a strange and illusive ship. The Wrights were stumped and curious. They coordinated this visit to check out the last survivor's story. Jess concentrated her view towards her husband. He had hesitated. She wondered what was going through his mind. The scope was on the table.

Derek ran his hands through his brown hair. He was nervous. It was very similar to opening Pandora's chest or entering a police interview room. A person never knew what they would find. He paced back and forth. The love-hate emotions entered the room. He stopped and took another deep breath after looking at his determined wife. Her mind was already searching for the writing on the paper. Jess trusted that the item was inside the scope. She was positive there was information there. He was doubtful.

He undid the segmented draw of the telescope. His strong hands broke the dusty seal. Carefully, laying the old thick lens down on the hotel notepad, his fingers searched. Slowly, circling the inner rim, he touched softness. The paper was fragile. The hotel pen was used to nudge the paper forward. Inside was a piece of old papyrus with barely distinguishable writing. The lens he laid on the table also picked up the light from the sun. Derek pulled the drape to stop the second reflection.

He wasn't sure why he was surprised there was an old papyrus inside. His heart pounded. Even more slowly, he unwrapped the fragile-yellowed paper.

Derek recognized the three different sets of figures which were coordinates written on the paper. He pulled up the three-hand-written coordinate sets on his computer and sent himself a note with the grid information. Copying the note, next, he placed the small paper back inside the telescope.

Jess viewed the three coordinate sets when her husband rotated the notebook computer screen in her direction. Neither were surprised by the destination. Derek clicked the map view to appear larger. The coastline of Africa came into their line of vision.

Jess looked Derek in the eyes. Her own pale gray eyes bright with excitement. Whenever she looked excited, they developed a warmer blue-violet color.

Derek grinned.

The anticipation reflected in her voice and a curve gently nudged her pink lips as she spoke. She took a bite out of the red grape she held in her hands and handed some to Derek. He popped several in his mouth and continued to watch his wife. Shifting in her chair, the white lace from her slip peeked out from her dress. He was amused. She was taking her time to respond. It always drove him a little crazy and she knew it.

"It's a very long way away," said Jess. Her long eyelashes blinked, looking up at him.

"Yes, it was."

Derek sat down in the other gold brocade chair so that he could be closer to his amazing wife. She was toying with him, and he liked her expression. He laughed with relief. It was his turn to tease her.

"Honey, are you in for our first enterprise in the diving world? It might be a rich adventure to search for sunken treasure in Dakar with our motorboat. Or we might have more fun high-rolling in Las Vegas. We could try poker. I'm pretty good with cards."

Jess raised her eyebrows.

"I know Dean always let me win. But I could try to win. Which adventure would you prefer? Or should we flip a coin?" He started digging in his pocket.

Jess smiled. "Stop, you know my answer."

Derek touched her hand. He knew all along which choice she would pick.

"I can find a company to move the motorboat to the harbor. There was an excellent firm from Dean Crain's list that is the same company that I would have chosen. Dean expected to help Louisa retrieve her family's jewels, only he ran out of time. It could be fun for us dipping into the ocean together. You can write the book you have always wanted. It could be a book about our adventure. I can help you with the underwater photos or any videos. There's lots of software for almost anything. Did I guess the correct answer?"

Jess hugged her muscled-six-foot husband's frame that was scrunched into the delicate chair. "Oh, yeah, most definitely. You read my mind so well."

She hesitated. "It might be dangerous. We will need to hire security and the experienced people that Dean Crain left on his other lists. He researched the divers for the sub and their backgrounds. That will be a good place to start."

"All right, but let's not even think dangerous or perilous. This is a simple case of vacation and exploring the ocean. We have great equipment and will locate those experienced divers. There shouldn't be anything to signal the bad guys or bring them into our sphere of treasure hunting. We will need to be careful and let people believe we are on a lazy, joyful mission exploring the Atlantic for a new book."

Derek thought about their past encounter with murderers and evil people with agendas of their own.

He started to worry a little bit. *Jess was a magnet for trouble in the past.*

He stood and looked out at the blue ocean and knew there was no way to stop the forward motion this mysterious adventure was headed. Ever since they saw the sub that Dean Crain left them, it was impossible to steer Jess away from their next project. She was already sold on the possibilities. At least, they were wealthy. Their worldly experience and great friends were valuable resources.

"It should be a great time," said Jess.

Derek laughed once more. "This adventure is going to be good. Any time alone with you, my lovely wife, was worth it. Most definitely can this be fun a thousand times over."

He crossed over to her chair, bent down, and kissed her. Their favorite calypso song was on the motorboat. It was a surprise for her when they returned to Los Angeles. It was re-recorded and changed. The song was at a slower tempo or andante. He loaded it as number 6.5. The knowledge that his wife would be pleased made him feel warm.

The surroundings around Dakar would become the beginning of very dangerous liaisons. It was one of those times when Derek would think back on his thoughts about the trip. The scene would feel like walking into a meta-universe. The bizarre people somehow leaked from their creature world over into earth's space. They weren't smart enough to build a space craft, but had maybe found a forgotten portal and were shoved through by a storm. Derek would wonder if their arrival was a mistake.

The bad guys would pile up higher than any sunken treasure. The board game their children played in Rome was nothing like the game the Wrights would become involved in. He would have to be vigilant and stay out of harm's way in the ocean and on land. He would protect Jess and his family always in his universe.

Derek knew the type of people that existed in his world. His work with the police and the investigation side of things meant endless contact with unsavory characters. It was the hidden con artists that were the worst. Their unpredictable actions created chaos and a crappy mess most of the time. He thought the terrible con artists belonged in jail or somewhere else not on this earth. In other words, he would have to find a way to send them back from the black hole they came from.

Derek started to make his phone calls to put extra people and security around the motorboat for the eventual trip. Covert was the name of their game. He contacted his motorboat captain about the possible venture and the lawyer about the necessary permits. Then he called his good friend, retired policeman, Jim Michaels. Derek would call in a marker or favor soon. Also, his new friend, War Julio, would be contacted about building a special crate for the freezer.

The Wrights were going to Africa. He hoped the new coordinates were possible. He wouldn't know that one of them was *dead on*. Derek was lost in thought, already calling contacts, and calculating the items that needed to be done. There was plenty of time to notify the Renaliere woman of their decision.

The old woman already planned on the Wrights choosing this exact path. She read it in the stars. The stars were those spreading over centuries of her ancestor's lives. The stars were aligned perfectly. The Wrights would find their way. The last plan was coming together.

2   Louisa's Story

LOUISA PARTED THE heavy navy-colored drape, clutching the soft fabric with her hands. It was a little frayed in the one place she always touched. She saw the Wright family exit their rental car on the street below. She looked around her small three-bedroom apartment with antique furniture, paintings, old crystal, and ancient Persian rugs. She loved her beautiful inspiring city of Rome. She liked her building even better after they installed an elevator.

There was no reason to meet the Wrights. They were unknowns to her until she met Dean Crain. She didn't want to meet him at all until Dean told her that he held her platinum diamond necklace in his hands. He needed to return it to her. She was enthralled by that concept.

"How did Dean know about her family's other gold necklace? He must have seen the Auction brochure. But why would he care about a painting and her platinum diamond necklace that was sold. The entire transactions were all legal."

Louisa remembered meeting Dean. He was gracious and a true knight. He was one in a million. That is why she had agreed to meet the Wrights. She was curious about them. Jess was the daughter of a special woman her family had known a while ago. Dean told her that she could trust them. It was hard to trust anyone. Her family shied away from people. It was that way with her family for a long time. People were kept at a distance. Perhaps she could trust again. Louisa liked Dean. He was a good person. She felt his heart and his righteousness. There was nothing hidden in his soul.

Her hand smoothed her black silk dress with red roses and black lace. She found the new dress at her favorite shop. The shop was surprised to see her, because she kept away for some time, stating her other clothes worked just fine. She didn't need anything.

Louisa wanted to impress her new friends, the Wrights. She wanted to be a woman, looking like she was in the current fashion zone. She hated to feel old. She avoided that feeling whenever she could. Her girlfriends would like the new look, too. The new hat that went with the dress was in her closet. Hats were required to keep the sun off the aged face.

The Dresden skin didn't adore the heat. Her luncheon women kept up-to-date on the fashion world. It was one of their weak vices and they all joked about it. They sometimes indulged in gossip which was their second vice. Their first was looking at the young male waiters. This hotel hired them faithfully until they moved on to better jobs. They loved this one hotel. It was an excursion into their fantasies.

Touching her gold key once more, Louisa decided it was time to share her secret. She reflected about the other person she told. Worried now about the consequences of her decision, she noticed the kitchen door was open.

13

"This was not the most auspicious time for the butler's son to visit his father."

Louisa saw the crack in the soul when he was a small child. The blood seeped slowly out of it. The color was not a normal red. Perhaps a bolt of lightning hit him when he played outside to create the crack.

"It was definitely a bolt."

She read that scientists recently created a new color which was called the darkest black. It was made of those carbon nanotubes. Louisa didn't have any idea what a nanotube was and didn't want to know. The color was black, almost as if a person were seeing an abyss. Louisa felt there was an abyss in the child's eyes as he aged. His eyes grew darker. Or rather, she occasionally saw the vast emptiness.

She wondered what dark happenings were part of the butler son's future. The decay that could happen made her reminisce about phrases her mother told her.

"Be watchful. Evil always lurked where the light dimmed."

That was when she locked a valuable item in her bookcase and carried her precious key with her.

"That look must be what a warrior saw when he encountered the enemy on the battlefield. The totality of darkness hid everything from view. Sound didn't rise out of the abyss. The trenches must feel like the abyss. The enemy's eyes and the trench were so dark, there was nothing. It was much easier to kill nothing. My family fought the evil people in the past and now I am here. I feel the trench is not too deep and I am all that is left to continue the fight."

She couldn't fire her butler because she needed him. He was loyal and did help her. She supposed it might have been better to hire someone else, but she was set in her ways. Change was an effort. The son would remain as a problem. Louisa sighed.

"Bad timing for everyone. Oh, well, the Wrights were here. I cannot wait any longer."

She saw the children exuberantly jump up the steps to her building in happy anticipation.

"They will love the elevator ride with its metal cage door." The elevator man was old and decrepit like the elevator, but fun to talk with.

"Today, I feel ancient," said Louisa to no person in the room. She was talking to herself and the air. The air didn't talk back. She liked the morning air best. It was full of healthy sunshine.

The Wrights were surprised to see Louisa employed a butler as they were led inside. The door to the kitchen was partially open and their daughter, Sami, saw the butler's son before he closed the door.

When they met the woman in the apartment, the little girl and Louisa became best friends. Louisa was old, but was real smart and efficient. She purchased the paste version of her diamond necklace set in platinum online. The Website sold mostly inexpensive old jewelry and refreshed antique tablecloths made of Irish and English linen. The San Francisco police gave the paste necklace, which sparkled like real diamonds, back to the adopted son of an elderly woman who was murdered in Los Angeles. The adopted son quickly sold it to an antique store because he didn't want to be reminded of the murder.

The Website was linked to lots of antique stores around the world. Louisa heard about such an item and went looking for the fake necklace every day until she found it. She already switched the necklaces, putting the paste one in her wall safe. Her real diamond necklace that matched Jess's necklace that was also set in platinum was in the vault at her bank. She entrusted the bank key to her lawyer with a new will.

Sami whispered to Louisa, "The man in the kitchen is bad. He didn't look at me right. He doesn't like children. I can tell because he gave me a mean look. You mustn't trust him."

Louisa told Sami, "You shouldn't worry because things were already covered. Yes, the butler's son has given me that same look when he thought I wasn't looking. Besides, I come from a long line of smart people, just like you do. I know how to be careful."

Sami smiled.

"Do you have a crown, too? My mom says you are a royal, like a queen."

Louisa laughed. The thought of a crown warmed her heart. Her family once owned a beautiful crown.

"Yes, my family did a long time ago. I've been told the crown shone bright like a star in the night with an eagle wrapped around its base."

Sami looked surprised. "Stars and eagles are my favorite things. I like to watch them through the telescope on our motorboat. I learned their names, the stars especially. My dad showed me how to be careful and hold the telescope just right."

Louisa told Jess and Derek. "Sami has a good spirit and is very intelligent. She was all right."

Derek thought the woman was talking about Jess's mother, Samantha. Jess knew she was talking about their daughter.

Jess said that one word, "*magical.*"

The old woman nodded. She saw insight into people and sometimes saw visions or dreams. She never understood why she did. It was just there, part of her personality.

Derek saw the nod and knew the word. Even Justin was hugged and loved by the woman. Louisa fused over both of their children. The old woman seemed to love having guests in her home.

She told the Wrights that she thought their friend, Dean Crain, was a kind and generous soul to return her diamond necklace.

"He didn't have to do that."

She explained why it was sold. It was a time when Louisa was down, and her bank account rapidly approached the red zone. She was lucky Dean found the buyer named War Julio, in Rio, and made a deal with him.

"It was a joy to receive my necklace back as a gift. The two of us talked about members of our family. We both lost people precious in our worlds. I liked Dean and was saddened by his death."

17

Dean was missed by all the Wrights' friends, especially Jess. Jess looked at Derek with her eyes watering. He squeezed her hand.

Louisa steered the conversation back toward happier notes. She loved family and she even mentioned family many more times.

Louisa liked the Wrights very much. The old woman knew how love looked on a person's face and how passion worked. She saw the way Derek looked at Jess and touched her. Jess was his sunrise and vice versa. It was what made the earth turn. The Wright family knew love. She could feel the rhythm of love surround them. She also saw their powerful passion for adventure and excitement.

Louisa knew her decision was a correct one. She wanted them on her side. Winning was now an option for her family. Dean had told her that sometimes a person needed to roll the dice. Louisa wanted to play. She wanted to roll. It was time. She took the gamble, feeling the wind swirl around her as if she was a warrior riding her chariot. It felt good to be in control again. The day would be a glorious one. She heard the church bells in the distance sending out their sweet music to alert the town that the time was one o'clock. The familiar chime was a comfort in her life. She would set everything in motion. Her story was major information that all the players wanted. Louisa would trust the Wrights.

Derek and Jess earlier in the week viewed the wonderful oil painting of the exquisite gold diamond necklace and *stuck* pin. It was the necklace in the

Auction brochure that the Renaliere's sold. They visited the man who bought the painting from the Auction House. Sami had drawn a picture with a pin that held the heavy clasp to one side. She somehow felt the design in her intelligent little mind and thought the necklace was somehow stuck.

Jess turned back to Louisa after nodding to her handsome husband.

"I know the necklace in the oil painting was the original master design which belonged to your great-great-grandmother. It was also the one stolen, along with a wooden chest with other family treasures, which are still lost to your family. Dean told us about the chest. To you, it probably isn't the current price or the diamonds, but memories. I know how important those memories can be to a woman."

"The diamonds in the necklace clearly were all larger stones. We know the quality of the stones were similar in quality to my necklace because the diamonds came from the same mine. The Renaliere's liked a very particular diamond company and kept going back to them for additional stones. The uniquely designed clasp is larger and does contain bigger stones on the face. The stones in the clasp were not diamonds, but were dark green emeralds, probably high quality, if the painter captured them accurately. The gold also looks heavy and awesome."

Louisa shook her head in agreement with the statement. Louisa's mother told her the necklace was magnificent. She looked at the two children playing with an old board game of some treasure island. There were little metal objects that could be moved around the map. The objects were costumed people, old ships, anchors, and cannons. The deck of cards was worn and contained scary pictures of pirates, skull bones, whales, and such. She remembered playing the board game. Enraptured in their game, the children were well entertained.

Turning back to her guest, she told Jess about the clasp before the man in the kitchen returned to listen to the rest of their conversation, slowly opening the door a crack.

Louisa whispered, "Inside the clasp were more precious emeralds. The gold diamond and emerald necklace, diamond pin, and diamond diadem were in a separate compartment at the bottom of the chest."

The old woman leaned closer to Jess. "I must explain to you where the release mechanism location is that allows access to the hidden section of the chest. It used to jam tightly shut so you might need to pry it open if the object is ever found. I'll tell you the rest of my story."

Derek and Jess leaned forward.

"The locked oak chest was lined with two layers of brass along with twenty coins that the family acquired. The coins would be considered rare today. The coins were probably from Syracuse on the island of Sicily where they were designed by the engraver Kimon. Artists were common back in those days and very well-trained in their craft. He was the finest of the ancient engravers and chose Arethusa on one side of the coin. I think he loved women, too, because his new engravings were etched a little differently and her hair on the coin was long and flowing. Kimon chose Arethusa because she was a beautiful and stunning nymph-like creature. He worked hard to capture the essence of woman and a sea creature in his design. That was the attraction today as well as the high silver content for investors."

"The coin, from the era of around 515 BC, was called a tetradrachm which is equivalent to four drachmas. A single drachma coin usually has about sixty-five grains of silver. The Head of Arethusa, the creature of water, was on the one side. If it was signed, then the value increased. Usually, there was a chariot with four horses on the back. The current day estimated price might be around one hundred sixty to one hundred eighty thousand dollars each. I checked online and called some coin collectors who verified the estimate. Because the coins were a collection and a part of known facts, the price would probably be higher for the twenty coins from my family's chest."

Louisa continued, "The robber who stole my family's chest fled the country on a ship. The ship was registered as a slave ship in 1725. But the investigator at the time, the great-great-grandmother's time, thought it was more a smuggling-type vessel of stolen goods. On the sunken, old ship could be the objects that belonged to my family or much more."

Louisa looked tired from unloading her burden of family secrets. Jess heated her tea in an old mug and put it back into the dainty cup for her. Jess brought back the tea into the cozy living room. Derek had lit the old fireplace when he saw the old woman shiver. He noted the thermometer was kept low, but the logs in the fireplace were freshly placed. An antique match holder held the long matches. The holder was a ceramic fully-rigged Spanish galleon ship molded into the front of the box. He traced the curve on its sails and wondered about the box.

Louisa saw Derek touch the holder. She smiled. Warmed by her medium dark tea that held a hint of orange spice, Louisa said, "The investigator thought the ship contained more. More something…a very valuable something. The Italians wanted to find that incredible lost ship a long time ago and searched around Freetown, now the Republic of Sierra Leone in Africa, for a very long time. I believe they have backed away from the search because of lack of funds and their frustration at not finding the doomed ship."

"Then the cargo was important and may still be," said Derek. He looked again at the match holder.

"The investigator was a good friend whose family knew our Renaliere family for generations. Both families trusted the other and helped each other in the past. He found additional information about the ship."

Old Louisa whispered to Jess and Derek, "We were told the ship just left Goree Island after picking up strong slaves which were needed to eventually unload the cargo. Some sailing trawler vessel in the area thought they saw a small heat spot and a larger bright spot that was a ship. Both spots disappeared, and they thought the ship went down."

"The fisherman, who saw the ship, was about a three- or four day ride from the port. They didn't check the ship out because a heavy wind storm approached rapidly. They already pulled up their trawl nets. Their full boat of fish and crew fled to safety forgetting about the ship until our family investigator friend questioned the crew member in a local pub."

Derek whispered back, "But Goree Island was off the coast of Dakar, the now Republic of Senegal, in Africa."

"Yes, that is exactly, correct."

Louisa motioned them closer. "The Italians possibly were searching the wrong area. The investigator friend gave my family a single-draw mahogany ship's telescope with a segmented draw tube which turned for access to the lenses. My family kept the old ship scope all these years hoping time would move technology down the road, so the ship could be found. Plus, we hadn't trusted someone enough to obtain help. Unfortunately, our friend was murdered on his way back to his contact person. My great-great-grandmother wasn't sure if any pieces of the new location reached the Italians. They didn't reveal the story because they were dealing with their own rise and fall. It was emotional times. Consequently, my family continued to hold the information secret."

Louisa removed a small key from an old gold chain she wore which contained a magnifying glass also. She walked to an antique dark mahogany bookcase with curved glass. She brought out the scope and gave it to Derek as a gift.

After they left, Louisa was lost in her dreams, falling asleep for her afternoon nap. There was happiness on her face. The last plan was started.

3   Butler's Son

WHENEVER "DIAMONDS" ARE mentioned, there are normal people who think romance and ever-lasting, or at least until the love factor wears out. Anyway, the woman is delighted to have something super valuable on her finger. The diamond is a status symbol of the high love that she has managed to capture. In other words, the larger the diamond, the better the man. It means she has conquered the best of the best. The guy doesn't care about the price of the diamond or where it came from, i.e. Africa, Russia, Canada or wherever. He wants to be on the receiving end of high love from his woman. Therefore, the diamond thing represents a win for the two people. Both are ecstatically happy. The love-love relationship works with diamonds.

With criminals or those with devious minds, the experience is the opposite. No one is happy until the diamonds are in their hands and totally hidden from view. The love doesn't happen until they are sold to the highest bidder. It doesn't matter that the gemstone was created from almost pure or pure carbon and formed into an octahedral shape. Eruption into the earth's surface from the mantle or a meteorite blast doesn't matter either. The crystalline item is real. To the criminal, only the money is real. Synthetics don't ever cross the minds of the experts. They won't touch the stuff they deem unworthy paste. Then there are the people who shouldn't be in the underworld market.

Stew Avery's head rose, ears tuned in, and there was silence. He had watched his father's employer, Louisa, cut out articles about diamonds from her magazines for the past month. He hated those magazines with missing pages. It really grated when he touched the ripped or cut edges. There was no way to read between the lines. He had tried the libraries and they didn't carry those strange gem magazines. It drove him more than crazy. Louisa was up to something. He just knew it. He could feel it. Then there arrived her new guests. They weren't her normal old lady friends. His father scurried out of the house to buy duck liver pate with basil, gourmet cheeses, vegetable cream cheese dip, cucumber sweet relish, green grapes and red pears plus homemade sesame and poppy seed crackers from a specialty shop for their afternoon tea. He saw the lumps of sugar decorated with floweret frosting in a bone china bowl on the counter. They were from another specialty shop. She never did that in the past for her other guests.

"Who were these Wright people from America?" He scrunched up his face when he saw the little girl.

When the door closed on his father, the butler's son, Stew Avery, listened to the conversation in the next room. He knew it was wrong and his father would chastise him. Stew didn't care. He listened and looked through the key peephole after closing the door.

Who was Stew Avery. He was a small figure. The man shouldn't have been anywhere near the apartment. Of course, the person listening was never one of the good guys. Small meant that Stew had a lot to learn and a long way to go to arrive at his destination.

When the Wrights visited Louisa, they knew there was another guest in the house. It was the butler's only son. They caught a glimpse but didn't meet him. Louisa treated the man as if he wasn't in the apartment at all. They also dismissed him.

Unfortunately, they didn't know the butler's son caught part of Jess, Derek, and Louisa's conversation that day. Trouble would move the scale of justice off-kilter sucking all players into the various games. But there was the important game which was the chase for the buried treasure. The treasure could be important. The questions were "Where and how big?"

Stew saw large on the horizon. He saw a way out of his current moneyless predicament. The butler's son was a true newbie con artist. His personality was malleable. It depended on the circumstance that blew his direction. This sneak-peak into Louisa's world could make him a rich man. He was disappointed that his own father was a butler, which meant slave in his mind. He knew his father wished that Stew was also someone different. Stew wouldn't settle down with some nice woman, but instead chased schemes. The son would fall someday into the hands of bad people. His father was out shopping and was not any influence in Stew's next move.

Stew knew that he was penniless most of the time due to unwise, and outrageous decisions. He was currently depressed with his life and unhappy. Unhappiness led men to keep dangerous friends. Dangerous was a mild term at describing the events that would unfold. Armed with enough information to begin a search for the worth-a-fortune diamond and gold necklace, Stew could leave Rome.

The butler's son, Stew Avery, wore the beginning baleful look in his con artist's eyes. Glittering much like the sunken diamond and emerald necklace had at its height of gentility and knights, the burning low flame showed.

Stew licked his cracked lips and dug the lip balm out of his pocket. It was cool in the house today in this old building. He was glad the fireplace was lit. He could feel the warmth. The air came through the grate into the kitchen. The oven would have warmed him, but his father had made the scones yesterday. He picked one of the delectable items from a silver tray and took a bite. He fingered the real silver tray and lifted it to assess its weight. He wondered how much he could get for that item. The scone still tasted fresh. He slathered the blueberry homemade jam on top. There was no butter for him. That stuff was fattening, and he wanted no part of it.

Stew admitted to himself the scone tasted delicious. His father did know how to make a decent scone. It was the only reason he came today. Stew bit into the thick slice of ham that he cut earlier. Food was required for energy. The food was free at the old woman's house. Avoiding the lettuce, carrots, and condiments in the refrigerator, he wrinkled his nose. He didn't need those green and orange things. Vegetables were to be avoided. Mayonnaise was eggs turned bad by a beater. He shoved the jar into the back of the refrigerator. Stew looked again at the old grate and thought about his choices. Money was what he needed. More money was a necessity now. He was glad that he spied on Louisa and saw the articles missing in her magazines. She had failed to cut out the bottom of the pages which held the title, Diamonds. He wondered about this new search and knew he would be successful.

This con artist's proclivity was moving toward eviler adventures. His mind began crossing to the opposite spectrum from knight. The search might be an easy one. From a distance, it appeared to be a simple plan.

The problem was that Stew looked like a normal nice guy. He never fit into the normal world. Hidden from view was a person with no heart inside. It was like his cracked soul was empty and devoid. He cared about no one. His focus would always be about himself. Psychologists would label him as a true narcissist.

As an only child, he was spoiled by a father who didn't have much. Stew hated the worn white shirts his father wore. Those shirts grated on Stew's mind. There was no expensive anything in his father's wardrobe. He carried a cheap watch that was gold-plated. Stew knew the difference about gold. Gold was soft and expensive.

Louisa's apartment held old items like real silver, and she wore a gold chain. He could tell she had once been rich. The old woman had airs and walked with her head held high like she was an aristocrat. He didn't think she was rich anymore because she had lived too long. The old woman looked worn out. She hadn't had her hair done recently until this week. He wondered about the why of the hairdo change. Something was more than up. Stew hated poor and worn out. There was no reason not to look stylish. He bought expensive clothes. Leaving Rome would be good. He needed real money because his credit card was maxed out. Stew hadn't told his father that he had been kicked out of his apartment. All his worldly goods were kept as payment for back rent. He was glad he had packed his clothes to visit his father. Otherwise, those items would be gone, too.

He also was no warrior and would have to hire newbie thieves for help. He felt there was plenty of time, and he could always abscond Louisa's diamond necklace with the platinum setting from the cheap wall safe for additional money. Stew overheard her talk to her friends about her jewelry. He was upset and mad the oil painting was missing from the apartment. The frame alone was worth about one hundred-fifty dollars. The money would have paid for some new shirts.

She had other things in her apartment that might sell at a profit in the pawn shop. He didn't like Louisa anyway and the feelings were mutual on her end. She stared at him too much. Stew felt uncomfortable around her. It was almost as if she could see his impure heart. He would need to be more careful.

The evil person, Stew, jumped to take the advantage, armed with his new knowledge of a possible sunken treasure. Unfortunately, he searched the wrong location for two years. Or rather the person he sold the information and his diving crew searched in Africa. That person was a con artist eviler and more psycho than himself.

That person smuggled diamonds, any, and all kinds of diamonds out of Africa. He became everyone's shocking worst nightmare. He was one of the highly experienced evil con artists. Years in the game meant power. Fear always worked. The Atlantic Ocean was his disposal site if people got in his way or cheated him. His name was Santan Chesin, and his job title was listed as diamond buyer. Within Chesin's organization were tribes of more con artists also working the game. Deceit was high on everyone's list. Other bad people would get pegged to enter the game. They would be in attendance for the private party at Chesin's home.

Stew didn't understand the hierarchy of predators that roamed the ocean and forests. He was walking into a mess. He was ill-prepared.

4   Planning the Search

A YEAR PASSED, and Derek was busy at work. The crime, for some reason, increased that year. Derek figured it was due to the extremes in weather in the Los Angeles area. Remnants of all types of criminals surfaced. A person had to ask, "are we having a border problem?" LA was a close haven for the unsavory people to land and hideout. Riches and Hollywood added to the enthralling pull for people to rebuild their lives. A new kingdom was what they desired. It didn't matter what dead body they needed to walk over to get their fill of glory and freedom. Stealing and drugs entered the mix to make the deadbeats high about their own power.

The Wrights' daughter, Sami, became ill with a bad ear infection. Sami fought recurring complications. Derek and Jess waited until after the second year before the start of their search for the lost treasure. That was all right because most of the permits to the countries they planned to visit took almost a year to receive.

They would arrive in Dakar, Republic of Senegal, Africa, in the middle of October when the rainy season almost ended.

Arrangements were made to move the motorboat on a special international transport ship. The company successfully moved boats all over the world for their clients. Most of the supplies and food they needed were stored on the boat.

The freezer was full, and they were guaranteed that within four hours, the power would be connected to save on the generators for the freezer and food storage area. All the freezer meat was vacuum sealed in clear plastic as were the freezer vegetables, marked with food type, and dated. Even the food cold storage area contained things in clear plastic bins which were dated. The dry goods were in clear plastic for assured visibility, dated, and sealed. It was easy to see what was in every package, nothing was hidden there in the food area.

War Julio sent them a specially designed crate that was lockable. The frozen seafood was in this crate in the freezer until something better could be placed there. If any additional perishable food needed to be acquired, it would be helicoptered in.

At the last minute, they decided to include Jim's fifty-foot fishing boat on the transport as a base for the divers to eat, sleep, and put their gear. Derek paid for the transport and extra insurance. The smaller fishing boat would be placed off the rear of the motorboat when they were at their dive location. They installed on the motorboat a specially designed winch cord that could easily be released and would snap back into the casing box.

Derek was glad there was the extra boat for additional safety in returning the diving crews to shore for their days off. He also liked the fact that he would have more privacy with Jess. She was the whole reason for this trip. It was something she wanted to do very much. He caught the way her eyes lit up when she saw the submersible and later met Louisa. Derek laughed. He had convinced Jess to christen the name of the submersible. It was *sub*. The name was perfect and much easier for her to write on her notes. He also saw the way Louisa took to his family and Jess. Louisa wanted to take the journey with Jess just like Derek.

Jess had a way of making the dull world disappear. She let the world delight her. Derek knew that look Jess did when she was delighted. It was the look that said, "Let's go get them." *It was her no fear look, charged up, and anxious to see what the adventure would bring which got them into trouble later.*

He felt everything was ready. Derek was also getting charged up. He was ready to roll, too. The motorboat and helicopter were heavily armed from prior episodes with the bad guys in America.

The same motorboat crew would fly to Senegal along with Derek when the motorboat and fishing boat were delivered to Dakar. Jim and Mary Beth Michaels, good friends, would fly with Jess and the two children. Justin was now ten and a half, and Sami, seven years old. The children would stay two weeks in Senegal with their parents for a family vacation.

The weather there was a tropical climate. They planned to do some sightseeing and visit Goree Island which was approximately one point eight miles off the coast of Dakar. It was the location of a fort around the

1700s. It was a place where ships sometimes picked up slaves or workers as additional crew.

The kids wanted to visit the Historical Museum to see the masks, statues, and musical instruments. The group also planned a trip to the market, which their children fondly called the Sand Market. But they would bring the protection squad for safety. The kids hoped to see anything at the market regarding the goblin shark, but probably wouldn't because it was rare.

The creature's elongated, flattened snout was different, and it inhabited mostly deep canyons and continental slopes. The shark reminded the children of spooky ghosts from some Halloween night when they saw pictures of the creature. But then they thought a lot of the creatures in the ocean were rather strange looking. They wondered about those facts as all children do.

They also didn't have time to drive an hour south to see the la Petite Cote area or the beaches bounded by steep cliffs of red rock. Their children saw them from the air when they left on their charter plane.

The sub divers and their wives who were hired would also meet them in Dakar. The first divers were named Brin and Jay Taylor and the secondary divers were Lorna and Gordi Anderson. Their experience in the Atlantic Ocean around Africa was filled with many years of dive sites. Also, two extra divers, who were Marra Childs and Josine Thorne, were hired.

Skid Peters was the underwater sub expert. He was the person with extensive knowledge of the African coastline and shipwrecks. He also knew about all types of diving equipment. He met with Derek and crew first thing in Dakar to discuss the planned diving sites. His skill and intelligence in managing a crew and dive site would be invaluable to the Wrights. Skid would become good friends with them.

All the diving crew and Skid spoke the French language as did Derek. Senegal, once owned by the French for many years, didn't receive her independence until 1960. A few of the Miami guys spoke Portuguese and Spanish which would also help with translation around some of the islands. Jess took French for six months to become proficient in the language.

Senegal's network connectivity worked from their hotel when they arrived. They were good with communication until the motorboat and fishing boat became available.

After two weeks, Jim and Mary Beth would fly with their children to meet with the Miami, Florida, cronies and their wives. They would stay in Curacao, an island north of the Venezuelan coast, until the Wrights' mission was completed. Some of the Miami protection squad were in Curacao and on the motorboat in Dakar. Derek asked for the sharpshooter and best weaponry men be sent to Dakar.

Jess asked, "How long do you think we will stay in Dakar?"

"The diving expedition alone might take approximately two months or a little more. Everything depended upon how quickly we can find any ships or treasure. After three weeks, I've planned to move to another coordinate site if there are no visible traces of a sunken ship. We will plot out grids for each dive site and work the teams to complete each grid. Weather could be a problem per our captain who sent me a note on the future forecast."

War Julio Samba, their friend in Rio de Janeiro, Brazil, had purchased a high-speed air-boat. He sent Derek a picture, which made Derek smile. The huge air-boat was painted black and looked like a pirate ship. He told Derek that he would move the air-boat to Curacao where his fishing business was located. His friends thought it looked like a scary ship. War Julio liked scary. Then, War Julio talked to Derek about his new special fishing nets that moved up and down in the water via the installed computers. He also had remotes that could be used from a notebook computer.

He gave Derek the name and phone number of a legitimate fishing company that he knew in Dakar if they needed extra help or more food. He wanted the Wrights to have good quality fish to eat on their expedition. Plus, the men at the company owed him a favor and would help in other areas. All Derek needed to do was make contact. Derek thanked him.

War Julio also purchased a building of condos in the harbor on Curacao. He was going to keep his air-boat close to his fishing business and docks. He currently renovated some of the floors of his condos, installing major equipment and security. One of the three-bedroom condos were reserved for the kids and the Michaels' visit. There would be a place for Jess and Derek when they arrived.

The large Curacao hotel on the island reserved the ballroom, catering staff, and bar for the dates Derek requested for their Masquerade Party. It was the place they had chosen for their annual party. The hotel provided a name of a company that would give them a discount on the large flower bouquets and palms Jess wanted. There was another local company that made fun plastic covers for the interior garbage cans.

The hotel reviewed Jess Wright's menu and thought it would be no problem. If Jess sent a drawing of the ice sculpture, they would give it to their chef to see if it was a viable thing to put together. The hotel did have a secured room near the ballroom for Derek's security people to use.

The limousine companies were arranged as well because parking in the area for their size crowd was a little impossible. They could only reserve two floors of the parking garage for the Wrights. War Julio and his people could hardly wait for the Wrights' arrival in Curacao.

Derek turned to Jess when she spoke.

"Our exquisite costumes and an overlay skirt were being made to match my red dress and a special headdress which I will wear for the masquerade party. Your costume is a red vest and black knit pants with a cotton silk blend white shirt and black cummerbund. The company couldn't do sequins on your shirt, but they can put some glitter on the ruffle edge of the shirt. I told the company that would be fine. The masks for the guests are a blended rainbow swirl of color. Our entire crew will have the red-colored masks. Ours will be the same red, but with more feathers," mentioned Jess.

Derek still seemed lost in thought. He wasn't sure about the black tights for pants. He would have preferred jeans. He couldn't talk her out of the knit stuff. She told him it was a period costume, whatever that meant. Derek sighed. He would have to do the tights and feathers. He needed to pay attention to his wife because she was still talking.

"Are you locked into our dance steps for the masquerade party after our classes together?"

"Thanks, on the update on the costumes. No, I want to do the dance routines again with only you."

"Oh, hide and watch. I can teach you some better dance moves with heavenly rhythm."

"That was what I hoped for. I will take heaven every time. Rhythm was what you are major good at, especially the slow kind."

Derek danced toward her with several slow intricate steps. Jess laughed. She now had his full attention.

"Our crowd will need a highly talented show," replied Jess. "Let's give them a show and contest of their own at the party."

"What type of contest do you have in mind, honey?"

"Remember the limbo?"

"Yes, I know the limbo. In the older times, the ships were built so that down below, it was very low in the cargo hold. The crew did the limbo and sang to themselves to overcome their claustrophobic fear until they retrieved the object out of the hold. It also was a way of staying fit on a long journey. There was no room on the boat for exercise equipment."

Jess looked sideways at her husband. Derek tried to do the limbo and fell on his knees and crawled over to her. He grabbed her feet. She screamed softly when he tickled her.

Jess was delighted he read a book she left out at their library at one of the Los Angeles warehouses.

"Let's do a limbo contest for some prize. What prize?"

"I don't know, but I do know you are better at games than me. You'll think of something. Okay, honey, how low can you go on the limbo? I would love to see that dance in your sexy, exquisite very beautiful red dress. But then I would enjoy you in champagne color also."

"No limbo for me, my dance moves were enough to drive the crazy husband even crazier."

"How crazy?"

She gave him another side-long glance and rolled her eyes.

He remembered that look when he took her to dinner in her champagne-colored dress in Napa and he smiled. Derek knew she picked up his mention of her other dress. He reminisced what happened after dinner that night had been real extreme in her hotel room. The words *hot, crazy*, and *wonderful* rolled into his brain. He knew their connection with each other would be just that. That's why he tailed her.

Jess smiled, too. She remembered the heat. Derek moved from her feet toward her leg and kissed her slowly, his kisses moving upward. Mystery and his loving arms were where he wanted his wife.

Jess knew where her husband was headed. She was headed there shortly but must make sure he received all the information.

"I forgot to mention something War Julio told me. There were some other conventions that same day at the hotels close to our hotel. People on occasion were invited to all three parties at the various hotels and that might work to our advantage if needed. Because of the difference in party themes, the blending of the groups of people would be a good disguise for their security."

"I know that fact. War Julio picked up more things for me that will coordinate with the other conventions. Both of us feel we covered any problems with my beautiful wife's additional insight. Plus, Jim gave us a few good ideas."

Derek was done talking. He reached her breasts and kept kissing her. He moved further upward onto her neck, softly seducing her. He held on to his wife and kissed her again, more slowly on the lips in case she didn't get his first message.

Jess received his messages loud and clear and let loose her passion to match his desire. They both were in the land of wonderful with the world totally locked out. Their excitement in the bedroom mounting with their passion for adventure.

Derek said, "Oh, yes, I remember the temperature and crazy wonderful."

Jess knew she held him in the palm of her hand. "I like the way you turn everything on. There is music playing in my head. I like the new version you did for me. Things were better, oh, yeah."

Later, they fell into an exhausted sleep, happy to begin their adventure soon.

XXXXXX

The next morning, Jess contacted Louisa Renaliere and told her their plans for the start of the diving expedition, but didn't tell her where exactly, but she knew the general vicinity. Louisa told no one. Everything was all right on Louisa's end. Jess gave her Jim's cell phone number if she needed any kind of help, because the Miami boys knew friends in Rome. They would be there instantly to remove her from harm's way, if need be. Louisa assured Jess that she felt all was well.

Shortly, things would not be well. The butler's son snuck into Louisa's apartment when his father drove Louisa to her monthly tea party with friends. She was gone all afternoon.

Stew Avery installed a small video camera earlier in Louisa's apartment, so he could read the old-fashioned wall safe dial when Louisa turned it. He removed the paste necklace from the wall safe. Louisa's safe remained unchecked for over a month after Stew's withdrawal.

His father wouldn't loan him any more money for his new schemes. Stew couldn't hide the fact that he was up to no good again. Stew needed the money to go to America. He thought the old ship's scope Louisa gave Derek might hold a clue. He sold the necklace and obtained the money from a fence he knew in Dakar, Africa.

The fence was a newbie and didn't know diamonds either. The newbie fence belonged to the red tribe group under Santan Chesin's group of diamond smugglers. The red tribe group reported their earnings back to Mr. Chesin in approximately two months.

Mr. Chesin's home base for his business was also in Dakar. He would not be pleased about the transaction. It would add to the other failures happening.

5   Diamond Smuggler

THE DIAMOND SMUGGLER, Santan Chesin, was upset that his diving ship was still anchored offshore from Freetown, Sierra Leone, in Africa. He was tired of being there. His diving crews checked the area's wreck sites for two years, barely scraping anything worthwhile off the ocean floor. Something was very wrong with the diving expedition area. Santan wondered if this whole business was a scam. He looked out at the Atlantic Ocean before making his decision.

He passed the word. "My boys should be on the lookout for Stew Avery who provided me with the information about the gold diamond necklace and potential underwater sunken ship treasure location. I paid Stew money for information that wasn't delivering." Stew would not placate him anymore with his flagrant tricks.

Santan had seen a forest of trees when he met Stew. It should have been a warning sign. Ill-natured creatures lived in the trees. Some of them were soft and pretty-colored, except others were dangerous. Even sneaking weasels were dangerous, one way or the other. He wondered if he stumbled upon a lying weasel. He hated liars who hid.

44

The only thing good about being in Sierra Leone was that English was the official language. He worried about that Ebola outbreak that happened there. That stuff scared the crap out of him and could lead to a low life expectancy at a high rate of speed.

"I'm scared to death of exposure and won't drink anything unless I or one of my trusted men open the container."

Santan ate only dehydrated food with distilled water to hydrate it while in the area. New clothes were purchased frequently, and the old ones were thrown away. He made his crew constantly wash his diving boat daily with antiseptic. Mr. Chesin wore gloves. He became an obsessive-compulsive neat-freak.

"I have worked hard to build my diamond smuggling business in the poverty-stricken African countryside. I won't let go of my profitable business easily."

Wanting to get back to Dakar, he made his captain turn the ship. He wasn't going to be in this vicinity for a long time. It was a fruitless activity.

"I have trusted my black tribe people long enough to handle my business in Dakar. The diamond money is always a temptation. Embezzlement was a word the black tribe knew in intricate detail. I'm a master and they have learned well. My top black tribe man is retiring, and the reins will pass down to the brother. I don't quite trust the brother yet. I will need to set up a meeting to clarify the rules."

Mr. Chesin preferred to be at his home in Dakar, Senegal, with his nice oceanfront view and secured brick wall and gates. His beautiful ladies were currently staying there. He loved all his ladies and lavished them with diamond baubles for their wonderful favors that they provided him in the evenings. He especially liked the ladies that were very, very good in bed.

Expanding the pool, he put in one of those dream infinity edges. His girls wanted the look and told him the expensive pool would expand his image to his business people. He could write the pool off as an expense just like the parties they wanted.

Santan checked with his lawyer and could expense the pool and parties. Happy with the business deductions, he even let the ladies pick the dark blue tile with flecks of gold. All the umbrellas were new and dark navy blue. The cushions on the chaise lounges were navy blue stripe. He put in a large rectangular bar with a tiki style roof. Extra-large plants were brought into the area in beautiful blue pots. Hot pink and bright yellow pillows adorned the chaise lounges. Soft Caribbean music played in the background. The pool area looked festive and happy. His home was perfect and soothed his mind.

He upgraded his secret video cameras and hired more security detail. New pavers adorned his very large circular drive with exotic trees and more plants camouflaged the house. Landscape lighting was strategically located. The garage was extended to five cars. His staff and minions stayed in cheap, portable, rented mobile trailers behind the trees. They were better than their last place of work and had air conditioning. The job of protecting the place was easy.

"I mentioned to my girls that my favorite female clothing was strategically placed lace and diaphanous outfits because we must be a little bit discreet at the house. My clients expect it. They must look beautiful during the day and evening. They get to live in my nice home and I do pay them. Plus, my girls get fringe benefits such as clothes, jewelry, and cars." Happiness flowed both ways or that is what he thought.

Mr. Chesin's very old voluptuous paintings in ornate gold scroll frames of women were all over his bedroom along with mirrors and cameras. It was a room few people were ever allowed to view. He made the ladies at his home take lots of showers and use special spray bath wands. Rain shower-heads were included. He made the girls that were his sexual partners take a medical exam once a month. He was also afraid of catching some other bad disease that was floating around out there in this part of the world. It was another thing to be avoided. His health was important.

Moving back to England or possibly the Caribbean frequented his mind. He let slip a few times to his girl, Ruse, that he would like to live in London, the hub of culture. It was his hometown and he had fond memories there. His eyes would tear just thinking about the wonderful city. Santan received some real estate flyers for flats in a specific area of London. Unknown to him, Ruse saw the flyers and read them. She read everything in the old man's bedroom. She knew every inch of the place and all the old man's secrets. It was her way of taking good care of herself. She could play both sides of a game.

47

"It is high on the need-now, right now, absolutely now meeting with this Stew person. There can be no more delay. I must give him a piece of my mind," said Santan. He summoned Jinx.

Santan Chesin paced back and forth, getting his blood pressure worked up even more as he downed the addictive fifth glass of his favored strong dark rum. His shiny bald head looked like a round turnip on his short sleazy body as he paced. He constantly scratched at what little dyed hair was left. With his linen handkerchief, he wiped the sweat off his face and was relieved when he saw one of his most trusted men, Jinx, arrive.

"Track that weasel Stew's every movement and report back to me."

"I will report immediately to you as information does become available," mentioned his security man, Jinx.

The weasel, Stew, became the hunted.

"Stew better deliver something soon to me or complications will arise."

Santan stood there staring at Jinx who started to sweat. Jinx knew what the word *complications* meant. He wondered if there was another job in Dakar. This one was getting awkward and precarious.

"Be off with you, then. We don't have all day."

Jinx quickly exited the room.

6   Stew Avery and Ship's Telescope

STEW FLEW TO Los Angeles. Having been there several times before, he stayed a month with a cousin. The cousin picked him up at the airport and drove him back to the small apartment in Santa Monica. It was not in the best part of town.

The cousin drove Stew nuts. The man wore faded blue jeans shorts and dilapidated tennis shoes with a holed tan-colored t-shirt. He couldn't tell if the shirt might have been white at some point in time and the cheap, nasty commercial dryers turned it to beige. The more he looked at the shirt, he decided that it was a yellow-beige. He had never seen this color in the stores.

The jeans were the same ones that the guy wore ten years ago, only they were a little more frayed. They looked like they had been through a street war with a gang. Then, there appeared to be specks of lavender paint on the seat from when he painted the bedroom of his apartment. He told Stew the color calmed him so that he wasn't a tiger in bed with women. Stew was doubtful of the accuracy of that description. The man was a pussy. There was one back pocket on the right side which was totally ripped off. The left pocket looked like it would go at any time.

He hated walking down the street with his cousin. The man talked to himself as he walked. People would stop and give him five dollars because they thought he was a homeless person. His cousin worked the system. He knew the tricks. It was panhandling. Stew didn't beg, ever. Now stealing was a different story.

Stew decided there was something wrong with a person who wore dread-locks after age twenty-five, especially if a beautician didn't manage the hair. His cousin looked like a bouffant, braided, drowned rat most of the time. Stew's hair was kept neat and short.

He next noticed the banana peel on the coffee table in the apartment. Stew wasn't sure if it was the same one that he saw ten years earlier when he last visited the place. The hippie furniture and ugly orange shag carpet were the same as before.

Stew sat in a derelict chair as far away from the coffee table as possible. He didn't want to touch the overfilled ashtray either. He bought his own package of eggs at the local market because he wasn't sure how long the other carton had been in the refrigerator. The gray paper carton wouldn't move when he tried to shove it out of the way. The egg whites sealed it to the glass shelf permanently. Stew looked for a chisel or screwdriver to dislodge the box and couldn't find anything. He gave up.

Stew went out for coffee. There was a reason for this besides the eggs. The cousin liked to make something that didn't quite taste like espresso. It tasted familiar, almost like chai tea. Then there sat the coffee mugs on an open shelf in the kitchen. Every single one had a chip and long crack where the brown stain was set permanently in the crevasse. Even the flies couldn't get the gunk out.

Those cups reminded Stew of bad memories. Stew once mistakenly ordered from a numbered menu in a dirt-water café along the coast near Mexico. The cup also had a chip out of it in the restaurant, much like his cousin's place. Whenever he saw a numbered menu that went past number 50, he left the premises. He wasn't going that route again. Stew rightly believed the place represented a health hazard. The only thing fresh to eat were the fried cheese jalapenos which were a side on 49 out of the 50 meals. A whole garden of jalapenos grew nearby the kitchen of the restaurant. They must have used good fertilizer because they were huge green things. Stew didn't get that they weren't jalapenos, but some other Mexican pepper called a Hatch chili.

His cousin kept small jalapenos in his refrigerator and ate them raw. A thought occurred to Stew. There was a defective gene in the cousin or the heat melted his brain. Stew worried about those facts. He started to wonder about his father who really liked the cousin. Perhaps his father was off his rocker, too.

The cousin knew some guys who would be glad to help him steal an antique ship's telescope. They were cheap. They wanted gas money and a case of beer for doing the job. Stew would pay them, only if they promised not to steal anything else. The heist operation planned for a quick in and out operation with his cousin. The other guys would drive the getaway car.

Their lucky day happened when a large bird flew into one of the bathroom windows of Derek and Jess's grandiose California home. The security boys turned off that section of the house's security and taped the window glass to wait until morning for the special heavy-duty glass to be replaced.

Stew and his cousin removed the glass and found the antique old ship's telescope in an unlocked glass bookcase in Derek's den. The security cameras showed the two of them clearly because neither one wore any kind of mask. The left blue jean pocket caught on the window seal as his cousin exited the window and tore completely off. The cousin reached for it, thinking that he could find some string or twine and resew it back on. They argued about it under the broken window.

Stew stuffed the ripped blue jean piece in his pocket and hissed. "You are in some freaking alternate reality."

His cousin would never get the normal stuff. He would need to explain the way things were now going to work.

"I'll buy you some new shorts. Just forget about it and stop making so much noise. You will wake the neighbors who will think you are nuts to be robbing this house. It is an expensive neighborhood and the jail term was always higher and longer in the pricey neighborhoods if we get caught."

The cousin finally settled down, but Stew looked over at the man's sad face. Those old shorts would be missed was his expression. Stew was exasperated and told him that he was absolutely a sorry-looking dude in those miserable shorts. He was surprised they weren't arrested already.

"This is a high-end community and might have celebrities living here. No one wore shorts like that in this neighborhood unless they showed a designer label on it."

Stew shook his head. His cousin might as well stand on top of the house with a megaphone announcing their arrival. Stew noticed the man's rear was falling out where the pocket came off. The crummy shorts were disintegrating, but not quite fast enough. Next, Stew pointed out that there appeared to be some blue jean fiber stuck to the window frame that would match his cousin's shorts. The faded blue jean shorts did need to be gone permanently unless he wanted to go to jail. Police could match the thread easily to the shorts.

His cousin rolled his eyes. He thought Stew was being a drag and told him so. Stew knew he must corral his cousin into the destruction that was occurring on this job. He told him how much Santa Monica would miss him if he were in prison. That did it. The cousin let him know his decision. The shorts should be a goner. His cousin accidentally touched the etched glass.

"Ow!" Quickly, the cousin grabbed his red bandana kerchief to stop the flow of blood. He used a corner to wipe a small spot off the glass.

"See, it's good as new."

Stew shook his head and rubbed his face.

"Shh! Haven't you heard about DNA?"

His cousin hissed back, "Do Not Accidentally take acid. Sure, I've heard of it."

Stew didn't know anyone who wore red bandanas and acted this way, other than revolutionists and motorcycle biker gang members.

"You have to stop the jokes. This heist is important." said Stew.

His cousin pointed at Stew and placed his hand over his mouth to hide the snicker. But he sobered and realized the banana peel would have to be a goner, too. Whenever Stew visited, the cousin took the black peel out of the freezer, knowing that it would upset him. A little trouble always stirred Stew up. The man went ballistic and his cousin enjoyed the show. Unknown to Stew, the cousin told his friends Stew was the nut job.

Next, the cousin rattled off the payment plan he now required.

Stew looked at his cousin. Frustrated, he groaned because his cousin argued with him while they were stealing goods. He should dump the guy. The man wouldn't stop talking. The flunky cousin wanted designer shorts, new shirt, sunglasses, and dark sandals. It was all because Stew had brought the whole idea into his mind. If the cousin must give up his shorts, he wanted to dress like the celebrities.

Stew just created a monster fashion boy. He could see him walking the streets with fake designer sunglasses. The monster boy was some slapstick movie waiting to happen. Stew would never do this again with his cousin. He realized they stayed too long at the broken window and worried there was a dog nearby. He agreed to buy the articles to get his cousin away from the area. The cheap heist would cost Stew too much and stress him out.

The cousin didn't care. He was heading to the malls to get free cologne. He had a date due to his new clothes. The cousin wanted to smell expensive. He already bought blankets at the cheap store to throw over the cigarette burns on his sofa. There was clearly spray put into the air to freshen up his apartment. His cousin was disappointed that he couldn't rent a sports car to impress his date. He asked Stew for money and was turned down. The cousin would check out everything that was free and enjoy trolling the mall. He later thought America was beautiful.

The two men finally hightailed it out of the pricey Wright neighborhood. The friends that picked them up drank most of the beer, and Stew drove the sleepy thieves back to his cousin's apartment.

There were pedigree dogs in the houses by the Wrights in fancy cages or rooms. Only one dog overheard the two men and its owners were not home. No one heard the barking until the owners returned home and watched their video of their dog's room. It coincided to the time of the break-in.

Derek and Jess received the video from the police and were notified of the break-in at their residence. It seemed like the thieves were at their house for some time. That was unusual. The thieves were obviously not professionals.

Derek was told that the antique telescope was missing. There were some blue jean fibers they would save. Per the police, the object seemed to be the only item taken. Derek quietly uttered foul language when he heard the news. He should have put the object in the safe. Jess would be upset with him about the missing scope and papyrus.

Notifying his people, Derek sent Jim Michaels and War Julio the video. The video was also sent to the Miami group. Everyone in their group would recognize Stew Avery when they met him. Unless, of course, he wore a disguise in the future.

7   Stew Meets Chesin

FINDING THE LITTLE yellowed papyrus paper in the scope, Stew was delighted. The telescope was old. Carefully, he unfolded the paper. The writing was faded, and he used the lens to read the numbers. He had taken a navigation class and recognized the three coordinates. He located the three coordinates on his computer just like Derek had done. Now he was excited. He left the antique telescope in his cousin's apartment on a shelf in his living room in his haste to get to Africa. He stuffed the papyrus in his wallet.

Later, Stew's father visited the cousin in Los Angeles and believed his son stole the scope from Louisa Renaliere. The butler dusted the thing for years once a month when the old woman would allow him inside the mahogany bookcase. The father would need to decide where his loyalty belonged. His son was not a good person.

Stew flew back through Rome, Italy, and then to Sierra Leone, with new information. He fingered the papyrus stuck inside his travel book about Africa. Meeting with Mr. Chesin in Africa, he provided him the new coordinates. Stew was confident until he was informed by Chesin that he no longer trusted him. He hoped it wouldn't affect the money offered.

"I don't quite believe some story about papyrus in a telescope. However, you gave me the papyrus and it did look old. Why haven't you brought me the actual scope?"

Chesin looked at the picture Stew's brother took and sent to Stew's cell phone.

"You forgot the telescope in Los Angeles? Didn't you know how valuable the telescope was in the scheme of things? Wasn't that a little stupid of you?"

Stew knew to remain silent and let the man lead the conversation. He was used to insults and chose to ignore the words for the present time. He slipped a little bit on the professional scale, but then he was no mind reader. Stew knew that he wouldn't be here if he owned that wonderful skill. His thoughts were rising at the idea of rich. He dared not smile. Las Vegas lights were showing in his eyes. However, his bland face showed no reaction for his error.

Santan Chesin was perturbed by the young man. His eyes looked strange, yet he kept his composure. The man was weird. He signaled his man to check online about ship's scopes. The timeline and age of the telescope seemed correct. His man verified it.

"The story was a plausible one and I will need to have my captain check the coordinates. Your story this time is more substantial, but you will not get the rest of the money until the treasure is found. I want no more tricks, or you will be swimming back to Italy from the middle of the Atlantic. I hope you are very clear with the rules. I must have rules to prevent trouble."

Stew shook his head in a positive gesture, because he now knew breaking of rules meant bad things for him. He wasn't a good enough swimmer to escape sharks. The gambling light disappeared from his eyes. He needed that money. He reached for the papyrus paper, but Santan Chesin lit a match to the old item. The papyrus quickly burned to nothing in the green glass ashtray. The man crushed the burnt paper to nothing. There would be no living person viewing those coordinates. Santan wore an evil large-toothed smile. The green light reflected off Stew's face making him look paler.

Santan told him a story about a person who displeased him in the business world. It was the kind of transaction that was unforgettable in Santan's mind. The test method must be used for troublemakers.

Rattled and not thinking about his next question until it was too late, Stew asked, "What's the test method?"

Rubbing his hands together, Santan lit his cigar. "The man was given the test method. We put him in a leaky rubber raft in the Atlantic because he obviously needed to leave. I remember the location was some distance outside the limits of fishing. The limits were about three miles at that time. But we felt the yellow rubber boat would get him to shore. Maybe the current was strong in that area. I forgot to ask my captain which was just a small, human misjudgment on my part. Mistakes do happen. We had to assume the man drowned because no one heard from him again. No yellow pieces of the raft were found. There were just a few rubber boat patches on shore, which surprised me. I thought we had removed those. You see, I just could not remember. It possibly was another mistake, or he must have run into bad luck. A person could say the test failed."

Santan rubbed a shark tooth necklace that he wore. The smooth gold at the tip felt cold. He chuckled because he saw recognition in Stew's eyes. It was fear.

Stew now knew the man in front of him was very dangerous and he would need to be extra careful while in Africa. Mr. Chesin was weirder than his cousin and he wished there was another universe he could rocket jump and get off this one. Stew's brain was firing away, like a small mouse caught in a spiraling drain. His body shrunk in stature,

Santan knew he clearly established himself. He saw Stew trying to assess his character. Santan felt at times that his personality did belong to the devil or a close relative. *That thought really should scare Stew a tad more*, thought Santan. He chuckled again when he saw Stew look over his shoulder for the exit.

After leaving Santan, Stew immediately contacted his cousin to request the expedited mailing of the telescope to him. Stupidity wasn't going to happen until after he disconnected from the evil shark man or found a safe place to hide. Stew would learn. He would not mess up for some time and would certainly hang on to the scope in the future. He wouldn't tell Santan that he kept it for fear the old man would destroy that item, too. Stew could sell the telescope in an auction market when things died down or whenever he was desperate for money. The papyrus would have added to the scope's value.

The cousin received Stew's message and didn't mail the telescope right away just to drive him a little crazy. His cousin told Stew about an appointment he must keep at the mall. The appointment was for his beautiful face to enhance his skin tones. It was a new beauty treatment designed for men. It was free. He also was dating a beautician who helped change his hairstyle. The cousin just didn't have time to go to the post office because women were also waiting.

Stew believed his cousin was feeding him more crap. He wondered what kind of woman would ever want to go out with his penniless cousin. Clearly, none of the women could speak very good English and Stew didn't know any other language. It was probably a correct fact that his cousin did. It was obvious his calls never reached his cousin. Communication was at a standstill.

Stew was irked that the money from the scope heist and the extra money his cousin finally wiggled out of him was behind this new image. The new image had to be a lie. Stew wouldn't spend money on fancy lotions. He shook his head to clear the thought. Stew would have to call his cousin many times before the old ship's scope arrived at his destination. Every time Stew called, a different woman answered the apartment. He was told that his cousin was at the *moll* choosing a free *mon's* bag that he won in a drawing. He figured out the woman meant man's bag at the mall because the woman called his cousin, *mon*. Stew became more frustrated with his cousin. His cousin was clearly falling out of touch.

Mr. Chesin headed toward Dakar and home for a little while before venturing out with his diving boat and crew. He was glad he painted the bottom of his diving boat dark navy blue. The boat was almost invisible in the water. It looked dark as night, inky dark. It was easy to disappear if a person was in a rush.

Santan Chesin reminisced about his lady friends. He wanted some lady comforts. He gave his crew a break and had his chef restock his boat. Santan Chesin needed time to rest. His ladies could potentially be his downfall, but he was oblivious for they were not that bright.

The women in his house knew the game and were not that loyal. They were bright enough. Their nickname for him when he was out of hearing range was not kind. Those words were always whispered because they knew where the hidden video cameras were in the house. They called him little Satan because he was internally conflicted and multifaceted, not in a good way.

Perhaps they were not well educated, but they knew men and their deceitful ways. This guy was high in the deceit scale, illegal as all heck, and off the charts compared to their old bosses.

Santan's ladies worked on their plan of exit out of Dakar. The money they received wasn't enough. They, too, wanted more. They had passed the stupid part a long time ago with him. They wised up and put their energies elsewhere. Living high was their name of the game and it could be with anyone better than where they currently were. They were ready to sell out.

8   Miami Wife Tami

THE SAN FRANCISCO ex-cop and now wife of one of the younger Miami Cortez brothers called Derek. Her husband was on the motorboat protection team.

Derek answered, "Hello, how are you, Tami?"

Tami Cortez let Derek know that she would also be in Dakar staying with an old academy friend named Rhonda White. When they were at the police academy, the women became good friends. Rhonda knew many skills and was in constant demand internationally on some police assignment. Rhonda was a freelance person in case Derek needed help. She was also good at catching criminals. She lived in Miami when she was off assignment and not dating some rich guy.

Tami went to Dakar to help her friend and be close to her husband. The two ladies would be undercover. Rhonda was involved with a current police investigation into some diamond smuggling.

"There was a huge quantity of diamonds that escaped the country and continued to exit the country. The police finally came up with a plan to catch what they believed was the top guy. The police always caught the lesser smugglers, but there seemed to be many groups or tribes of smugglers involved."

"The police were currently watching this one person who purchased a large ocean view home in the area and installed a brick and mortar fence around the property with strong steel electronic gates. There were numerous expensive cars. The guy also purchased a seventy-foot diving boat. Next he painted the bottom of that boat dark blue."

Derek commented, "Yes, I believe our captain heard about the dive ship on the radio while talking with some other ships."

"Evidently, more unsavory sailor-type people came to town. These people were obviously his divers and talked pirate language at the local bars. The divers even mentioned the word *diamonds* and *treasure*. Mr. Chesin also owned some fishing trawlers that were in the harbor."

Tami snapped pictures with her super camera lens of the diving boat when it came closer to the harbor for supplies. She would send them to Derek and ask him to look at the photo images.

"The rich man that owned the home has been out of the country with his diving boat. His business was listed as a diamond buyer. Therefore, the police weren't sure why he wanted a diving boat. The police tracked him down and he had been in Sierra Leone. The police couldn't go there so decided to create a trap for him when he returned."

Derek frowned and told her to continue. He wondered about a diving ship in Sierra Leone.

"Mr. Santan Chesin, who usually acted mesmerized by all kinds of beautiful women, was the target. The plan was for us to become friendly with some of his women so that we would get invited to one of the house parties. There were lots of great food and huge quantities of rum at these parties. The women would then search the house after the party when the power went off for a little bit. The power lines seemed to be a problem whenever the wind picked up. Mr. Chesin hadn't gotten around to installing a generator yet."

Derek said, "Watch yourself because this diamond smuggler has worked the system for some time. Dangerous was the name of that game."

She told him that she would wear her red dress from the Los Angeles set up with her special platform shoes and other high-tech gear. The two women were a good team in the past. Some of the younger San Francisco cronies were staying close to the girls for their protection and would attend the party as their dates.

Tami asked, "Will this rich guy with the diving boat present a problem for you in the way of competition for any sunken treasure? His only name on their files showed the name, Santan Chesin, and he is now back in Dakar. Mr. Chesin restocked his boat and he might be headed out again soon."

Derek started feeling edgy. It was the trouble he had worried about when they talked of their trip to Dakar.

Giving Derek the location where she was staying and phone number, she next gave him Mr. Chesin's residence address.

"The name of his boat was *Nuit Vaisseau* or *Night Ship*."

Derek said, "That is interesting for a name. He might as well have used the word, Cloaked. We'll try to stay clear of the ship and mystery man. Thank you, Tami."

They developed a code name for the *Night Ship* diving boat, which was *freebooter or pirate* and *old scratch* for any reference to the man, Mr. Chesin.

"There was one more thing. One of the undercover local police is named Jinx," said Tami.

Derek thanked her for calling and gave her their motorboat's phone number directly to the captain in case she needed anything. Most definitely was Derek going to request a tail be placed on Mr. Chesin. It was important to check him out. Derek's superiors would handle things on their end.

9 Toy Company

SAYING GOODBYE TO their children, Derek and Jess saw them leave Africa. Jim and Mary Beth took off in the small chartered airplane to a safer area in Curacao.

While the children were there in Dakar, they did eat at fun restaurants in the French area of town. Both children enjoyed shopping at the market in town that they called sand market. The children found pirate outfits because they saw War Julio's high-speed air-boat. If they looked like pirates, then War Julio might take them out for a ride.

When their children were at the market, they also found twelve-inch size plastic floatable goblin sharks that swam when the small batteries were installed. A small compartment inside the shark body was spacious enough to hide something.

Derek picked up the toy shark and turned it over. Interested in the toy as a water diversion for party games, he asked the salesperson, "Do the sharks swim straight, and if so, how far on one battery?"

Derek was assured that they did move straight, and the sharks could travel thirty or forty feet on new batteries. He bought ten more in case they wanted to do competition games with the goblin shark at their annual party.

Derek called War Julio and gave him the name of the toy company. He knew the guy loved all kinds of fish and tasty morsels from the ocean. He knew that War Julio would have fun with them and might be able to use the toys in his advertising commercials.

War Julio did contact the toy place and ordered twelve plastic coelacanth sharks. It was another deep-sea shark that long ago possibly moved on land. The toy contained a small plastic lung inside that lit up, large jaws, and its fins moved like human arms. Scientists thought this type of fish were possibly extinct, but then one washed up on the coast of South Africa in the late 1930s, rising like Lazarus. War Julio always liked the Lazarus story because his grandmother would read it to him on a Sunday morning. It was her favorite. It was too bad the coelacanth shark didn't jump out of the water a little bit. Oh, well, it would still be a fun toy.

In paleontology, a Lazarus was a taxon. It could disappear and reappear years later, having been raised from the dead. War Julio bought two for the kids and ten for Derek, plus he ordered batteries and other items per Derek's instructions.

War Julio read online about the motorized large, gray, huge, top-surfacing shark fins that moved in a circular fashion and then moved counterclockwise. He bought four of them. He saw the life-like plastic Japanese orange and cream-colored spider crabs that were motorized. He became fascinated with those toys, too. He was like a kid in a specialty toy shop. The legs of the spider crab moved, and their bodies lit up at night. The toy was guaranteed to add an eerie glow to the surrounding water. He knew some jellyfish glowed in the dark from a green fluorescent protein in their body.

He checked with the company and they didn't have any jellyfish, but thought it was another great idea for their future toy line. They were thinking about the jumping coelacanth, too. War Julio asked if the toy company had the toys he wanted with remote controls. They did. He bought four of the eight-foot size spider crabs. He thought Derek and Jess's kids would like to play with those items when they arrived plus one each for him and Derek to compete with in a race.

Then War Julio saw the motorized air-boats and bought two of those. The motorized air-boats sirens made noise and fake guns sent sparkler light outward. He knew Justin would like that item. War Julio bought rope to teach Justin how to tie all the knots that he learned in a boating class. He signed the roster to retake the class with Justin.

He bought a large treasure chest for Sami and filled it with fake jewelry, pearls, crowns, masks, silk scarves, hats, and miniature satin old-world dresses, capes, and shoes for her to enjoy. His boys made a heavy white cardboard castle and bought colored markers and stencils for her to decorate it.

War Julio signed Sami and Mary Beth up for a cookie class with his wife while Jim, Justin, and War Julio took a snorkeling class. The females signed up for a fencing class with Sami having her class with the fake plastic sword.

Jim, Justine, and War Julio learned how to use underwater diving gear and spear fishing guns practicing on fake bull's-eyed shark targets. If there was extra time, the females could take a snorkeling class while the boys went fishing.

They went for a ride with War Julio's wife on his special high-speed air-boat touring the harbors and island shores. The Miami guys provided them protection along with his Curacao people. War Julio didn't have many toys or friends growing up and was glad when the Wright children arrived with the Michaels.

His new Miami wife helped him with everything. She believed the cookie class worked, because small people liked sweet stuff. She thought the children would take to the spider crab toys. Friendships were instant between War Julio's wife and the children.

10   Head Out to First Coordinates

FINALLY, THE MOTORBOAT and Jim's boat cruised out together from Dakar to the first dive site and the first coordinates given on the small papyrus. They lost two days diving when a monsoon storm blew in. After they were past the harbor entrance, they cranked the engines higher to move the boats at a fast clip.

Anxious to drop anchor before nightfall and hook the winch to the smaller boat, their coordinates would fast approach on their guidance system. Extra gas and oil were put onboard the fishing boat down in the hold in special tanks and compartments. This dive site was the farthest out than the rest of the coordinates from the coast.

Derek, Jess, crew, protection team, and their divers watched as the peninsula of Dakar disappeared in the distance. This body of water was the second largest of the world's ocean, the Atlantic Ocean or its other name, Sea of Atlas. The floor of the Atlantic could reach depths of twelve thousand feet or more and the ocean contained high salinity on the surface water. The salinity was higher than the other oceans and hence, made things deteriorate fast.

The people on the motorboat saw hundreds of small, long, and narrow boats called pirogues leave shore. The pirogues, led by African fishermen and their families, would cruise out four miles from the coast and throw out their green nets in the hope the catch that day would be sufficient to take to market and feed their families.

The fishing ban for pelagic fish was extended to twenty nautical miles in Senegal. The coastal pelagic fish inhabit water up to six hundred or so feet in depth and include fish such as swordfish, tuna, mackerel, sharks, anchovies, sardines, chad, and other predatory fish. Only some of the large fishing boats were allowed licenses by the government to catch the bigger fish in their territory. It was an attempt to control the fishing industry around Senegal's waters.

There were also the international oil company ships that were working blocks of boundaries licensed to them by the African country. The motorboat saw some of these large commercial ships in the distance as well as many other ships carrying their cargo. Derek was sure some of those cargoes carried illegal items. He talked with his captain about some of the ways ships hid cargo.

Then Derek laughed because if they found any treasure, they would carry hidden objects onboard his ship. He wondered how many fish were kept illegally anyway. The unreality of legal and illegal hit him. It just depended on whose viewpoint, which government was involved, and how people could manipulate things. He was a good manipulator.

The motorboat dropped anchor and Jim's fishing boat was secured to its special cable. The chef made their favorite soup called Bouillabaisse Seafood and Clam Stew. There were homemade sea-salt crackers and pepper cheese breadsticks. Bottles of water were opened as they ate wonderful white sponge cake rolled with lemon sauce inside.

All the divers sat down on the main deck and relaxed when Skid Peters told them the story about one of the possible African coastline shipwrecks.

Skid talked, "The Dartman ship sank in May of 1788 or was it 1787? No, no, it was 1788. I need to warn my audience that I'm an experienced shipwreck storyteller, but there are so many that I sometimes forget and must shake the water out of my ears. You see, the water clogs up my thinking.

His audience whistled, cheering him on.

"I do sometimes embellish things. My audience must first understand that wet-eared deep-sea divers are never considered humanoids."

The hook worked, and he gained their attention. "Humanoids could be beings that resembled humans. Were they real or not? Could they disappear? Were they good or bad?"

The divers wondered what the creatures of the deep thought of them. They didn't look human with their masks and gear on. Their bodies were camouflaged in dark suits. The diving crew previously went to the museum in Dakar and saw some of the artifacts from the sunken ships. Some of the divers had been with Skid before on prior dives and admired his intelligence. He also was tenacious and untiring whenever they needed to work under the ocean. They were willing to be entertained.

Skid put his water bottle down.

"The ship, owned by a British East India Company, was the style of boat called, what else, the East Indiaman. The ship which was one hundred fifty feet long by thirty-eight feet wide by sixteen feet deep weighed nine hundred sixty tons. A fully rigged ship of one hundred fifteen crew and twenty-eight guns ran aground off Cape Verde on its second voyage. It was a total complete loss for the company as the first voyage was not profitable either."

"No one knows for sure what happened to the minds of the crew. Some thought it could be stress, overwork, fever, tainted rum, or just plain the stupidest newbies around. The crew on that ship became belligerent and refused to do their work. There was no teamwork. Nothing got done. A person can't count on this lazy crew. It was a sad day when the captain chose them. Someone should have noticed the nothingness expression in their eyes."

Skid took a drink of his water because he ate too many salt crackers earlier. "The officers did the work. This made the captain nervous and then mad. The captain told the crew to move the water barrels. When nothing happened, he turned the command into an order. Still nothing. The frustration level was very high in both arenas. Hence the captain made his decision and arrested four men. But over half the crew still refused to obey the work orders. The captain refused to give them food that evening. He would give them nothing for nothing."

Skid asked his audience, "Are you still with me or did you fall into a dark sleep? I do see something in your eyes which I'm glad to see."

"We are with you," responded his audience.

"When a crew doesn't obey the captain, what was the word that popped into the brain?"

Skid stopped his narrative. They said the correct word.

"Mutiny."

"Yes, that was exactly what went through the captain's brain. Fear caused the man to make a bad decision."

Skid pointed, "What was that bad decision?"

"The captain turned the boat around," said the divers in unison.

"Due to the weight of the cargo, the ship sat lower in the water. Instantly, the ship hit the runaway reef. The ship, Dartman, made it in the history books forever. The ship was now nothing but broken pieces of wood in the salty ocean. Humanoids brought that ship down. In 1789 or a little thereafter or maybe it was later than that. Anyway, some smart divers recovered some of the ship's salvage in their underwater, *let's search for sunken ship treasure* bright minds."

His diver friends knew where the story continued.

Skid asked, "How much did those wonderful bright diver friends find?"

Skid looked at his audience and felt confident they knew the answer. He said, "Hoorah, what were the inanimate objects?"

The audience responded, "Eighty-five thousand three hundred silver coins."

"Thank the audience, my witty comrades. I was told to keep the story short, because there is much work to do in the morning. My next story will be longer. The show was over, and now it is time to say adieu."

The divers boarded the smaller boat for the night.

Derek's crew and protection team set up their guard schedules. Derek and Jess went to the master bedroom.

"Don't you want to try the third bedroom like old times instead of the master bedroom as it is currently empty?"

"No, but I will take a long shower with music and could go for a glass of champagne."

Derek raced to the kitchen for the bottle, glasses, and opener and went back to the master bedroom and locked the door. They would drink a little bit of the golden liquid. After making wonderful love, she told Derek, "It is good to be on the motorboat again. I'm happy you wanted to go on this expedition. I feel fascinating feelings going on in my brain."

"I know other places you have that are fascinating. But I love your brain, too, even if it works strange sometimes."

"You better watch out. I know where you keep your handcuffs."

Derek hauled her off the bed with the top sheet and pretended he was going to throw her overboard. He took her to the third bedroom instead. After they were satiated from their fantasy dream in their familiar domain, they were filled with memories of their past.

Jess told him, "I miss our children, but did receive a note from Jim that they arrived safely. They were going for a ride the next day on War Julio's boat. Our children called it the pirate air-pop machine. The children were fascinated by the photo on your cell phone, but were surprised at its size when they saw it in the harbor."

"I wish Dean could have been on board the motorboat and gone with us to Curacao. He enjoyed War Julio's antics."

"His spirit definitely was on board. He would be on the top deck and hollering orders." said Derek.

"Yes, he would have done exactly that while wearing one of his captain hats. Oh, I forgot your present," said Jess.

She took the object out of her drawer and put it on his head. It was a captain's hat from Senegal.

"You now look official. By the way, Skid was an imaginative storyteller."

"Thanks for the hat, honey. I love it. The crew will like it, too. Wait until Skid told everyone about the Aguamala ship. He likes to play with the storylines."

"Oh, dear, I read a book from Louisa's collection. Out of an average guess of eighty or so shipwrecks around the African coastline, he picked that one."

11   Sub at First Coordinates

FIFTY MILES OFF the coast of Dakar were the ten volcanic islands called the Cape Verde Islands where many diving groups each year congregated to go scuba diving. The best time for arrival was February to April. But that timeframe didn't fit into their plans. They wanted as few divers as possible around them. The area was not that busy when the motorboat anchored carefully. They stayed in deeper water away from the islands. There were over fifty shipwrecks around these group of islands and they weren't going to be included in the number.

On their day off, some of the Wright's divers went to the capital, Praia, at the Republic of Cabo Verde, to see the shipwreck artifacts there. They took along two of the Miami boys who spoke Portuguese for any protection from the African and mixed European heritage people. Unknown cities presented a problem on occasion with diving teams. They were cautious to stay out of the low-income bars. The locals thought that divers were rich with all their priceless gear. They didn't know that the gear was occasionally all they really owned.

The Miami boys picked up a package close to the airport that Derek ordered. It was a special digger arm that would fit on the sub. He told them to handle the object with great care. They needed the arm due to the heavy sand on the ocean floor.

Dean Crain bought this wonderful diving submersible. The sub's capabilities included descent of one thousand feet and could hold two people. The first dive site was only five hundred fifty feet down and the rest of the coordinates were much less than that.

The sub contained two detachable manipulator robotic arms and was an exceptional piece of equipment, probably overkill, which was their typical Dean person. He always bought the best because he could afford it. The battery pack could last eight hours, and it contained up and down thrusters as well as fore and aft thrusters. There were extra battery packs onboard. Five external halogen lamps were on the sub and VHF radio for surface communication.

There was room enough on the sub for extra life support and gear. Made of glass and lightweight epoxy composite, it could travel two to eight knots. It was fast and could ascent at six hundred fifty feet per minute. The sub included all the standard instruments and the depth, temperature, and pressure gauges. There was magnetic compass and a guidance system receiver. Dean also installed spear guns hidden in side panels to shoot anything strange that might appear that acted threatening toward the sub.

The crew traded off during the rest of the week exploring their gridded coordinates at this location. The divers were enthralled with the sub's electronics and mechanicals on board. Everyone that drove the sub felt a high when they came off their shift. Brin and Jay Taylor were moved to the second team of sub experts. Skid and Derek were the first team on their daily dive schedule. Skid taught the rest of the crew how to handle everything. Even Jess drove the sub and took lessons. The crew checked out the other equipment on the motorboat.

Dean also obtained a smaller scuba craft vehicle that could cruise two to eighteen knots and descend capability three hundred fifty feet. The scuba craft could take a maximum of three divers to operating depth one hundred FSW (feet salt water). They would only use two divers on the craft. The vehicle was prop driven and contained two of the two-hundred-forty-volt batteries. The battery life was approximately ninety minutes. The scuba craft would require independent scuba equipment to breathe. The craft would be used later for the shallower water dives if needed or as an intermediate drop off any smaller cargo to bring to the surface.

All the gear was the latest in high tech and top of the line. The tanks were various mixes of oxygen and nitrogen with some of the tanks for deeper diving filled with a trimix to include helium. Various types of rebreathers were on board which could recirculate exhaled gas for reuse, so a diver only needed to carry a fraction of gas. A rebreather added gas to compensate for compression when depth increased and vented gas to prevent over expansion. The closed-circuit rebreathers produced no bubbles and less gas hissing which was perfect for entering sunken ships.

After no luck on the first coordinate grid site, part of the dive crew took two days off and then the two boats met at the shallower second site. Derek and Jess relaxed for the first time. Their pace had been hectic and a learning experience for the Wrights.

"The diving teams did a thorough job at the first coordinates. It was great their friend, Dean, selected the best diving teams for this area. We could still be on the sub wandering the ocean floor. Plus, you shot some great underwater photos and started part of your video recordings at the first site. Do we want to add the narration and sound now?"

"I want us to wait. The write-ups are done, but some of the write-ups will change."

"How do you think the write-ups will change because I read them? The starting tone of the book is great. You nailed it beautifully."

"I feel strange. I cannot explain it. Somehow, I dreamed about Louisa who seemed troubled."

Derek knew to listen carefully to Jess. "What was the dream?"

"Louisa forgot something."

"Oh, no." Dreams or visions could mean something good or anything else.

Derek, being a mere mortal, knew to wait. He knew Jess was knowledgeable in ways that he was not. Sometimes women knew things and saw things way differently. He trusted her totally now. Derek hadn't in the past. Dean pointed out to them one day that they needed to do just that, trust each other.

He looked at Jess and knew the answer immediately. "We need to wait until later to add narration and sound."

"I think waiting is a wise decision. I wonder what she forgot?"

Now Derek worried. He scanned the ocean as far as he could see.

12   Santan Chesin's Party

SANTAN KNEW A large motorboat from America was in the area with divers searching for sunken treasure. There was someone always searching, but this motorboat was large. It raised suspicion and curiosity in his brain. "The American's motorboat looked expensive and contained a helicopter" was the information provided by his captain.

Expensive meant rich. Rich was the attraction for Santan. He wanted to know who these people were from America. They traveled a long way to reach Dakar. The Americans must know information. He needed to find out what they knew.

His network of people extended to the islands around Cape Verde. His men checked out the background of the rich American couple who moved their boat to Dakar on a transport ship. They were supposedly on vacation as they were seen in town with their children in Dakar. Santan didn't believe the vacation story. They were on a business venture. He could feel it. He knew he was correct in that assessment. He was always correct.

"What were they up to?"

Santan itched to have a party and his girls were pressuring him for one.

"Why not party? Digging for sunken treasure could wait. If he didn't find any, maybe he could steal it. He was tired of looking for objects underwater."

He felt in a good mood and would even let the girls have their beloved reggae music. Everything could be bought. Santan knew how to purchase items locally and from far away. Airplanes flew into Dakar all the time. There was no place other than his supreme pleasurable home for the party. A party right now was up his alley. Santan could hardly wait.

"My girls will fawn over me. Their thankfulness was what I require. I have plenty of time. The Wrights just arrived so I can delay my activities for a few days more. My coffers now are all right. The weather will be perfect. No storms on the horizon yet. Besides, it's an expense that I can deduct. Bring on all the beautiful woman. They don't need an invitation. Or I can send them a simple invitation. They will love the invite. They will want me. My business associates will feel honored to come."

Santan felt ebullient. There was nothing that he couldn't buy. He was full of himself and anything his diamonds could buy. The party was buoying him higher and the dismalness feeling vanished. He was the god for the evening or week. Santan knew that he was king over his empire.

Caterers were hired and extra hogshead (barrels) of rum were ordered. His black tribe members who were for night security were given invitations. Some of his girls snuck invitations for the two undercover female cops, Rhonda White and Tami Cortez.

Jinx, the undercover detective, would also be at the party. He really liked one of Santan's girlfriends, Ruse Blake. She was a redhead and fascinated him, but it was too dangerous to talk with her very much. Santan's cameras were everywhere and the boss was protective of any advances on his women in his house.

Jinx checked his ammunition just in case it was required for the party because Santan had asked. There was a drug smuggler from Africa who would appear for a short time at the party. Jinx must watch him per Santan's explicit instructions. Jinx would continue to follow his boss at the party and hang close. This was someone Santan feared. It was this specific man. Jinx had only seen the man once before. He was a big man. Santan knew the drug smuggler was more powerful than himself.

Most of Santan's guests arrived in their glittered finery and old jewels and new jewels. A huge nautilus ice sculpture overflowed with champagne. There were tables filled with mangoes and other melon fruit.

Dishes consisted of dried and flavored peanuts, salads of green beans and tomatoes, plus anchovy or sardine appetizers with massive quantities of shrimp and tuna. There consisted very special cooked chicken on bamboo skewers. They were organically-fed chickens from a special farm in Guinea. In other words, they were expensive. Rolled breads and sweet dates (flown in) waited on a tall glass tower that spiraled in steps to the table-top.

The cake was a delectable chocolate cake in the shape of a four-foot monster shark with pink frosting for his girls. The shark was on a bed of large palm leaves and white orchids. His girls swooned when they saw it, walking around the special table brought in to showcase the shark. The top was aqua-blue glass to imitate the ocean. They had heard about the wealthy African guest coming to the party and believed the cake was made to impress the man.

Santan's half keg of rum and the two extra kegs of rum that were delivered were not rum, but the hated whiskey. This was not good. He must have his rum. Sending two of the black tribe men to town to get the required rum, four of them went. Those four men were picked up by the cops who found a small stash of drugs in their vehicle. Consequently, security for the night became a little lighter.

Santan conversed with his narco drug trafficker friend from Guinea-Bissau. He dared not call him the African. His name was Sphinx and was a real scary person to talk with, so Santan wanted to keep things light. It was, after all, a party. He let him know he was disappointed his new beautiful friend was not at his wonderful party. He enjoyed the man's choice in women. Perhaps she could come to the next one.

The Sphinx told Santan that he needed to talk to the new black tribe leader and then he would leave. The Sphinx hadn't come to party. He was not in the mood. Santan watched the drug trafficker walk away. Santan knew how the predator hierarchy worked. The Sphinx was higher in the chain. Turning toward his other familiar guests, he saw the young woman in the red dress. She was talking to his man, Jinx. Jinx next moved toward Santan.

"You must have stopped her briefly for interrogation because you never bother my guests. Of course, you're attracted to her, too. The woman looked amazing with matching red satin platform shoes and my favorite hair color which is blonde."

Santan strolled over to her with every blood vessel in his body in a heightened erotic alert mode. Smelling her expensive cologne five feet from her, he inhaled flowers. Rhonda saw the little guy approach and knew that expression on his face was not good. It was his bedroom-crazy look like a shark circling its prey. One of his girls had warned her about that look. She looked at the shark cake. Santan wanted her friend, Tami, for the evening all to himself in his very large bed with the brazen, super-vulgar female paintings. Santan was the shark. The cake was just an imitation.

Santan approached Tami. "I'm Santan, the owner of this extravagant piece of real estate, and I wondered who the beautiful creature was across the room that entered my strong fortress. I very much came over to talk with you."

Tami also knew the look. Blond she was, but dumb was not one of them. This person thought he was important, but not on her highly-tuned scale. She knew she could handle him. Tami knew the type. Miami was full of the critters. They were demented deviants. She thought to herself, *jail bait*.

Tami turned graciously and said, "My creature name is Tami. I love the very pretty ice sculpture, Nautilus, which was the same name as Nemo's ship long ago. The gold-flecked pool tile is extraordinaire. I also love the poolside flamboyant navy and blue colors. They help accentuate the spectacular pool. Strong fortresses are a draw for beautiful women. Always a good choice for an impressive person who is in twenty thousand leagues of their own. You must enjoy this wonderful, expensive oasis."

Rhonda took a sip of her drink to stop her laughter. Tami was always good at assessing a creature or man. She accurately assessed the creature in front of her.

Santan was a goner and hadn't even drunk his normal quota of rum. He knew this girl was sexy, more beautiful than that expensive pool, and her depth of knowledge was vast. He loved educated. She knew big words and that meant smart. He could be entertained just listening to her. He wanted to love wonderful her and feel extraordinary.

He needed smart people to join his team. She fitted into his number 1 gold tribe. Tami spoke with this strong voice and looked very tan. He thought she was absolutely an outside girl. Her image would be an upgrade in his group. Encouraged by her comments, he wanted to impress her.

So Santan said, "My expensive lifestyle included owning this deep-sea diving ship that matched my flamboyant navy poolside oasis. My ship is navy-colored and large. We will move to another diving expedition soon. Would you care to join me?"

Santan saw her hesitation. "I graciously gave my crew the rest break they required and I decided to throw this party in the interim."

Santan decided to inform her of his first coordinates so she would see that he was knowledgeable about such things.

Tami smiled. She had checked his Website. Not anything good was happening there.

Santan smiled because he thought that he had impressed her. Santan was clueless. Tami could hardly wait to exit this scene.

"You could stay aboard my ship during the dive as my guest. I can show you more than impressive. I could buy you flamboyant. I love fortresses, too, and the Nautilus. Unfortunately, twenty thousand leagues are beyond my mere ship. But I can always try. Anything you desire is worth trying."

Rhonda was moved closer to Jinx to tell him that she needed help. Jinx slid over to his boss and distracted Santan.

She wanted to move Tami out of there fast. Jinx had noticed the important narco drug guy move toward the door. Santan was alerted about his other guest's pending departure.

Tami smiled at the little sap, Santan.

"Not this time because I must attend a previous engagement. Perhaps I can get with you another time. Everything is worth trying."

Santan kissed her hand and let her go. There would always be another dive and an opportunity to meet with Tami. Tami had moved him. He couldn't explain why. There was salty ocean filled with sunsets and rum with her. Santan relished the thought. He turned to his other extremely valuable, scary guest. His man, Jinx, was watching his back by being prudent.

Rhonda talked with Tami outside as they left the party. In the car driving back to the girl's apartment Rhonda said, "Don't ever go on the diving boat as you will have no protection. The only way you can be safe on that boat is to have a bazooka gun that was invisible."

"Weren't we supposed to try and get into his safe tonight?"

Rhonda told her that Santan didn't drink enough liquor. His staff and friends, however, enjoyed the whiskey too much. Rhonda told her the police would try again soon, but not today.

"Where can I get an invisible shoulder-fired bazooka? I want the heat-type warhead. Did they make a nuclear one yet? No, way too much blast. The fallout crap would go everywhere. How about a laser one? Pin-point the villain within a millimeter. Was a surgical millimeter one and the same?"

Rhonda laughed and told her that she was as crazy as ever. Tami laughed because it was fun being around bad boys again. The adrenalin kicked up a notch. That was an amazing high. Tami loved her part-time jobs.

The guests left, and Santan went to bed. Jinx went to the security room in the house to relieve the other guard who went to the kitchen to eat some of the leftover tuna and party food. Then the security system went down. Jinx went out to the power box and flipped a few switches and the power came back on.

It was enough time for one of the girls to open the safe in Santan's room. She drugged Santan so that he would be out. She pulled her cell phone from her pocket and quickly took pictures of the three pages of documents for an upcoming diamond heist.

In the hall, she ran into Jinx who noticed her cell phone and guilty expression. Jinx said, "Hello, Ruse Blake, why were you in Santan's room and why are you leaving so quickly?"

Ruse knew Jinx liked her. Ruse decided that she could tell him part of the truth. She said, "I forgot my cell phone in there."

"It is all right because I won't tell our boss."

Ruse would ask the girls later if they should let Jinx know their plans to rob Santan. She wet her lips.

"Would you like to meet me for a drink sometime?"

Jinx liked Ruse's red hair and wondered what she was hiding. Jinx accepted their date and told himself that it was because of his police work.

13   Second Set of Coordinates

THE MOTORBOAT AND other boat were anchored and battened down for the night when a bigger storm, a freak monsoon started around the Cape Verde area. In the morning, they checked everything for minor damage and they were just fine. Their new anchor system held. A couple snaps came loose on the canopy on Jim's boat. They heavily taped the corner until they could get a new strip of canvas replaced there.

They used the sub again due to the large number of schools of fish in the area after the storm. It was a good thing because they ran into a few sharks which were coming into shallower water to feed. The ocean water was still murky from the storm the first day.

After twenty-one exhaustive dive days, they were done with the second grid and didn't find anything worthwhile. Some wrecks farther south issued no reward as they were pretty much picked clean of any valuables. Derek and Jess gave the crew four days off. Skid would stay on board.

Their crew was going to take Jim's fishing boat back to Dakar for more sightseeing in the morning. Derek selected a time and rendezvous point to meet again before they went together to the third set of coordinates.

The weary group ate dinner and settled down for popcorn and light beer before turning in for the evening. The divers put ice in their cups of beer to dilute it further.

Derek brought Jess a bottled water. He showed her the champagne opener hidden in his hands. Jess laughed. She told him that she wanted to try the ice-cubed beer with a little tomato juice. He groaned and thought it was a crime to put anything in beer. She knew what Derek wanted to do after the show. He was buoyed up about something, probably her.

Skid asked, "Ready for another sunken ship story? I warn you this story is longer than the last one so please get comfortable. I assume by your enraptured faces, you are ready. Oh, yes, you are ready. I see the nods. This one is about the Spanish frigate ship, *Aguamala*, and its shipwreck. Do you know the story about this ship? No more nods, I want to see the hands."

All the divers knew the story and raised their hands, wiggling them back and forth.

Skid raised his hand and there was a rubberized plastic, fake, barnacled-looking glove all the way to his elbow. He wiggled his hand.

His divers laughed.

Derek whispered to Jess, "Be ready for crazy and spooky."

"Who names a ship after the word jellyfish? *Aguamala*, seriously? Why not *Sea Wasp*? There are so many other super words which can be used to describe the ocean's body or its creatures. Maybe they should have named the vessel, *Beach-in Boat*. Think about it. Soft-sand beach means pretty women, blue skies, coconut-flavored rum, music, and fun times. It would have been a more positive, forward-thinking name."

Skid's audience was wondering where he was taking them on the story.

"These jellyfish are water, like probably 95 percent. What were they thinking? It makes a person believe that maybe their mind was running at 5 percent which was truly considered subliminal level."

Skid sighed.

"The jellies are known as a strange gelatinous and bell-shaped, tentacle celled-stinging invertebrate. It belongs to the Scyphozoan class. Doesn't that word sound like psycho? The Spanish, who were sailing in the *box jellies'* favorite waters, did not realize the name was a bad idea."

"Box jellies can be killers. Why? They are invisible or very transparent. Divers have a hard time seeing them. Perhaps they thought it was a good name, for the invertebrate has been around over five hundred million years. Maybe they liked to think they were invisible. But then, so have beaches been around since forever. Beaches, however, don't usually disappear. They are cloaked in rotting seaweed mostly, especially after a storm. Once dried, the seaweed is great for a bonfire. I do digress. Fish are good to eat at a bonfire. It's like eating a filleted wiener on a forked stick. But am I making any sense?"

His divers agreed. They were enjoying the riddle.

"Alas, the name most definitely was never a good idea. Psycho reigned supreme on the *Aguamala*. The ship, launched in 1805 with thirty-eight guns weighing one thousand forty tons with one hundred fifty or so people on board. The ship did run aground on another reef in October 1814 which was around today's country, Mauritania area. Yes, we know the box jellyfish live there. We don't know if anyone got stung. Perhaps it was daylight when they hit the reef. Jellies sleep then. But we do know this ship originally was headed for Dakar."

Skid pointed in the direction of the African coast.

"The same type of problem occurred as the other ship story."

Skid turned back to his audience and whispered slowly, "Human annoyed. Yes, it was a humanoid problem."

Jumping up and down, Skid crouched. "Another not so good idea was a person's name. What villain's name rhymes with life?"

The audience responded, "Dian La Vida."

"What type of high-ranking job did the man hold on the ship? I'll give you a hint; he wore a uniform."

His friends groaned.

"You didn't like my hint?"

"Captain!" His team cried in unison.

"It was a classic case of inexperienced newbie plus possibly a really scared, helpless, or inane crew. Perhaps this shows us an example of a good time for the crew to find courage and go forth with the illegal deed to get them back to land." Skid pointed to them.

They responded, "Mutiny."

"Correct."

Skid went on to explain. "Navigation and weather concepts can be difficult to learn and grasp. Pearls of wisdom do not always reach everyone. Too late do they start measuring the depth of the unforgiving ocean? The crew notice the larger waves are replaced by tighter little waves. The captain told them to not heed the ocean. Who does not heed the ocean's warning?"

The divers shook their heads because they paid attention whenever they dived in all depths of ocean water. It was critical to their survival. They were careful and constantly monitored their gear. The divers knew that they wanted to live and enjoy their off-boat time chilling on the beach with their friends. They had been on dives with arrogant people. They knew to avoid them.

"The ship had arrived in the land of the forever-known precarious zone. It was called in layman's terms, *shallow water*. What mostly exists in shallow water around these parts? We know fish or sea urchins would be a good answer by a land person. You know what lies out there in the shallows. We try to avoid them, too."

Skid held his hands together in a large circle and danced in a sideways line like the true actor he was.

His diver friends responded, "Reefs!"

"Exactly right. Long and large, dark reefs are there, silently waiting. The reefs were ready. After hitting the shallow water reef, the ship tilted. It was stuck and became a beached whale on a barren hard ground. This was not a good place to park a ship. For it truly was parked and showed large holes. The ocean sloshed in and out of the doomed ship."

"In those days of old, a busted ship can go nowhere so the crew must build another one. Wonderful idea, but the crew wasn't very good at building anything. Nor parking. I wonder how they approached a dock. Threw the lines, jumped, and prayed probably. I digress. The real problem was time. They had mostly spent their time elsewhere in the local pub. Navigation and now boat building concepts were too much. No engineers were on board to build a smaller ship or bond boards together and carve points. They could have dropped the cannons as anchors and put the bonded pier boards into the water locking them to the canons somehow. Then a floating tiki hut could be built on the supports. There were plenty of tarps for the roof. There were nets. Fish were plentiful in the shallows. There were many crew members available to try fishing. They could have carved sticks and somehow used the cannonballs to build a fire pit. See, fish on a stick! Next, there possibly could appear another ship to rescue them. Or just send the launches who, once they made it to shore, could send a relief ship. Then they suddenly remembered how to make small rafts. Seriously, a raft? The older men wondered about rafts. They asked the question: *don't rafts leak or sink?* But the captain and his officers influenced the crew to pursue this course of action. They asked themselves, how hard can building two rafts be? The men ducked into the bottom of the ship and dragged out the saws, hammers, ropes, and more nails. Man-cave tools were in their burly hands. They were in seventh heaven."

Skid took another sip of water, shook his empty bottle, and placed it beside him.

"Heaven or the opposite was nearby. There were approximately eighty men counting the stowaways who created two rafts. Half were put into each makeshift raft. They wave goodbye to the skeletal shape left of the helpless, doomed ship. It would not last throughout the night. The tools were thrown in the salt water to rust away along with the useless cannonballs. They surely wouldn't need them. Space was needed for the essentials. The weight could tip the raft. The old men hated to see the cannonballs sink. They glumly felt the weight of their souls fall with each ball."

Skid chucked the plastic bottle in the trash, hoping to make a point.

"The plan was for the launches from the ship to tow the rafts to shore forty miles away. Small sails are put on the launches to help speed the journey and the tarps are hidden from the raft people. No, they won't share those tarps. The items were good for a shield against the sun and rain on the launches. A few torn sails were given to the rafts to figure out how to resurrect them. You're thinking. Not fair. I see it in your expression."

Skid looked up at the clear night sky as did the divers. He put his finger in the air. The divers knew what was coming.

"Not such a good idea to do rafts. They hurried. The food wouldn't last forever. Fish was a diet that might have worked if they could have caught some before leaving. They worried. Another storm could really sink their launches and rafts. It was better to go. How far was the distance? Too far. A gale did blow across the ocean because it was the monsoon season at that point in time. Everyone here knows about monsoons. Who was in the wrong place when the storm hit?"

Stew stopped and folded his arms like a college professor standing at a lectern.

"How strong was the gale on the Beaufort scale in this monsoon? We don't know because the measure from 0 to 12 wasn't implemented until years later. Ship navigators don't use wind speed numbers or additional scales until the twentieth century. Was it a slight gale or one where no sail could withstand the wind?"

Moving his arms to show a filled sail as any actor would, Skid continued. "We are told that what appeared on the ocean were monster waves, worse than any Halloween nightmare. Those launches feared for their lives and did a sinister deed. They tossed the ropes back to the two rafts, setting them free. Who was free to live? The captain, of course, and his group quickly sail away in their safe launch. The two rafts separate in the storm. The one raft broke apart and disappeared forever. Maybe the tools would have helped. Anyway, too late to think about that. Its crew did not live. No life or beaches for them. They joined the box jellyfish world."

His audience looked sad.

"The old saying, *only the strong shall live*, was true for the second raft. It was the strong who lived, only those that were friends who lived, and only one's necessary were kept on the final adrift raft. If the huge ocean waves didn't knock people off the raft, the humanoids did, especially anyone breaking the rules. Those old and ill quietly slipped in the water because they couldn't hold on anymore. But then they shouldn't have thrown anybody off the raft because suddenly, they were in a dead zone in the ocean. It was almost as if a hundred or more bullets were shot around that raft for fifty miles. All the wine and food eaten. No water, no land, only madness and salty ocean exists. There was nary a fish in sight. There was nothing but the still ocean for thousands of more miles and tropical, hot, dry heat. Soon, people on the raft began to look at each other as not good friends. After twelve very long days at sea, their number was decimated to six men. A pall envelops the final scene on the second raft. Would they disappear, too? How deep was the ocean where they are? Does it matter? They aren't going to feel anything when their bones reach the bottom."

Derek reached for Jess's hand. He knew the story. Jess shook her head. She was waiting to reach the conclusion.

"Finally, the half-baked, half-gone skeletal men see a ship's frame in the distance. The men sit on the raft and do not move. It seems pointless to hope for a rescue. Next a fish jumps out of the water awakening them from their trance. Electrified into action, they try to wave and flag her down with a small piece of tattered sail left on the rotting raft. My friends know the Portuguese ship named *H. Azores* was sighted in the area and does a dos-a-dos dance. The ship maneuvers back and forth and dips like a goshawk raptor around the Azores Islands."

Skid turned to his friends. "What happened to that lifesaving ship? Think ghost-like, my friends, my very close and knowledgeable, good diver friends."

The friends clinked their iced beers together and said, "Disappeared."

"Now a very low cloud surrounded the raft. The half-men, half-skeletons know they are doomed. The raptor-named ship moved out of range and there were no more Lazarus fish near this raft that was going to revive or save them. Perhaps it was that mention of the one single word in last minute prayers. The word was Lazarus. Do they know about Lazarus?"

"Yes, they did," responded the diver friends.

"A heavenly wind rippled the water ahead of the Portuguese ship. Not the tiny zephyr wind, but a strong wind. The ship was forced to turn and heeled over when it caught full wind. Its sails strain to push the heavy ship quickly. Her back-to-back dance complete, the *H. Azores* ship, glided over the ocean with amazing speed. The lookout men on the *H. Azores* were true hawks who saw the barely standing dead with their long scopes. Saved by the large ship, the small group of men on the raft go home to tell the horrible, cruel tale."

Skid picked up a pair of binoculars and viewed his audience. "Now my extremely knowledgeable diver mateys, what is your verdict? I know you're bright because you know about goshawks and Lazarus."

Skid looked at his audience over the rims of the binoculars, scanning their faces.

The divers replied in unison, "Guilty".

"The ship's captain was tried by his countrymen and found lacking in many ways. The captain was negligent in his duties to protect ship and crew from harm. He complained the men didn't use their heads to survive. The courts did favor the gentry. Yet there was concern that the captain did pick his crew. He should be made accountable for those facts. His sentence for his lack in judgment?" asked Skid.

"Two years," said his audience.

"That is correct. Two measly years were given for loss of those human lives. His sentence should have parked him on an empty island with the stonefish and jellies. Flip a coin, food or poison could have been on his menu every day."

Skid told them the story ended. "You decide. Select your captains, but be wise and careful. Fairness in the world was sometimes naught. Be safe while under the deep and on earth's surface."

He saluted his team and bowed.

The divers clapped and turned in for the night, happy to be on the Wright's ship.

Jess told Derek, "Definitely felt spooky madness."

Derek received the call from Tami after the divers turned in. Tami let Derek know Santan would be at their third set of coordinates in four days' time. Two competitor boats would be at the same location at the same time.

Derek didn't want to place Jess that close to this Santan person. Tami told Derek how intrigued Santan was about her appearance at the party in the red dress and how he invited her to the current dive. Derek warned her that would be extremely unsafe. Derek didn't want Tami or Jess near this bad guy. He knew all about compulsive, obsessive people. Tami and Jess looked very much alike.

Derek looked at Jess and said, "Trouble." They went to their bedroom to discuss the situation. Jess grabbed one of the larger paper chart maps.

"What if we were wrong about the three sets of coordinates? Perhaps the three sets of coordinates were meant to cause confusion. What if the actual shipwreck was located dead center inside the three coordinates?"

Derek looked at Jess. "That was entering the realm of unbelievable."

"Unbelievable but possibly believable. A minute possibility. Or the other concept is that they are real close. What is that expression—only a stone's throw away?"

They looked at the maps and the ferryboat crossed over their new imaginary fourth set of coordinates.

"But the ferry wasn't there when the ship went down."

Derek commented, "That was probably why no one checked this area because of the ferry. What if people passed over the treasure for years? Or was there another something hiding their ship? Like perhaps a newer ship on top or a ridge. The ship could be hidden under a ridge. That can explain why the ship was never found. It must be hidden. Dean's special high-tech metal detector should be mounted on the scuba craft."

"We should drop the motorboat anchors some distance away. We can use the scuba craft at the depth listed on the charts."

Jess told him if they found anything heavy, they could put the bucket on one of the robotic arms to move anything off the ocean floor faster. Derek and Jess brought their maps up to the bridge with the captain of the motorboat to discuss movement of the boat. He informed the crew to mount the metal detector.

Derek reminded his captain to wait until morning before moving the motorboat. Derek would join the captain on the bridge. He would notify their divers about the different rendezvous point in the morning.

Derek asked Jess, "What if the third set of coordinates is the actual winning ticket for the sunken treasure and Santan Chesin's group find the valuable haul? Tami told me their competitor's coordinates. It was mysteriously identical to one of ours from the papyrus. I believe this was not a coincidence."

"Yes, an unlikely coincidence. Someone has Louisa's telescope. Santan is connected. We will just have to figure out a way to steal the treasure back if he finds it."

"You are one of a kind." Dean told him Jess was way ahead of everyone else. Then he remembered the Santan guy.

"No. I would have to figure out a way to steal it for you."

Derek couldn't believe he said that, but he knew sometimes his thoughts about his wife drifted over to unreasonable. Plus, he hated the bad guys barging into his vacation. Glad he would have four days without the diving work and some of the people, he wanted to be together with his wife.

Jess came over and hugged Derek.

It was going to be a good night. She braided a piece of her hair and wore this gold barrette. It was the same gold barrette she had worn in Napa, California, a long time ago when they met a second time. Derek enjoyed the memory of their time in Napa. She was more than the exotic creatures in the deep. Strange, but magical.

"Hold that thought."

When he came back, she told him that the kids were fine in Curacao. She next told him about the wonderful toys War Julio picked up with remote controls on some of them. War Julio's friend hooked up the remotes to his computers.

"I'm glad everything is fine in Curacao. Yes, War Julio bought the remotes. But you are waiting. I hate to keep you waiting." Derek smiled.

"I am waiting and really need you."

"I very much need you, too," said Derek. He danced back to Jess and hit the number 6.5, Calypso song, on their superior sound system. He turned it down low to play only in their bedroom. He took her into his arms. It was where their beating hearts worked well together.

14   The Dolphins and a Deal

THE NEXT MORNING after they ate breakfast, War Julio called Derek and told him that their daughter, Sami, insisted he call them.

The message she received from Louisa was "Look where the dolphins run."

Louisa forgot to tell them that information. Sami and Louisa talked on the phone the day before and then Sami forgot to tell her parents.

After the phone call, their captain alerted them to the unexpected dolphin run off the bow of the motorboat. That morning, just a small distance, five hundred fifty feet to the west of their second set of coordinates ran a pod of dolphins. Derek thought there were about thirty dolphins. There was a whistling sound escaping the dolphins who were feeding on something.

Jess told him about phenomena known as a super pod where there existed thousands of the mammals traveling together. Or even a mega pod could exist. The small group was probably staying together for mating. He knew they could travel speeds over thirty miles per hour, so they needed to stay back from their run.

Jess and Derek were on the bridge watching the amazing sight of ocean churning with dolphins sometimes leaping fourteen feet.

Sardines were their meal May through July when the schools of dolphins ran through, so to see this sight was unusual. Perhaps it was an unusual sight back then by other ships. Derek knew the water temperature must be just right and the sardines followed the colder water northward. The sardines were usually traveling in bait ball shapes, but then the other predators followed such as sharks. Derek didn't see any sharks nor predator birds above.

Jess mentioned echolocation where the dolphin emitted a sonic pulse to locate their prey. The prey were probably mackerel, cod, herring, squid, and shrimp. Maybe not a large enough school to attract the sharks. Dolphins were intelligent and rounded their prey up much like a cowboy herded his cows in a circle to take to market.

Then they came in for the meal. Dolphins didn't chew. They would take larger fish down to the sand and break it into smaller pieces to swallow, expelling any water.

Derek knew there must be sand below their run. Sand would hide a sunken ship for a long time and a reef. He remembered the charts. The dolphin display was a perfect example of survival of the fittest. The downed ship members hadn't, however, survived their run.

Skid joined them top deck to see the end of the dolphin run. Derek put Jess's expensive camera and lenses down. She told him to take the shots. She wanted to watch the show.

Finally, the dolphin feed frenzy subsided.

Derek contacted his captain.

"Turn the motorboat and move a little past the dolphin run. Skid and I are going to take the sub down. We need to check things out."

He handed Jess the camera equipment. Derek was excited. It was a stone's throw away if you knew how to skip a rock properly. Derek could visualize it. He always won the skip.

So much for relaxation.

Skid and Derek found a submerged old ship under the dolphin run. The ship laid in the gulley part of a ridge, buried in sand, almost hidden for centuries. The wood was rotted and looked ancient with corrosion on any metal.

"Honey, we have found a sunken ship."

She could hear the joyful thrill in his voice.

"The ship is almost totally covered in the ocean floor sand," he told her on the submersible radio.

Derek also installed a new video camera inside the sub. Jess could faintly see the broken ship in the water when the underwater lights hit the small piece of broken hull. There was an underwater camera that Derek used for outside the sub to take photographs.

"Pointing the video camera around the sunken ship site now. It looked untouched. I'm going to move around the site to get the lay of the wreck and take close photos. We can assess them later. Can you see clearly on the video feed?"

Jess said, "Yes, pretty much."

"The dungbie or narrow flat stern of the ship is mostly missing, and the small remainder looks heavily burned black with charred broken pieces. The ship most likely was engulfed in fire. It probably took water fast and the fire may have been the cause for the ship's demise to its current resting place. The crew probably didn't have time to lower the launches. The ship appears to have broken apart in four places having descended to the ocean floor quickly with its heavy tonnage."

Derek talked with Skid.

"Per Skid, there appears to be a lot of jagged boards perhaps broken by cannon ball fire. Hitting the ridge, it fractured the upper two-thirds of the ship, leaving just the bottom to fall in the gulley. Those top boards of the ship also show charred wood. It must have heavily burnt before going down. The ship lay pretty much flattened here for almost several centuries. The sand and silt covered it well. We will need the sub digger. The ship's masts and shrouds rotted away, and her cannons are rusted. There are eerie-looking lumps that I think are crates. There are smaller lumps, possibly chests or trunks strewn around. Most of the crates are lying broken in the silt and sand."

Derek found two small lumps. He nudged the bucket into the sand, so the edges were exposed. Derek used the bucket to scoop the two fragile chests and decided to put only one at a time into the bucket on the sub. There were eight smaller chests around, and they would have to come back for them.

They moved the metal detector over a group of the eerie larger flattened crates that were near the bottom center of the sunken ship. Suddenly, one of the larger crates set the metal detector off.

Derek looked at Skid and said, "With a miracle, we may have found the missing Italian ship, *The Cathar*. Or it is a mystery pirate ship with metal that set off the detector."

Skid grinned and nodded. "Do you think we'll have time for another search of the area? There might exist a second ship if this one fired their cannons and hit the target at close range."

If there existed a second pirate ship, Skid would have a new story to create and tell much, much later. He loved pirates.

Derek looked at Skid. "A very good idea, indeed."

XXXXXX

Before their trip, he met with the Italians about this diving expedition with his motorboat in Dakar to search for sunken treasure. Derek told them his proposition that could be a benefit to his business and theirs. He didn't tell them about the small chest of silver coins nor the jewelry that belonged to Louisa Renaliere.

The Italians told him the name of their lost ship was *The Cathar*, a galleon style or the French called it a nef, just under five hundred tons. It was a smaller, faster ship that was designed after the larger and slower carrack ship. The Portuguese and Spanish used the galleon ships a long time ago for oceanic travel and to explore.

The Italians informed Derek that if he found the ship, they would be glad to share a huge reward because some of the objects were priceless and rightfully belonged to the Italians, or they rather did, sort of.

The Italians disclosed to Derek information about three smaller trunks that contained new plates for a newly commissioned coin with three dancing Arethusas. The three trunks should also contain a total of one hundred fifty stamped and signed silver coins never seen by the Italians other than parchment design drawings. The charioteer or quadriga design, which could have been on the back side of the coin, was changed to a newer design of one very strong war horse with rider in a single chariot, charging along the great sea with water splashing into the air.

The designer was not Kimon, but a young new designer that they found to make the two-faced coin. The designer went by the name of Leonardo Alexander who was a passenger aboard the doomed ship along with two of their people for protection. The die plate was signed on the obverse or the head which was the three women side of the new coin.

Also on the ship were two hundred four-pound ingots of gold from either Mexico or Peru, which the crew picked up from another Italian ship that somehow intercepted a Portuguese ship. But we don't want to tell anyone that because it could present a problem. Now the other issue with the gold was that there were no markings at all on any of the bars. So therein lied the problem, because if found, anyone could probably grab them and run.

Derek said, "In summary, we have gold bars from a Portuguese ship that somehow miraculously landed in the Italian's hands. The gold bars were unmarked. These bars secretly became the valuable bounty in the hold in a crate on the Italian ship, and there were also small chests on the now sunken ship. The four-pound bars of gold could be from Mexico as possibly part of the Hernan Cortes stash obtained from Montezuma or possibly from some other group, Peru or Bolivia or wherever. The fact that there are no markings means anyone can claim them, if found. Next, we have very precious die plates from a design that was extremely new and would now be considered very old and exceptionally rare. The signed and stamped silver coins were from that same never-seen-before plate, again very old and exceptionally rare."

Derek cleared his throat to complete his final pitch.

"What we have, gentlemen, was an investor's dream come true. They also have a sunken ship with that huge something cargo laying on the ocean floor, up for grabs, because the sunken ship never had been found. Let's be discreet together. It's a gamble, gentlemen, but at this point, I propose we go for it."

The Italians knew Derek was not stupid.

Derek went on to explain to the Italians, "My expensive costs to move the motorboat across the ocean twice plus the smaller boat, permit licenses, my crew and extra protection, food and drink, diving equipment, cost and bonus for the divers, sub and boat maintenance plus depreciation, valuable time, etcetera, added to a significant amount."

The Italians were experienced and knew Derek might have a fairly good idea where their ship went down because he had approached them. If Derek knew anything, then other people knew something. The Italians' fear was that the other someone would be the band of unscrupulous con artists. Their fear was that the entire ship's treasure would totally disappear leaving them with nothing once again. It was a gamble, but they already decided to do the business venture if ever approached by a reasonably sane individual.

Quickly the Italians made the deal with Derek because they checked him out and found he was clean and trustworthy. They hoped he would find the treasure for them and would offer their assistance if needed. Derek would receive one-third of the gold bars and one-third of the silver Alexander coins. Any other items would be his for locating the ship. He told them the ruse for his adventure would be that they were writing a book. The Italians liked the idea. They moved one of their ships closer to Dakar, just in case their new partner became lucky.

15   Louisa's Chest and the Rest

THE FIRST TWO chests contained small ivory carvings and a porcelain tea set. Derek's crew put the newly purchased digger arm on the sub. With the digger arm, they pushed the ocean sand away. The third and fourth chests contained jade jewelry and more jade carvings. The fifth chest contained what was once a lady's ivory hair brush set and boudoir ivory jars and the sixth chest was corroded silverware.

They approached the crate that set off the metal detector alarm. Using the digger arm, they cleared more sand until the crate area stood alone. Derek and Skid managed to retrieve some of the gold ingots or bars in the other robotic arm. They took them back to the motorboat. They hadn't yet found the name plate of the ship. Derek knew it was the Italian ship, *The Cathar*. After drying the gold ingots with no markings, they knew their mysterious sunken treasure was an awesome find.

The three of them alternated to bring the other four small chests on board for Jess to open and the two men returned to work on collecting part of the gold ingots. The men stopped for another school of dolphins running through the area.

Derek moved the sub upward and took underground photos of the beautiful creatures. He took photos at the other sites of the sharks and schools of fish. Jess wrote lots of notes inputting them into the computer along with the photos. Their book about their adventure was more than halfway completed.

Of course, the real treasure was always found last. The treasure would be in the last four small chests. Jess opened the seventh chest, which contained the twenty silver coins which belonged to the Renaliere family. She put the Renaliere coins in a tub of solution and moved to the drawer.

Jess found the release on the now fragile wood and corroded brass chest and hit the button.

The bottom drawer released, but stuck. She picked the special hard rubber screwdriver to try to move the drawer. The drawer fully opened. An aurum or gold necklace with large diamonds and clasp of emeralds was there. The diamond pin and diadem were also inside.

Jess carefully washed them and then moved to the clasp. She took her jewelry tool and touched the clasp.

"The additional emeralds remained inside the artfully designed space all this time."

She washed those emeralds and then put them on the display. "Esmeralde, how big and beautiful. The chromium content is high and the stones a clear, deep green. Good transparency."

Louisa told her it was sometimes called the holy gem, and in Rome, green was the color of Venus. The emerald was chosen by her great-great-grandfather because it represented the goddess of love and beauty. Plus, it was one of the gems royalty loved to wear. Jess read about the stone and knew Cleopatra in Egypt supposedly owned emerald mines.

Jess touched the stones. "I congratulate you, Cleopatra, after seeing these stones. You were right on about building mines. You must have felt beautiful wearing the precious gem. The green color goes well with gold. I am impressed by this collection. It has high bling!"

Many pictures were taken of those three items and pictures of the twenty silver coins that were the Renaliere's. Then she sat quietly for half an hour before she contacted Derek on the radio.

Jess said to Derek, "Where are you?"

Derek told her they would be back shortly.

As soon as Derek was out of the sub, he knew Louisa's family heirlooms were found. The coordinates were *dead on*. Jess wore a smile wider than the motorboat and she hugged him. Then she did a little dance, giggling like a child at a party winning the piñata.

"We did it. The treasure was real. Louisa did good, holding her secret. The sunken treasure is beyond totally amazing. It is a one-of-a-kind find, super quality bling. Money, money, very high end."

Jess did another dance.

Derek grabbed her to stop her craziness. His own heart was jumping up and down.

"And there is more."

Derek responded, "I love that there is more. Tell me." Her excitement was contagious. Skid was watching his two bosses and felt their energy.

She opened the last three chests and showed him and Skid what was inside. Then they moved to the eighth chest. This chest contained Alexander's coin plates and tools plus thirty of the original first stamped silver coins. The ninth and tenth chests contained sixty Alexander-stamped silver coins in each chest. Jess put them in a different tub of cleaning solution.

They unloaded more of the gold ingots. They left the larger balance of gold ingots and rest of the cargo for their divers to help pick up the booty when they returned.

They took pictures of the separate piles of gold ingots.

Derek said, "The ingots were called shining dawn a long time ago. It is also another name for gold."

"Another name should be dolphin dawn."

"I like the sound of that much better and told you we should use the name for some of our photos. It could be aurum dawn, shining dawn, silver dawn, and so on."

"Good choices."

He grabbed her and tickled her. She laughed. It was another good day. Helping Louisa was important and her pleasurable excitement toward her husband were immense.

Derek felt super and in a high ecstatic state. "Yes, we did it and found the ship."

They snapped pictures of the Alexander silver items. Derek took some of the Alexander coins as agreed by the Italians and the gold ingots. The Miami boys helped to store part of the sunken treasure find, which would eventually yield one hundred forty gold bars and a hundred and five Alexander coins for the Italians. Derek's share, the sixty gold ingots and forty-five silver Alexander coins, would be hidden in the closets on the motorboat later.

The Renaliere coins were hidden in a closet. Five of the silver coins from the Renaliere chest were left out to give the divers per Louisa's instructions as their bonus. The rest of the Renaliere jewelry were hidden as well.

The two women, Marra Childs and Josine Thorne, left the boat after the first dive to join another diving boat. Due to their departure and contract terms, they would not receive any of the spoils.

XXXXXX

Derek radioed the other on-shore divers, "Head toward the second set of coordinates again at our designated time as the motorboat will be anchored approximately five hundred seventy-five feet or a little more than that. We are in location, off to the west from where we were."

Their other teams of divers returned after their days off. Everything seemed normal with the crew so they setup their morning dive schedules and went to bed.

Derek kept the discovery as a surprise until the next morning. The treasure was a game changer for the divers. He gave Skid his silver coin earlier who hid it within his bag of scuba suits.

Jess said, "Louisa's generosity of giving each diver a silver coin from her collection is a wonderful bonus. The divers would know the monetary value and they would not talk about the valuable sunken treasure find until their coin was secure. Louisa was pretty smart."

Skid knew it was the largest bonus he ever received and was grateful because Derek already paid him well. Plus, there would be two more weeks of pay for Skid and an additional bonus week. Skid thanked him again and asked, "When would we get rid of most of the precious cargo?"

"My Italian contact was called, and they radioed a boat in the vicinity. They congratulated us and our expedition team upon finding the wreck site. The Italians theorized the cargo was a lost one forever. They are excited and look forward to seeing us. I set up the date and agreed rendezvous point with the Italians to transfer the extremely valuable portion of the cargo to them. The Italians agreed to wait outside the limits from Senegal for the lesser valued historical artifacts. A salvage ship will pick up the rest. The arranged rendezvous date is in twenty-eight days. I allowed an additional seven days to the rendezvous date which meets approval with the other diver's plans."

Jess joined Derek and Skid and gave them an update.

"I informed the captain and chef in case we need to send out for more supplies. Our food supplies are fine as is their crew with the arrangements. Since the diving crew is okay with the change, I let War Julio and Jim know about the extended delay in arrival as well. Fortunately for us, our masquerade party date worked into our return plans. The transport will pick up the two boats on the date requested. The charter plane is rescheduled. Things should work out fine for the extra time delay for their departure."

"Thanks for doing that for me. If we can't bring the cannons up, no problem with the Italians. It is all right to leave them for their salvage ship. In a month or so after our departure, this dive site will be swarming with boats. I'm glad our motorboat won't be around all those crazy obsessed people in such very close quarters."

"Yes, we've had enough of crazy and totally obsessed people. I will be glad to leave African waters and the Atlantic, too," commented Jess. She has waited all these years and given up her bounty.

16   Sunken Items and Rendezvous

DEREK WISHED THEY could turn the video for an inside view or install a small camera in the sub to capture the first set of diver's faces. There was no time for changes. But the sound from the sub was very clear.

Jay looked at his wife, Brin, when they approached the sunken shipwreck.

Jay said, "There is a deathly pale ghost ship in the misty dawn water, broken on the salty sand floor of Atlas, with old decayed strewn cargo. Strewn cargo meant we are the first team to find her lost soul. Lost dreams for some, but not for us. For us, it is different. That's what we call jackpot, baby. We definitely will have your nice three-week beach vacation after all."

The other divers, Lorna and Gordi were watching the video feed on the motorboat, jumping up and down hugging each other. Derek, Jess, and Skid were laughing.

Jay said, "Dauphin du Cameroun, Sousa teuszii."

Derek told him, "Wait until the Atlantic humpback dolphin school move through."

"Oh, yes, humps and elongated dorsal beautiful fins. No taxon here, infraorder Cetacea, this is a mammal. Avast, my matie, to his sleepy wife."

Brin said, "Stop speaking French and quit the pirate-hold fast jokes. Dolphins have exceptional hearing, and I don't have time to entertain them. It is too early to be sociable. I'm worn out entertaining you. We have much work to do. I like the vacation idea, however."

"Yes, my Olympic mermaid wife. My sweet woman. You can have anything you want. We have work to do. But not too much work, no, never too much. God, I love you. This feeling here with you and the treasure is the greatest."

The group on the motorboat was entertained by their comments. They acknowledged where that conversation was headed.

The divers worked the next few days, giving the three of them a needed break. Then the team coordinated to recover items in a twelve-hour day. After the rest of the gold ingots were retrieved from farther down inside the ocean floor, the divers took a break. Some of the other crates must have held silk because there was nothing inside. There were two crates of Chinese porcelain dishes and another crate of old silver.

They pulled the ship's wheel and found it contained a corroded plate with the boat name. Other chests contained gold jewelry and possibly clothes at one time. They found slave shackles on some boards. There weren't much of anything left but corroded instruments. They saved two small cannons, but would leave the rest and the larger guns for the Italian salvage ship.

The work days for the diving expedition went fast. They were five days away from their rendezvous. Skid and Derek were going farther west to see if there was a second ship. They needed to survey the area now that they had time. If nothing else but to satisfy Skid's obsession with pirates. She agreed it would be fun. She reminded Derek of the words Louisa mentioned.

"What are the words Louisa mentioned? I can't recall, but knew women remember every little thing."

He smiled at Jess because he knew she remembered the words.

"The fisherman saw a small heat spot and a brighter spot."

"I remember now. Thanks, I will pay attention when we are in the sub."

XXXXXX

"Do you think we miscalculated the mark?"

Derek looked at Skid. "I'm not sure. The software is supposed to be accurate. If we don't find it, then we made the error. We should go back soon."

"There is something in the distance. Let's get closer before we turn." Derek rubbed his eyes.

"I see it now. We didn't miscalculate. We're on top of it. Turn her around slowly in an arc." Skid aimed the outside camera and took more photos.

Derek notified Jess and the other dive team, "We found the second downed ship. Heavily burnt with large cannons mainly remaining. That's how we found it. We followed the ridge and saw the tip of two of the rusted cannons. There are massive amounts of sand in this area. The last storm that went through the area probably moved the sand just enough for us to find it. It would take us a day to dig it out."

Skid told him his experience with pirate ships was that they were essentially a fighting machine and quickly emptied their cargo. If they found any treasure, it would only happen, because the pirates stumbled into the Italian ship before they could unload their last haul.

Derek was glad his lawyer put in an additional clause on salvage and any additional ship finds in his contract with the Italians. He hadn't even anticipated such a thing occurring.

It took an additional amount of time to find the rest of the cannons. Skid turned over the camera to Derek. He shot photos around the pirate ship from the beginning to their discovery of the hold area of the ship. There was no name found on the ship. It was an unregistered pirate ship. On their third day, they found broken barrels full of silver coins. The pirates didn't have time to empty their cargo and were greedy in their desire to hit another ship. Pirates hid coins in their water barrels in the hold.

Derek and Skid looked at the pictures on the computer of the pirate ship with the sand pulled away and they compared them to the downed ship, *The Cathar*, pulling their maps of the area.

Skid pointed.

"Did you see the right side of the pirate ship in the photos? The major damage is here, starboard, broken by heavy cannon fire. *The Cathar* shows that it is heavily damaged on the left or wharf side. I mean port side and the stern."

The two men looked at the maps and pin pointed spots where the wrecks were found. Then they put a point on the map for the fishing boat. Skid drew out the imaginary routes of the two ships from their starting point until they encountered each other.

Skid spoke, "I figure the larger ship was headed south when it saw the pirate ship. The captain slowed the large ship a little to assess the other ship's country of origin and noticed the large long-distance cannons. He realized his mistake in slowing the ship. It turned west, out farther into the ocean, possibly because there was a shift in the wind from the bad storm and the heavy ship needed all the wind it could keep in the old sails to escape. The lighter weight pirate ship caught them a crippling blow in the stern because they carried the same large, longer-distance cannons on board. The larger ship was now with fire which accelerated across the top of the ship. The fire was fueled by the heavy wind. The sails probably caught fire which slowed it so that the pirate ship came alongside."

Derek shook his head in agreement.

"The pirate ship continued to fire its cannons at the portside. *The Cathar* kept firing its heavy guns, hitting their mark. The heavy typhoon wind fueled the fires even farther on both ships until there was destruction. The two spots are the final view of the ships before they went down in a burning descent to the ocean floor."

"That sounds good. I've inputted the data into the computer," said Derek.

Derek played the scenario on special software he brought onboard so that the divers could see what happened. They thought it was probably an accurate series of happenstance. Bad luck and the wrong circumstances caught both ships in the ocean's grasp. The wasted remains of the doomed ships were a vivid picture of their lost dreams.

Jess raised her hand.

"What is it, honey?"

The divers liked it when he called her honey. His voice and posture changed. He became the adorable guy. Anyway, that's what the women thought. That's what the men thought, too.

"What if?

"Oh, no." Derek remembered those exact questions in Las Vegas, Nevada, when they planned to catch the evil con artist, the poisoner.

"Perhaps the pirates knew the valuable cargo that existed on board the wonderfully loaded ship, *The Cathar*. They may have followed the larger ship from the fort place after it picked up additional required crew. In which case, the larger ship was targeted by the pirates who owned pre-knowledge. The question must have arisen to the Italian's, by whom was the cargo known?"

"It may have been a total set up. If the larger ship hesitated, it could have been an arranged meeting with a different ship for a different transaction. Multiplicity was common back then. The captain looked in the scope and saw the wrong ship. He may have been in on the other transaction. He may realize the triple or double cross, and that was why he ordered his crew to continue shooting. Revenge could have placed both the ships in the fiery doom."

Derek remembered Louisa's story. "The investigator was murdered trying to reach the Italians' and that person, the murderer, was now, hopefully dead. The possibility existed for multiplicity or duplicity. So, greed equated to more greed. Revenge may have factored into things plus the elements. The unfortunate ones on board were caught by evil con artists. Louisa's thief also chose the wrong ship to pick his escape. It's odd fate. The scales tipped and re-tipped in our favor. We are the victors of a tremendous booty."

"You are absolutely correct. I thought it would be a good idea to include the scenario in our book. We could use the software demo in our video. It was too bad we didn't know the name of the other ship."

Derek laughed. "We can call it *Night Ship*."

"Why don't we call the pirate ship, Unknown Pirate--*Doomed Night Ship*?"

"It sounds perfect to me." Derek told her the name of their competitor's diving ship from Africa.

The divers were fascinated how Derek and Jess bounced their ideas in their communication to each other. They thought that there may have existed a conspiracy. The idea was plausible. They felt the eerie silence of choices under the deep, especially after finding the second unknown ship. The carnage that cannon-balls reeked was visible.

Derek and Skid backtracked on the map to the approximate position of the actual start of battle boundaries. Derek said, "We need to verify whether the estimate is correct. There still is a little time to check more things out."

They thought they would take the submersible out one last time.

"All right, everyone, we are at the computer's estimated coordinates. We used the digger and scooped up the silt. Some of the cannon-balls were found in the first scoop, the second, the third, and fourth. We don't have time to check the entire floor area. There exists in the deep a huge quantity of cannon-balls. The partial stern of the larger ship rested on top the ridge. It was stuck for centuries with burnt edges just waiting for retrieval. We need to complete a second trip to retrieve the stern section of wood wedged into a crevasse of the reef. The software version of the battle seems to have been real."

The idea that they found what the computer generated was exciting. All people in the diving expedition were amazed by those possibilities.

Derek knew it was Jess. Her intricate mind engaged into the con artist's world and the players that created evil disaster. When they ran a match test on the cannon-balls, they would find the corrosion rate was a match in time and the objects would match those found on both ships. The stern wood found at the starting battle site would match the pieces of wood from the downed ship, *The Cathar*.

It was a fun and adventurous dive to add to their resumes thought the diving teams.

Derek and Jess would be delighted when all the final tests on the found objects were revealed. The scientific evidence would impact the authenticity of their sunken treasure find and final book. They would have a bestseller. They would be heroes in the dive world. The investors would pay big money for the treasure because of the accuracy and notoriety of the story.

The entire diving teams alternated earlier to bring the additional silver coins from the pirate ship on board. Later, Derek and Jess gave their diving people one hundred coins each as a bonus. Skid received three hundred silver coins as his bonus. The coins weren't as valuable, but enough to bring their extra winnings to two hundred-fifty-thousand dollars per diver with Skid receiving four hundred thousand dollars.

Skid talked to Derek, "Could I have two of the cannon-balls? I want to give Louisa one in this plastic box. I thought she might like to be reminded what brought the Italian ship down. I know a friend who makes the boxes any size. I like the words you mentioned previously and believe it would look good on a brass plate with engraving of *Unknown Pirate Ship*."

Derek smiled because he knew some other people who might like the cannon-balls. "No problem, help yourself. Thanks, because it gave me an idea."

Jess also wanted some cannon-balls for their masquerade party.

The time arrived for them to rendezvous with the Italian ship, and the exchange was made quickly toward the early night time per the agreed distance from shore. The second ship find was a surprise and they were delighted. Derek thought they knew about the second ship or the possibility of its existence.

No ships were within sight nor visible on the radar screen. The calm seas made the exchange go smoothly. The small cannons were put on Jim's fishing boat and then hoisted aboard the Italian ship in nets with this large automatic crane setup.

Surprised how efficiently everything went that night, the final Italian papers were given to Derek for his ownership of the agreed balance of the sunken ship treasures and any additional small items later found. The Italian ship headed back home to Rome.

The motorboat cruised back to their last coordinates, which was their dolphin run. They moved slowly with Jim's boat following in their calm wake in the stealth of night. They anchored at last.

The next midday, it was time for the diving group to leave. It took a while to assemble everyone's gear. The divers were given lobster and crab sandwiches, homemade chips, and small wine drinks for later from the chef. They each grabbed a bottled water from the bar. Everyone hugged. They said their goodbyes on the motorboat.

Derek told them, "I would hire all of you, any day of the week, if they ever needed a job."

They told him they would crew anytime on his beautiful ship.

Jim's boat brought the divers and Skid ashore. Their rare treasured coin, extra silver coins, and final paycheck safely stored in their gear. Jim's boat was left at the harbor for later pickup and final transport to Curacao. Two of the Miami men were left to guard Jim's boat.

The motorboat cruised into the harbor later as well awaiting the transport ship. Their private chartered plane was on its way to the airport. Everyone remained silent about the dive expedition and the two found ships. Even Louisa was left in the dark about the find until the items were secured.

17 *Nuit Vaisseau (Night Ship)*

SANTAN CHESIN HIRED Marra Childs and Josine Thorne to get information about the American motorboat and check on their success at finding the sunken treasure. The women told him about the sub and scuba crafts, plus all the highly technical diving gear. They talked about the first dive coordinates and Santan bristled that the weasel, Stew Avery, sold the same coordinates to Mr. Wright and him.

They mentioned that the owner, Derek, was more interested in taking pictures of the dive site and fish in the area for some book that he and his wife were writing. That's when they made the decision to leave. The two girls were into finding sunken treasures. The Wright's ship was playing, and they didn't have the time to waste. They felt sure Santan's boat would deliver.

Santan's diving crew was at the third coordinate and found an unregistered sunken ship with very empty crates, which probably were originally cotton. There wasn't much retrievable valuable cargo, but Santan made them strip the boat of everything. The amount of money that he could get from the salvaged relics was just enough to pay for his expenses. Santan was not a happy person. He kept thinking about Stew Avery and the wasteland he gave him. His ship moved toward the next set of coordinates.

The Italians would pick up the rest of the salvage from *The Cathar* site. Another ship would be parked on the spot when Santan finally arrived at the last set of coordinates on his list. He would be late to the party. This ship would provide Mr. Chesin no information other than their name, Ernesto's Salvage Operation. Large buoys and nets were placed around the site by the salvage ship's crew. This prevented Mr. Chesin and his diving boat from dropping anchor very close to the recovery.

Ernesto's crew were large, burly men with scars and tattoos. The men gave Santan's crew no notice. A closer look showed some of the men with guns strapped to their legs. His captain told Mr. Chesin the meaning of the word, Ernesto, which meant *battle to the death*. Santan moved his boat a distance away and watched the ship for several weeks in his telescope. He didn't want a battle at this moment. He didn't know what was down there. It probably wasn't worth the bother. The items brought up were wrapped in green tarps and heavy rope nets, so he couldn't see very much. The Italians retrieved just about everything and were almost done. Only the ocean floor and a few boards would remain by the time Santan's divers dropped into the water.

Mr. Chesin was late checking his red tribe accounts. He forgot about them, but had time now that his ship was displaced. He might as well review the books while he waited. Jinx delivered the leader to his boss on the deep diving ship while at anchor.

Santan asked the red tribe leader, "What was this entry: two-hundred-fifty-thousand dollars?"

The leader swallowed and knew this one was going to be a tough call. Mr. Santan could believe him or not. If he believed him, he could be shot. If he didn't believe him, he could be shot. Or he could be fed to the sharks immediately with no explanation. The red tribe leader must set up this conversation carefully and Stew Avery became the fall guy. The leader knew that Mr. Santan called people he didn't like weasel.

The red tribe leader said, "It was a transaction with the weasel."

"Which transaction and which weasel has dared appear on my books?"

Santan had glimpses of a forest. The forest now was burned to the ground in his mind. He knew which weasel but wanted his man to explain.

The leader responded, "For the diamond necklace set in platinum owned by Italian royalty that you suggested I purchase."

"And the weasel?"

The leader said, "Stew Avery."

Santan became red in the face and filled his glass with more rum. Santan asked, "Then there is a two hundred forty-eight thousand five-hundred-dollar negative entry. This entry must be an illusion in someone's mind. Explain that one."

The leader bravely stepped closer to Santan and said, "The transaction was a trick. He lied to you."

"Who lied about what?"

The red tribe leader moved even closer. "Mr. Avery, the dirty weasel, lied to you and the lie showed that the necklace is cheap paste set in platinum. The platinum was to fool you. The platinum made the diamonds shine."

"Some dirty weasel fooled me with a cheap paste necklace worth only one thousand five hundred dollars?"

"Yes, he fooled you with a lie. Like I told you, it was a lie from the bad vermin weasel, Stew."

"Then I have caught two weasels or Mustela vermin in the chicken coup. I don't need nor want either one of you there. I've been victimized, and now the necklace was another huge waste."

Santan balefully said, "The red tribe is responsible for anything bad that happens to my business world. Your utmost task is finding the evil vermin weasel. If you don't find the weasel, I will deal with you. I'm extremely angry. Reckless wasteland is what I have been given, ugly burned stumps."

The red tribe leader was confused about burned stumps. Should he ask about them? No, that would be unwise. He saw how red the boss was in the face. His blood pressure was up. He would leave the dead forest theory alone.

Santan continued to remain agitated. "Did you understand the word *extremely*? The ocean is part of the extreme solution to anymore extremely sticky situations. One could think of the ocean as a place to pour leftover salty chicken soup, which also contains fresh weasel meat. Sharks will love that extreme combination. They are smart and know meat is meat. They aren't fooled by the shine."

He rubbed his shark's tooth necklace that was dipped in gold. "They even eat dead dull meat. Bones are bones. There are always choices. I get to choose yours. Listen and follow my advice. The red tribe leader should move far away and out of my sight. You will find Stew Avery or else the Atlantic is where both of you will end up. There will be no yellow raft."

Red tribe leader left quickly. He hated the yellow raft story and sharks. The dead forest was a new one. At least, he knew that he would not die today.

Santan became angrier and angrier drinking more of the strong rum. Not even his girls could make him happy. The girls stayed clear of the little guy because someone just pissed him off. They were glad it wasn't one of them. He called his man, Jinx.

"The red tribe is going to hunt Stew Avery down for swindling me. When the red tribe does find him, I want the slimy weasel, Stew, brought to me immediately, to face me. And I want the red tribe leader in the same meeting. I'm mad. Time and money wasted."

Santan stopped and looked at Jinx. "Do you understand the immediacy of that request?"

"I do and will readily inform you as soon as we find Mr. Avery."

Santan counted on finding a profitable sunken treasure. There was no profit in the enterprise. He paid a weasel. "No, I paid a shiny-furred weasel that stole my green money."

Santan sighed and set down his glass. It was time for business. He needed money now and made the decision to move ahead with the African diamond heist plan.

Stew was still in Dakar and heard Santan was looking for him and hopped a vessel heading to the Venezuelan coast. Stew dared not return to Dakar or Italy ever again. Stew's father called and told him Louisa reported her diamond necklace stolen from her wall safe to the police. Louisa suspected him because she showed the police her own hidden video. It showed Stew taking her necklace.

He speculated if Curacao didn't work out, he could always return to Los Angeles and stay with his cousin. Stew scrunched up his face at those thoughts. The last time he talked with his cousin, he was playing Hawaiian music and having some coconut oil party. He also didn't understand exactly when old Louisa installed the camera in her apartment.

18   Return of Necklace to Louisa

JESS AND DEREK saw the large motorboat and Jim's boat finally loaded onto the transport ship. The gold ingots and Alexander coins were removed from the hidden closets and placed into the specially built section of the locked food storage box that War Julio sent. The special box stayed in the freezer with the leftover frozen food placed on top.

The Renaliere gold diamond jewelry and silver coins were secured in a special locked case as they boarded their private chartered airplane and flew to Italy to see Louisa. The Miami boys hung around a week longer in Dakar with some of the other Miami people and their wives. His crew flew back to Los Angeles and met with the Wrights in Curacao when the transport ship was a few days closer to arrival.

Louisa answered the door because she gave her butler the day off. After tea, Jess placed the beautiful, professionally cleaned necklace with diamond pin into Louisa Renaliere's small hands. The diamond diadem also lay in her lap.

The old woman closed her eyes and remembered the painting as she touched her family's jewelry.

"I can't remember my great-great-grandmother, but I've known all the wonderful, rich, old stories. It is an amazing love story. I will tell them to you and Sami someday. Then the family stories won't be lost."

Louisa opened her eyes and exclaimed, "It is exquisite, truly more beautiful than the painting. The stones are bigger. The jewels must have felt impressive when my great-great-grandmother wore them."

Touching the emerald clasp, she felt proud of the Renaliere family. "The journey was hard and long. Two ships went down. There was so much destruction. One of the coordinates was the two spots seen by the fisherman in my family's story."

Derek and Jess agreed.

Then she looked at the fifteen silver very rare old coins. Louisa nodded, "It was the dolphin place, wasn't it?"

Derek replied, "Yes, it absolutely was under the dolphin run. You can see for yourself the amazing mammals."

He unwrapped and brought out the photo picture made just for her. It was the school of dolphins swimming with the light filtering the water. They chose a special ornate gold frame made for the photo. Then Derek pulled up the short video with sound that he redid on his cell phone just for Louisa. It was the dolphins whistling. Louisa was pleased.

"The second ship, a pirate ship, was also a surprise we hadn't known about and contained coins. We brought you four hundred silver coins." Louisa held some of the coins in her hand and knew the pirates failed. She was glad.

"What did Derek know about each of the divers? I received a thank you letter from each diver personally for their rare coin."

He verified the authorization from the divers to provide their personal information fact sheet of why the Wrights should hire them for the dive. Louisa was impressed with the experience of the crew.

They took Louisa to her bank where she put the gold jewelry in velvet pouches that Jess brought. The jewelry went into the bank box in the bank vault along with the coins. Derek explained to her their potential financial gain from the spoils and the Italians' gain in the valuable expedition.

Louisa smiled. "My family's investigator friend was one of the good guys. The ship scope, passed for generations with the valuable coordinates, held the papyrus. The remembered story held the revealing disclosure of the dolphins. My mother told me every word in the story must be passed to the next generation."

Derek and Jess invited her to Curacao to their masquerade party. The old woman declined. She was too old to party and travel so far. Jess gave her a photo album of pictures taken while on vacation with their children and those taken at the second dive site. There were even pictures of Louisa's sunken treasures.

Derek and Jess left the apartment. They flew to Curacao.

The old woman told her butler to buy a special notebook for her, and every day, she wrote down in chronological order her great-great-grandmother's love story. The notebook was addressed to the Derek Wright family in Los Angeles, America. She locked the notebook in her mahogany bookcase.

She looked at the dive photo book often.

Before they left, Derek said, "Some of the diving team were planning a trip to Italy and want to visit with you."

"I would like that very much. Do any of the divers know any good sunken ship stories because I like to read? I own lots of old books filled with the ancient ships."

Derek and Jess laughed and told her, "Skid is the incredible storyteller."

Skid and the others visited Louisa for a whole day, regaling her with adventure. He brought her one of the cannon-balls from the pirate ship that he had encased in a plastic box with a brass plate, *Unknown Pirate Ship*.

Louisa loved it. They planned on coming back the next year for a visit. Louisa made new friends.

Skid told Louisa his dream about moving to Los Angeles or San Diego and his desire to set up a small surf shop. He was getting older and it was time for him to get out of the diving business.

Derek shared with him a name and address of a nice surfer guy near San Diego that could show him the beaches. The surfer person used to clean pools in Napa, California. He also told him that the surfer person married a girl from this nice family who were also into horses. Skid knew all about horses having grown up around them.

Louisa wrote to Jess, "Skid reminded me of my son that is now gone. I outlived my family. But I'm happy because I've found new friends and families."

Jess smiled when she read the letter. She and Derek made the correct decision to visit Louisa. She believed it was her deceased friend, Dean, who nudged them toward their next adventure. She thought it ended well.

19   African Diamond Heist

SANTAN CHESIN CALLED his drug smuggler friend in Guinea-Bissau to let him know the deal was on. The girls at Santan's house believed the plans they stole at his party were for a diamond heist. Well, it was a dual diamond, drug-type heist, very common in many circles of the con artist world.

It always was that confusion thing so that people never knew what type of business a person was in, either the good guy or bad guy, and at what level. The level could be from newbie to very experienced evil. There was no turning back from evil once it took hold of a person. There would be no release. They would go down, but just didn't know it. In the meantime, it was grab everything or go frame someone else. Santan chose to go make money. Illegal always worked in the past. His African friend could be useful to him.

The diamonds were coming from Sierra Leone. Santan put up the fence money for the black-market purchase of the diamonds, which would be sold to a rich French diamond investor in Dakar. Some of the diamonds and the diamond money from the Dakar deal would be kept by Santan and that money partially reinvested in drugs purchased from his Guinea-Bissau friend.

This friend, the Sphinx, sold the drugs, making way much more money than the diamonds ever did. His drug friend received a cut on the purchase and the sale side of the transaction as would Santan with the diamonds and drugs.

The whole thing worked just like the real estate market with the buyer and seller side of things, only the con business had a few more risks. But the rewards were so much better and higher, making all the players in the diamond-drug heist game rich, except for the conned. The conned (people who owned the diamond mine) were meant to lose and would always lose. It was because they owned the precious commodity. Riches were always up for grabs.

Santan purchased the smuggled diamonds and put them in his safe. He knew exactly how many diamonds were required for this new deal. He dropped the contraband on the market slowly, like a writer dropping bread crumbs throughout a story to appear as small ripples of disturbance. The police were not even aware of any part of the transaction until much later.

Whenever he stole diamonds, he always bought his girls diamond baubles to celebrate. The girls knew this and brought Jinx, the undercover cop, into their own robbery of the diamonds from little Santan.

The police were alerted along with their two-hired people. The Santan girls waited until nightfall to steal the diamonds only to find Santan had disappeared. The diamonds were missing from the safe also. There was nothing in the safe. He already made his exchange with the French man and received his money. Part of the money had been given to his friend for reinvestment.

Santan eventually returned home and the police raised their hands in disgust because they couldn't arrest anyone because there was no viable evidence. The hidden cameras were deleted of their video images while Jinx was out.

The Santan girls arrest records would be shown to Judge Daken who always considered them unreliable witnesses. Santan would say he was talking about a diamond proposal with someone and not necessarily was it ever a real deal. He would venture that the business of legally selling diamonds was too complicated for them to understand. The paper documents didn't really have enough information in print to pin him down for a crime.

So, Jinx installed listening devices in the house for the police. Santan's friend in Guinea-Bissau bought and sold the drugs and wired the money to Santan's special account which Santan quickly wired to an untraceable account. Santan celebrated his victory and got drunk. He spilled the friend's drug heist to the girls while he played with them in his bed.

The listening police first went after the Guinea-Bissau guy. Santan received wind of this horror through his network of people and knew his girls were not to be trusted. He warned his men who quickly fled the area. Santan believed the police would come after him as an accessory so he quickly sold his diving boat to an old friend who would help him.

Then he began to worry about someone named the Sphinx, his scary Guinea-Bissau friend.

"What if the scary friend believed he had been sold out by me? He would believe that I set the frame up. The great Sphinx would come after my body."

An old friend of Santan's sold the property for him in Dakar and wired his money to a different hidden account. Santan disappeared on a repainted fishing boat. His old friend repainted, renamed, and re-licensed the large diving boat and sent it on the international motorboat transport ship.

Santan's large boat was on the same transport ship along with Jess and Derek's motorboat, and Jim's fishing boat headed for the Caribbean.

The raided house revealed that only the girls and Jinx were there. The girls left the house and Ruse went to live with Jinx. Ruse told Jinx that she thought Santan would eventually end up in London because he talked about that city. Jinx let the authorities know. It was one of Santan's police friends who misplaced the London message.

Santan was relieved and looked forward to reaching Venezuela. He was ready to hunt down Stew Avery. He received a tip that he possibly was in Curacao.

Some of his diving boat crew went with him to Curacao. He met with his red tribe to find out the status of the search. They didn't have a clue where Stew was located and needed to make up a story. The red tribe leader told him there had been diamond jewelry stolen at the parties in the homes and the hotels in the area. The thievery was not by any of the red tribe because they always followed Santan's orders. That was what the leader told him. Santan worried it was another weasel story.

Apparently, the local cops in Curacao would be watching strangers in their area. Santan was glad he was prepared.

After Santan picked up his boat from the transport ship, he would move the ship to this potential customer's dock. He would be safe while there. The company wanted to view his large diving boat which was up for sale. He was pleased his man found a potential buyer so fast. The diving boat would be a dead giveaway for the Sphinx to locate him, so it needed to be gone.

20   Arrival in Curacao

JESS AND DEREK flew back to Curacao, the island on an international trade route of the Atlantic Ocean in the Caribbean owned by the Dutch Netherlands. The island contained many captivating beaches and was filled with quaint European-style buildings and charm. Tourists flocked to the area and the capital, Willemstad. The area was situated on the outer fringes of a hurricane belt. Therefore, they felt it was a reasonable safe territory to visit.

Many hotels and places offered vibrant Creole restaurants, shopping, and golf. There was a local casino built around an old fort site. The harbor was superb with depths of sixty-five feet and was a natural harbor formed approximately ten thousand years earlier. Some of the languages of this part of the island were Dutch, Spanish, and English, which helped make many of the tourists feel like they were home.

They arrived at the harbor condo and were happy to hug their children again. They made smaller pictures of the dolphins for Justin and Sami for their rooms on the motorboat. They were welcomed by Jim and Mary Beth as War Julio had flown his helicopter back to Rio for routine maintenance. Some of the Miami cronies began to arrive. Everyone swam in the

149

private pool that looked out toward the crystal blue waters. The children showed their parents their new snorkeling skills.

War Julio's chef made them Creole food for dinner. They ate crawfish ettouffee, red beans and rice jambalaya. Dessert was praline ice cream with praline pecans and heavy whipped cream. There was much white wine. Everyone went to bed except Jess and Derek who stayed in the double chaise lounge watching the sun disappear from their three hundred sixty-degree view.

"We were very lucky to have participated in a wonderful dive expedition with our amazing crew, protection team, and diving teams. I will also remember Louisa's help. The discovery of two ships will set the diving world into frenetic activity. All the people with money will be parked in Dakar hoping to retrieve some similar find. Our estimated value of the found sunken treasure before expenses is approximately ten to twelve million depending on the investors who want to purchase our find. I think it will be on the higher end. This sum does not include the Renaliere items."

"That is totally an obscene amount of money. We never dreamed of finding that much," said Jess.

"Yes, it was a pretty good sum. It was a chance we took that worked."

Derek and Jess were quiet. The toll in human life was huge for those on board the old fiery ships.

"I look forward to the masquerade party to celebrate Dean's annual passing. It is what we need right now to slow things down."

They agreed that Curacao was the place to be located. They invited Dean's old crony friends from San Francisco, Los Angeles, Miami, Rio, and Curacao to their party. The fireworks were approved, and the party arrangements were falling into place. Derek didn't think things were going to slow down. He looked at his wife.

"Happy to be in Curacao?"

"Yes, I'm happy to be where my husband and children are located. I want to stay here close in your strong arms. You are what makes me happy. The bonus is our friends in Curacao."

"Absolutely correct. I am glad you like my strong arms. I work at our gym every day to stay ahead of the bad guys. You make me happy, too. God, I love you as well."

That made Jess even happier. She moved out of the chaise lounge and touched his muscled arms. Then she danced in front of him, moving her sundress straps down a little bit at a time.

It didn't take, but a moment, for Derek to get out of the chaise. He wasn't going to waste any time. He learned fast. He took her in his arms, touching her straps a little lower. She felt smooth, soft, and warm. It was what they both wanted, each other. Nothing was wasted. Time was a precious thing.

The fires were burning high. No wind was required to fan the flames. The flames raised higher, hearts beating, kisses spiraling the two fires into one. Both knew they were on safe ground. The pressure mounting between them was like a tropical cyclone.

The sustained power ramping the ecstasy speed from category 1 to 5.

When he released her, she said "More?"

"Maybe a little later."

"I don't want to wait."

"I won't make you wait."

Later was not a concept in her vocabulary once the spark of passion was lit. He started singing an opera song he knew, gently touching her in all the known, familiar places to make her eyes turn to misty pools again. Their rhythm matching the swaying, swirling fire. The fire yielding to their urgent need. They held onto each other for a long time letting the fires rebuild before Derek took her hand and led her from the balcony to their room.

Both knew how important this trip had been. It was fun working together again on an outside project. Their bond and love became stronger. The sunken treasure finds added to their wonderful life.

XXXXXX

Jess worked on the draft of the book, and the two of them decided the final photographs. They selected their narration for the video and book. The draft was ready, and they sent them to their publisher, happy to release the story to the editors.

The family rented bicycles the next morning to tour the town, expelling everyone's energy in play.

They ate dinner that evening with War Julio and his wife. There were oysters Rockefeller, shrimp remoulade, more rice, and bananas Foster dessert. War Julio let Derek know that he owned two helicopters now and kept one at each location. The one in Curacao was in a hangar at the airport for now.

Finally, the international boat transport ship arrived to unload the motorboat and Jim's fishing vessel. War Julio and Jim would meet at the docks with him to watch the boats unload.

"I'm relieved our motorboat arrived and we can stay there with the children. It will free up the condo rooms for other guests in our group."

"I will be glad to be on our motorboat, because it is more private. Our crew is very good about disappearing for us. We can be alone again. I need more time with you."

"Yes, more is always good." Her eyes told him she remembered last night.

Derek smiled. He knew she liked those important moves. It wouldn't take him long to get there.

"I recognized that you needed more time as well and asked War Julio's wife if she could help recommend a place to hide our motorboat. Of course, she told War Julio that we need privacy."

"Smart move, honey. You are a good wife."

"Of course, I want extra time before our normal life returns." Jess knew she would be in trouble if she said the word more again to Derek.

"Women are really good at helping other women. It must have been a wonderful bonding experience with War Julio's wife. Then War Julio and I can bond because of our newly found site to moor the

153

motorboat. It will be close to his fishing warehouses. This will be a win for everyone."

"We need to find a way to thank them for their generosity."

"I know the perfect gift that is about Montezuma and the peacock."

Derek explained to Jess that War Julio always liked history and the gold find was more than that. Jess told him his idea was awesome. It was the perfect gift.

"I informed the police of the large party ahead so none of our group would be on any suspicious watch list. Anyway, that's what I hope," said Derek.

"It was a good idea to invite the dignitaries to our party. They know War Julio paid heavy taxes to the city from his fishing business. His wife was friends with many of the wives. I always liked her easy grace in communicating with people. Her father trained her at an early age the art of marketing."

"Yes, there is graciousness in her every movement. It was a good match. Did you know Dean dropped his name and put in a good word for War Julio with her father?"

"No, I often wondered about that. I knew she didn't plan to attend the other party and then she flew in at the last minute. Dean also invited War Julio to the motorboat celebration. His plan worked."

The motorboat crew also arrived and two of the Miami guys stayed on Jim's boat like they did in Dakar. Some of the Miami protection team stayed on the motorboat. Tami and her Miami guy arrived and moved into the condo with Jim and Mary Beth.

War Julio kept two empty rooms at the hotel for late arrivals. His family stayed at his renovated completed condos in the same building. They waited for the San Francisco group and some more Los Angeles people to arrive later in the week.

21 Unloading the Boats

THE INTERNATIONAL TRANSPORT crew unloaded Jim's fishing boat first and Jim smiled as he was a happy camper to have his tub back. He sent up a thank you to Dean Crain who was in heaven or somewhere close. His boat was boarded by the able-bodied Miami boys who knew which dock slip to take the boat.

Next, they unloaded Derek's motorboat much to Derek's relief. His crew was at the boat dock ready to hold her fast and quickly steered her out of everyone's way. They would move the motorboat to War Julio's shipping docks for a special package to unload. Derek turned to leave with War Julio and Jim to check out their special package.

Derek turned back to see the next ship and stopped dead in his tracks.

"I know that ship. Let's pull up the images Tami sent me. I have the shots from Dakar on my cell phone."

He looked back at the ship's hull. "Unbelievable match."

The boat was repainted white with a red stripe and then black bottom. Derek said, "What the heck?"

He showed Jim and War Julio the cell phone picture and nodded toward the transport boat.

Jim said, "Sitting in its brace for transport was the competitor diving boat."

The crane swung the ship over the water. "It was the same darned boat for sure. No doubt about it," continued Jim.

War Julio looked at the name and said, "*Bleu Crabe*. That meant blue crab, didn't it, but the boat was black, white, and red. What sense is the name?"

"No sense at all if a person was an African diamond smuggler and narc interchanger, part of the bad guy collection in this world."

War Julio said, "That meant big trouble."

Jim and Derek nodded.

"Perhaps Curacao is a wrong place for the party." But then he remembered what Dean told him. Wherever Jess went, the thugs would arrive and lead them to the gates. Derek wasn't sure he could do the gates. Dean told him that he could, for his wife. He knew that he would. He hadn't been quite prepared for Santan Chesin to arrive under what looked like a new disguise in Curacao.

"What could possibly bring him to this exact place?"

"I agree with Jim. The bad guy, Santan Chesin owns this boat. I informed the rest of my boys of his name and ship while you were in Senegal's waters," said War Julio.

Derek asked, "Would your company's fishing and dock boys ask around about the diving boat? Find out the owner's name to see if he changed it and where the dock is located for its mooring duration here in

Curacao. We need to figure out what the man is up to now. He may know about our cargo and attempt to steal it. We can't let that happen and need to move fast to ship the treasure out of Curacao."

"I will get on it," said War Julio.

Derek told the boys, "We should secure the special package from Dakar for delivery and heavily change the plans. It was good the rest of the protection squad would arrive shortly because they must attend a meeting and involve the police. Jess will need an update and the children should be moved temporarily to Rio. I know Jess will want to be involved in the plan to catch the con artists if they are here to cause trouble."

Derek must come up with a plan to protect her and his family. War Julio was already making plans to fly the Wright children and his precious and now-pregnant wife out of harm's way.

They drove to War Julio's fishing docks and opened the special box in the warehouse when the workers were off on their lunch break. The less people that knew about the cargo, the better. The package was still safe. Derek unlocked all the hidden closets and they began assembling the precious cargo into the thin wooden crates that would be shrink-wrapped and hoisted into a secure metal container. But first, the items in the freezer box were shown to his two friends. Jim wasn't surprised by the special package being an old history buff. The treasure had been an excellent discovery.

War Julio asked Derek, "Could I hold one of the gold ingots?"

Derek told him, "Sure, they weigh around four pounds each."

War Julio was fascinated by the gold and Derek told him about investors and the estimated price range an investor would pay. It was a whole learning experience for War Julio. Derek explained the coins to him, but he wasn't as interested.

War Julio looked wistfully and said, "I wish that I could have met this Montezuma person."

Jim and Derek laughed. It was what they needed to come back to the real world. Montezuma was probably not one of the good guys either if the gold bars were from his mines. Or some of his friends were snatching the gold on their own. No one would ever know, other than the ingots existed.

The treasure from the motorboat was loaded with the appropriate weight for a shipment of frozen fish. They put the frozen shipment also in the metal cargo box, sealed it shut, and addressed it to a secure shipping dock in Los Angeles. War Julio's workers returned to deliver the box to the airport for transport. They were used to shipping items to America and didn't think anything about its contents. They assumed it was fish.

Derek's men would pick up the cargo with the first and second truck of guards. The cargo would be placed in his heavily guarded freezer warehouses in Los Angeles. The security was ramped up until the investor payments were received. Everything sold quickly on the privileged, hidden investor market.

The motorboat cruised to a dock leased by War Julio. After the lines were secured, Derek and the two men drove back to the condo. Derek dreaded telling Jess about Mr. Chesin. She would dream up some plans to catch the guy. He knew the masquerade party plans were completed and she would be full of the details to share with him.

Derek let his superiors know about the whereabouts of Santan Chesin and the new ship name, so they could check that out and get with the local authorities. He talked with Jess.

"I'm understanding of the situation because we have a known character whose elusive nature is questionable. We have been here before. The bad guys are in the vicinity, highly likely a band of diamond smugglers. Why is it always about the priceless gem? Their sparkly brilliance is part of the lure, but others love the money the diamonds bring to the game."

"Yes, money was the name of that game."

XXXXXX

Derek frowned when War Julio informed him of his problem via a phone call. He had run into massive resistance from his pregnant wife. His pregnant Miami wife was daughter of the king of kings of all the Miami cronies. She told him, "You need to stop right there. There was no way that I'm going to miss this wonderful annual party because my husband was afraid for my safety."

She let him know that she was used to this kind of action and had been protected all her life.

"Who do you think those strange men are that follow me everywhere? It is part of my father's protection squad."

That stopped War Julio in his tracks, because he and his people never saw her father's protection squad.

"My husband had better get on board because there was no one who entered her world that the king of fathers hadn't checked out at a high rate of speed."

Derek talked into the phone, explaining about pregnant crazy women hormones. He saw Jess smile, remembering her pregnancies. Derek recommended Jess's plan.

"Let your wife go to the masquerade party and stay until right around ten or so in the evening. Then remove her to safety when the show would really begin. Nothing bad ever happened early." Anyway, that is what they hoped.

War Julio learned to stay at peace with the wife. Then he hired more of his protection teams for his wife so as not to be out done by her father. Shortly thereafter, War Julio received a call from his wife's father.

He mildly told War Julio that he would be on an airplane, first class, with a second group of Miami sharpshooters to help protect his daughter. His accommodations were at one of the larger hotels. He needed invitations to the party that his beautiful pregnant, beloved, only daughter wanted to attend. His daughter told him about the diamond smuggler.

"Familiarity with that class of thugs was the reason I want to personally be on hand at the party. I informed my daughter the number of invitations required were now thirty-five for myself and my family's protection crew," said the Miami father.

War Julio learned about the Miami crony version of protected family. War Julio made sure the rest of his condos were completed on their renovations before the party. He called his wife's father and offered his amazing condos to him and their protection team.

The father liked War Julio and accepted the close accommodations to his daughter and her nice husband.

22   Plans for Masquerade Party

JESS ORDERED HUNDREDS of Caribbean battery-lit, turquoise-blue paper lanterns. There were tiny blow toys that looked like the pufferfish, which silently popped multi-colored streamers out the end for the men. She thought the men would get a kick out of the concept. The toys would add to the noise level in the ballroom. The women would receive red bags with a small bottle of cologne bought from a perfume shop in the Penha building and mini yellow paper fans. Larger multi-colored fans and gold streamers hung from the ceiling. Royal blue garlands were strung around the buffet tables.

Extra-large pieces of driftwood placed in the live, potted, lighted palm trees gave a festive island flair. Large fishing nets were strung by the doors and hung with bright sea-shells. The place looked similar to a colorful carnival in Trinidad with paradise thrown into the room. The metallic confetti on the tables added to the glittery world.

Jess told Derek, "A party is all about the senses of sight, sound, smell and taste."

Derek walked into the ballroom. "Your magic touch has been taken to the maximum. I'm blinded by all the color. The excitement is in the air surrounding us."

She laughed. "Maybe it is a bit much, but I did want excitement. Yes, I can feel it in the air."

The Mambo Steamroller band were hired to play reggae, Caribbean, and modern music and would be on a higher stage in the ballroom. There was room on the stage for Jess and Derek to perform their specially arranged calypso dance. When the band wasn't playing, they would turn on their softer slow music.

The fountain of champagne was an ice sculpture carved into a five-foot Queen Sea Nymph taken from the Greek story of Calypso and would stand in the very middle table. Derek saw pictures of the sculpture earlier. The design drawings matched.

The invitations sent were special gold scrolls. Large bouquets of white flowers were placed upon heavy four-foot-high pillars and showered the edge of the room with their scent. Even the garbage cans contained special plastic covers that looked like dolphins that fit over the tops.

Each banquet table was ordered. Table 1--blue tequila with zest of Laraha tree fruit which was like an orange and full bar setup. Table 2--lomito or small pork slider type sandwiches with dim sum and egg rolls. Table 3--stoba or beef and papaya with funchi or polenta bites.

Table 4--keshi yena or soft creamy flavored Gouda cheese stuffed with fresh thinly sliced vegetables and cooked chicken with hot pasta on the side. Table 5--seafood with massive quantities of shrimp and crab. Table 6--Caesar salad with exotic dressings and fruit with special fried potato chips for topping. Table 7--small yellow sweet-glazed rum cakes with chopped dried fruits and nuts for the topping. Jess made sure there was plenty of extra cut meat available at the tables for the hungry men.

Teams of hotel and their own security patrolled the party plus the extra Miami group. The hotel allowed Derek to set up his own security cameras that fed to a secure room with computers. The police monitored the premises to help traffic flow and keep the riff-raff out of the hotel.

Their children saw the paradise ballroom and ate some of the prepared food in the hotel kitchen and then they were flown to Rio where they could go horseback riding and dune buggy riding on War Julio's estate for the next three days. It was now only two days before the party. Derek, War Julio, and Jim set up the outside security measures.

The other two parties consisted of space and pirate costumes. One of the companies sponsoring the party was a vendor in technologies that were used in outer space.

The other party was a local pearl diver company. Their group would wear pirate costumes. War Julio obtained some costumes that would fit across all three parties.

The Miami group received the pirate outfits and some more of the Miami group and the detectives wore the space suits. The wife's family of War Julio would be dressed in Miami finery. The Curacao boys wore their flashiest Caribbean outfits. War Julio and his wife were pirates with lots of gold color and gold-and-blue striped shirts. Jim and his wife were space officers wearing silver costumes. Everyone at the door received masks if they wanted to wear one.

Jess would perform as an exotic dancer and Derek was her partner. They planned a performance of Jess's favorite number 6 calypso dance. It was the sixth song on their motorboat and home sound systems. They practiced their routine for a long time, perfecting every move. Jess even recorded the song on her cell phone.

Jess put her red ruffled satin costume outfit on for Derek and hit the calypso song on the cell and turned it up loud. She exited the room with her sound machine, and Derek quickly picked her up. He twirled her around and told her that she was the most incredible sea nymph he ever saw.

"Now you've enticed me way enough. I'm no longer your prisoner. You have convinced me to stay on your island."

He hauled her into the bedroom, making their kids laugh. Justin and Sami chased after them dancing their own version of the thirty-two-count calypso beat. The bedroom was filled with a crazy dancing family.

"Paradise was the perfect place. It was a great runaway place to play," said Jess.

Paradise would arrive at the start of the masquerade party, but then chaos and confusion would enter via all the bad guys in the audience who purchased or stole invitations.

Finally, Jess made Derek and their children leave the room. She changed clothes, because their family planned a couple hours at the Old Ship Museum. They wanted to see something that looked like a Nef ship. The doomed ship, *The Cathar*, was similar in structure.

23   Smuggler and Red Tribe Plans

SANTAN CHESIN CHANGED his name to
Mann Nisee in the hopes that the African wouldn't find
him. He planned to dock his diving ship, *Bleu Crabe*,
in the Willemstad harbor at a Curacao company dock.
He warmed to the idea of being in this city with its
friendly atmosphere. He even liked his new name,
Mann Nisee. It was like he was the main man again.

Walking with confidence on his ship, he looked
down at the deep-water channel, St. Anna Bay, leading
to the busiest seaport. Things were all right as his ship
passed under the Queen Juliana Bridge. Mann didn't
want to be trapped in a harbor, he would rather be out
in the ocean. This week Mann must do his business
here.

He saw the white and blue ferries taking people
from Punda to Otrobanda. Although Mann was here to
escape Dakar and find Stew Avery, he waited a day
before talking to the red tribe leader.

He would stay on the large dive boat for now.
Having heard about the three upcoming parties,
invitations were obtained to two of the parties. The
parties were close to each other. Evidently, the
masquerade party was private and exclusive. It was just

fine with him because he was flush with money and didn't need to steal any diamonds for the moment.

"I do, however, need some companionship and will ask my bodyguard to search for pretty ones. I also need more rum."

His bodyguard combed the area for temporary entertainment in the strange island city.

Mann was perfectly content to wait. All his paperwork was in place and he felt safe. This trip would be like vacation and then he would sell the boat and move to London. His buyers were coming this afternoon to check out the ship that he could dock at their company. Perhaps he could get his money from the sale of the ship and do a leaseback of the ship for a month or two.

"That was exactly what I have planned, exiting the area when I want. I will appear as just another nice businessman in this town. My cover was solid."

Santan's or Mann's red tribe hadn't been exactly honest with their boss about the whereabouts of Stew Avery. Unable to access any information regarding Stew's whereabouts, they only fled to Curacao to distance themselves from Mr. Chesin, now Mr. Mann Nisee's employ.

The red tribe leader would have to create another story about Stew to tell Mr. Nisee. One of his red tribe members belonged to a group of relatives in this area. That is how they arrived here. They were surprised to hear the diamond smuggler was in Willemstad. It was the strangest of coincidences. The red tribe members must be more cautious. Perhaps it was too early for them to flee to Venezuela which would have been a better location for the lazy group.

The red tribe hadn't also been exactly truthful to Mr. Nisee about stealing the diamond jewelry from hotel patrons and homes in the area. They were those thieves doing the stealing. The red tribe hadn't sold any of the goods yet because that would be too risky. They would wait until they reached Venezuela or possibly Los Angeles. Los Angeles was now looking better due to the great distance and they felt the pay for their stealing efforts would be higher.

They planned to hit all three parties because they were part of the garbage crew. The red tribe wasn't going to steal jewelry at the party, but they would pick-pocket wallets to get the rich peoples' identification cards and cash. Then robbing their homes later was the easiest route for stealing jewelry. The thieves would have their personal information. The wallets would be dumped in the trash for later retrieval. They would have to rob those last homes quickly before they exited the area.

The red tribe group thought they were real smart thinking up their party heist and plans.

The red tribe leader met with Mr. Mann Nisee. It was hard not calling his boss, Mr. Chesin. He must not slip on the name or his boss would get mad. The red tribe leader's confidence must show when he spoke. He puffed up his chest, swallowed, and walked the gangplank to the ship. He saw a burned forest in his mind. He had no idea where the image came from. His chest deflated; fear started rolling in. This idea must work for him.

The red tribe leader knew how to sell his old boss to an idea, even though it sounded a little far-fetched when he rehearsed his lines. He told his boss that Stew would certainly appear at one of the three parties. He would appear somewhere at the parties that were taking place at the three hotels due to the high volume of diamond jewelry those people wore. Stew was a weasel, but also a thug who previously stole before.

"I figure you are onto something. Stew now has increased knowledge of real diamonds having learned the hard way about paste. The vermin weasel will appear the evening of the three parties. Congratulations on the excellent idea. You will create a plan to catch him," said Mann.

The red tribe leader left the diving boat having hidden in a place some of the prior stolen jewelry on the ship. That was one plan put in place. The leader went back to his tribe relieved. The red tribe leader knew he needed to get more creative for the second plan and thought a long time. He would hire someone that looked like Stew, rent another space rental costume, and give the actor his girlfriend's ticket to the party.

That would keep Mann off their tail because he could take a picture of the actor and send it to Mr. Nisee. The temporary holding of any bad feelings at bay was the goal. The actor escapes and they are off the hook for a bit. He already put in place the plan to set Mr. Nisee up by planting some of the stolen jewelry on the diving ship. Mr. Nisee told them where the ship would continue to be docked. Then the police would mysteriously be notified after the three parties were over or they had stolen enough wallets. They weren't sure on the timing of that angle. That would eliminate their first huge problem for the tribe. That problem was Santan Chesin, aka Mr. Nisee.

With the extra cash from the three parties and a little more thievery, they could leave. If they accidentally stumbled upon Stew, then they could shake him down for more money. It would be a totally win-win situation.

Mr. Nisee sold his ship the same day to the buyer of that wonderful company. The company would give him a cashier's check early the next day if they could have the dive boat immediately. Mr. Nisee agreed. The next day, he and part of his crew went to the hotel that was holding the pirate party. The rest of his crew departed to their homes. Mr. Nisee sent a couple men to find pirate costumes to rent.

When he checked into the hotel, he asked, "Clerk, do you have four packets of needle and thread?"

The hotel clerk gave him the packets.
"Where is the nearest bank located?" The clerk showed him the building close by.

Two gold scrolls were in the hotel clerk's pocket. Mr. Nisee asked, "What are the funny objects?"

"They are special invitations for a party in the hotel across the street. Two of their guests couldn't make the party so they left the invitations with him. It should be the grandest of all the parties in the area. He would keep the tickets for himself, but had promised his mother a trip. He couldn't use these gold scroll tickets, because it would cost him to cancel the other one."

Mr. Nisee wanted the gold scrolls because the red tribe thought Stew Avery may attend one of the three parties. He needed access to the third party for the evening. The gold scrolls were of high importance to him. His luck was turning.

The hotel clerk thanked Mr. Nisee and pocketed two hundred dollars. The gold scrolls were missing from the hotel clerk's shirt pocket when Mr. Nisee left the lobby to find his room. Mr. Nisee could attend the more prestigious and grand party if he wanted with his bodyguard. They would blend into the three parties very well.

Mr. Nisee was happy and walked toward the bank to do a wire transfer. Then he could drink the precious rum while he sewed before the women arrived in his room.

24   Stew Hiding in Curacao

STEW AVERY WAS in Willemstad working as a pool person. Normally, he was not inspired to work, but needed the money and a cover. This job was made-to-order, a perfect place for him to live. He didn't clean out the pool, but handed the pool towels, umbrellas, and extra chaise lounges during the day to the never-ending string of guests. It was a no-brainer job. His girlfriend worked in the kitchen of the same hotel that was catering the space party.

The two of them could find invitations. As a matter of fact, some of the people threw their invitations in the garbage and Stew retrieved them for their use. He also sold some of the tickets to strangers in town. Stew went out and rented a space outfit and an extra one for her in case she could get out of the kitchen early.

His life here in this town was just great. His girlfriend didn't mind that he was cheap. Stew liked her, and the sex worked fine with him. He told her that he had this poor cousin in Los Angeles that he must wire money all the time. Stew easily lied to everyone because it was fun to con people.

He never wired that idiot cousin any money, but put it in a special hidden place in a flat body pouch in his room. Stew did call his butler father once a week. He decided to tell her the truth about that important fact. So, she thought he must be a good person. Stew was, however, not one of the good guys.

Stew didn't tell her about a lot of things like the single open airline ticket, already bought, and a new identification card if he needed it. These he kept hidden inside the bottom of the hotel lamp wooden base which he could unscrew with his knife. Yesterday he stole the identification card from one of the waiters that looked approximately his height and weight. He wasn't sure the guy even missed it, because he paid everything in cash. Pay day was a good two weeks away.

His girlfriend knew Stew's type. She found the flat pouch with money and decided that she liked him anyway. She wished she could go live in Los Angeles if he left. That was probably what the money was for anyway. Deciding he was the one person for her, she wrapped his true character in layers of delusional goodness.

She was one of those insecure women who needed someone all the time. When she didn't have someone, her life was in a depressed-wreck mode. She was afraid if she told him about finding the money, he would leave.

His girlfriend knew he wanted to go to the hotel space party. She informed him she would be off at eleven o'clock in the evening. But then another kitchen worker had quit, and she would have to work until the party was over. She didn't tell him. Stew would be upset with her and spoil her evening. He might even make a scene. Her job was her major and only source of income. She couldn't mess with the important job. It was one of the better ones on the island.

All the players congregated within proximity to each other and were disguised as to their identity. The con artist game began as one by one, they all recognized each other. Before that happened, a little partying and thievery occurred. That was the kind of action that Dean Crain, the Wright's deceased friend, would have enjoyed. It was what the Wrights were used to and all their crony friends. That's why the masquerade party was heavily guarded.

25   Guinea-Bissau Friend Arrest

MEANWHILE, SANTAN CHESIN'S drug trafficker friend from Guinea-Bissau was arrested and handed over to Senegal. In court with his very rich, powerful, handsomely paid, mastermind lawyer, he stood before Judge Daken from Dakar. The Guinea-Bissau friend was named Sphinx Reeker.

The judge peered at the name. He took out his reading glasses. The judge turned to his clerk who gave him the tissue of lens cleaner. Rubbing his glasses, "Why do the papers show the man's name as Boyd and not Sphinx? Could the lawyer for Mr. Reeker be succinct about this problem?" wearily asked the judge.

His lawyer explained that Boyd took a trip to Egypt.

The judge bit his lip and said, "Okay, that explanation is a little bit too concise. Continue."

Per Sphinx's lawyer, he fell in love with Queen Hetepheres II so then changed his name, legally, of course, to Sphinx. His lawyer handed the judge copies of those legal name change papers. The judge shuffled the papers and checked out the document. He felt that mystery of a name change unraveled itself. He liked legal documents. This was a valid legal document. He handed the paper to his clerk. The court proceedings could now begin, and the evidence could be scrutinized.

The judge cleared his throat. He looked at the suspected felon and saw disdain in the man's eyes. The judge wished this mythical androsphinx, human man-lion, sometimes winged freaking jailbird stayed in Cairo or Guinea-Bissau with the organically-grown chickens they raised there. He wished the Sphinx wasn't in his court. The man made him uncomfortable. It was the criminal eyes. The judge could see past the cornea. Transparent were his thoughts. Empty was more the case of what existed in front of him.

The judge turned to his clerk who gave him a small plastic bottle. The judge ate a few of his anti-digestion pills. He hadn't taken the pills for a month now.

The judge noticed the other name on the documents, Santan Chesin. Now the judge thought about that piece of slippery slime and band of reprobates. Santan Chesin exited the area about a month or so ago when the police needed him as a witness to this supposed drug heist case that was before him. He was so glad that man left his town. The judge hoped he was on the other side of the earth. Let the moron take his corrupt world somewhere else, bothering some other judge.

Santan Chesin's people were constantly in and out of his court due to their vicarious crimes and quickly were released due to Chesin's highly-paid, over-achiever lawyer. The group of thugs, thieves, prostitutes, narcs, screwed-up hippie divers, drunks, and every other kind of criminal for a thousand miles entered his courtroom daily while Chesin was there. It was amazing the way the lies rolled off their tongues. The judge knew ten thousand fake, delusional stories from all those tribes or groups that were part of Chesin's little empire.

That business didn't even count the alleged diamond smugglers and illegal fishing group. Then there were the marijuana-smoking caterers. Plus, some illegal liquor men on occasion. It was enough paperwork to give Judge Daken an ulcer and heart attack. He thought about his wife's family in Venezuela and wondered if it was safe there. Venezuela was looking good right now.

The judge reviewed the evidence. "Is this all the facts the police obtained on Boyd, err, let me see. Yes, the name is Sphinx. The facts on Sphinx Reeker look thin? I'm sure both lawyers received my message regarding that one word. Unless they didn't, my thinking is quite simple. The case before me is weak."

The opposing lawyer knew what thin and weak meant. He shuffled his papers. He told the judge that they had two witnesses. The judge motioned to bring the show forward. The first one was Jinx, the detective.

The judge asked, "Did you actually hear or witness Mr. Chesin accuse Sphinx Reeker of the drug heist?"

Jinx said, "No, I did not, but was told about those facts from Ruse Blake, one of Mr. Chesin's girls."

"The video tape of this supposed conversation of a drug heist is missing. In the paperwork, it states the witness did not see the tape, and now there appears to the courts that this same witness was a party to only a hearsay conversation. Are the lawyers clear about those two points?" The judge shook his head. "Where was the next witness? Maybe there is more credible news on this case from the second person."

Both lawyers agreed to the judge's assessment. Ruse Blake was placed on the stand.

The judge looked at Ms. Blake. "Hello. Ruse, how are you today?" The judge smiled.

"Ruse, why are you in my courtroom again? Your prolific attendance within the halls of this building on both sides of the law amaze me. Haven't I seen you enough?"

The judge knew that she would not be considered a credible witness due to her many arrests and other prostitute offenses. "Ruse is the only person whom Mr. Chesin talked with regarding a supposed drug heist while Mr. Chesin had been drunk and in his own bed. Therefore, it is her word against Mr. Chesin. The situation is precariously weak. Mr. Chesin isn't here to defend himself unless someone in this courtroom knows where the man is currently."

The judge peered over his glasses at the two lawyers. The lawyers looked blankly back.

"I thought that no one would know where the man exists. Mr. Chesin is the missing key witness corroboration for me to be amenable to the situation the lawyers have dragged into my courtroom. I'm sure Mr. Chesin's documentation is secure. He has also appeared here many times and appears to be a savvy businessman." The judge almost said *slippery*.

"I don't want this precarious situation brought before the court again unless the words thin and weak are removed."

Sphinx turned to his lawyer and asked what the judge meant by precarious situation. Precarious meant uncertain. His lawyer explained that Mr. Chesin could corroborate Ruse's story. Sphinx still looked unsure. His lawyer, tired of the whole business, wanted to go back to his cushy life. He had a golf game shortly. He told Sphinx he could go down and live permanently in jail-hell if Mr. Chesin appeared anywhere on the face of the earth.

The great Sphinx received the message.

The judge wanted this whole affair to end. He was too tired to play golf.

"I will venture a guess further to explain that a man's prurient nature would cause him to say anything to a very pretty, delectable woman. A man sometimes embellished his business savviness to that woman to get her into his bed."

The judge looked directly at Ruse and smiled. The judge scowled when he turned to the lawyers. The only lawyer smiling was Sphinx Reeker's lawyer. The judge got out a few more of his pills and banged his gavel.

"Case dismissed, insufficient evidence." The judge exited the room in relief. He hoped to never see the Sphinx in any court room where he resided as judge.

Sphinx Reeker thanked his lawyer. He smiled at Ruse. She was safe. It was Santan Chesin he wanted taken down permanently. There was no sweet jail for this enemy or any of Sphinx's enemies.

Sphinx was one of the con artists that no one wanted to out-maneuver. His successful business was full of clients who never made it into a courtroom like Chesin's pals nor any deluxe jail. The reason was because they just ceased to exist or were dead by some other means. He knew Chesin would sell out the Sphinx's business to save himself.

He made the call to his friend to set up the hit on Santan Chesin or whatever piece of crap name he thought up. Sphinx's man would track him down.

26   The Three Parties Began

THE FIRST PARTY started in the space ballroom in the hotel around the corner from the other two hotels. It was the smaller of the hotels and was the closest to the ferries. All the high-level techies were there along with the managers, marketing people, and administration. The owner of the company and his wife were there early.

They were invited to all three parties and felt it was going to be a grand, exciting evening. They hired a professional photographer to take pictures at all three parties to show their children and use at their next "Rah, Rah, Let's Get Creative" company meeting. There were tables of displays of their newest technological toys and products.

Arriving at the space party, the red tribe men met with their Stew-actor friend. The boys took a couple of long-distance photo shots on the leader's cell phone and checked to make sure the image would be hard to discern even if a person increased the magnification. They were happy with the photos and paid the actor.

The red tribe men moved inside to their other positions at the pirate party and had to wait another hour for the Wrights' masquerade party to open, which would be eight o'clock in the evening. The special dignitaries went to a cocktail party at seven-thirty at the masquerade party and they knew not to be close to that many government guns and heightened security.

The Stew-actor stayed at the space party. He was in the room at nine o'clock when the real Stew stood in the doorway. The party was so compact by then that neither one saw each other. Tami, who was dressed as a space person, saw the Stew-actor, and she alerted Derek who alerted the Miami boys at that ballroom.

The Stew-actor exited the party to take a short walk and smoke his marijuana stash. The Miami guys followed him.

Mann and his bodyguard arrived at the space party with the rest of his partial crew waiting close by outside. They drank their first drink and stopped for the buffet at nine-thirty when Mann saw the real Stew in a space costume. He couldn't see the man's short hair except he recognized the face of a weasel. His weasel was here.

"I would know that creepy weasel anywhere. Bodyguard, we must get closer."

The owners of the space company asked the photographer to take a last picture of this large and short pirate. The owners of the space company left to attend the pirate party.

"Inform my outside crew to take down the photographer in the red madras plaid shirt right away. Tell them it was not the flowered red tropical shirt person. They need to steal the photographer's camera and destroy the memory card because it contained my picture."

"Good idea, boss."

Moving from the doorway to the next table, the real Stew picked up a small meat sandwich, ate a couple bites of the sandwich, and turned. He saw Santan or Mann and his mean bodyguard approaching. Stew saw the evil shark killer look in the man's eyes.

Stew couldn't believe it. He knew why they were here. They were after him because the diamond necklace was a fake. Louisa tricked him and now the diamond thug was after him. It wasn't his fault. It was the old woman's.

Stew ducked under the table and escaped to the pirate party. Mann and his bodyguard followed Stew and entered the pirate party. Mann's remaining crew moved along outside to the next hotel shadowing their boss. Some of the other Miami boys at the pirate party recognized the bodyguard and began to follow him. They forgot to alert Derek in their excitement.

Mann watched Tami enter the pirate party and knew he must leave because she would recognize him and possibly alert the police. His girls whom he didn't trust anymore brought Tami to his party in Dakar.

"Tami looks strange in her space costume. I can't see her gorgeous figure very well and am disappointed. It is an odd coincidence she traveled to Curacao," said Mann.

Stew didn't like the food at the pirate party which served many different flavored oysters and sushi. He hated raw fish. It gave him a rash. He snuck through to the kitchen of the masquerade party because one of the kitchen girls knew him and let him inside.

Mann and his bodyguard saw Stew duck in the kitchen entrance. They entered the exclusive and private masquerade party. The dignitaries already left fifteen minutes earlier. When the police were alerted to an outside camera theft incident, they left to check that out. During all this back and forth activity, the red tribe stole quite a few wallets and money.

War Julio's wife and father left the masquerade party as planned, and a large contingency of the Miami protection family also exited the ballroom. Jess and Derek were standing on the stage talking while the band took their last break. It was now ten-thirty at night, and at eleven o'clock, the fireworks display would start outside.

Many of the island people heard about the fireworks and were jamming up traffic and parking where they shouldn't. The crowd wanted to see the fireworks because it was supposed to be a spectacular one. This activity kept the police further occupied.

Mann saw Derek and recognized the affluent American with the diving motorboat from Dakar from the papers he was provided.

"Why were the Americans in Curacao?"

He realized this ballroom was their expensive party. They were snobby rich and could afford a party. He saw the Queen Sea Nymph ice fountain. Mann knew the story about Calypso. Next to the fountain was a table of old rusted cannon-balls in a large plastic display box with a brass plate that read, *Unknown*

Pirate and then a large blank space which seemed strange.

"Who brought cannon-balls to a party, part of the theme? The food is exotic and very good. The woman did her research of the country."

He picked up a pufferfish toy and handed it to his bodyguard who blew it up. The belly expanded, and the thing popped. The confetti landed all over Mann.

"Sorry, boss."

"Get me some of those cakes. I can smell them." He wiped the spray of paper off his clothes. Mann ate a rum cake and then another one. He started to get a little dizzy. The rum in them was probably high quality. Mann felt he was dizzy from working the maze of tables at the three parties. He stopped to rest and looked around the heavily decorated room. Next, he worried that the Wrights saw the large diving boat on the transport ship. But he wasn't sure they ever saw the original boat in Dakar.

"They probably did not see my boat because they seem happy."

Then he really looked at the beautiful woman beside Derek in the red dress with violet-gray-diamond necklace and a red headdress. She took her mask off. Her diamond necklace suited her skin and soft, pretty, blonde hair. She wore some shimmery glitter around her breasts. The glitter rubbed off Derek's costume during their dance.

Mann knew a good female body and nodded. Her eyes sparkled violet gray when she viewed the colorful room. He was more impressed. The dress flattered her delightful goddess figure.

"She was close to my Tami girl, only better. Tami was the princess, but this woman is a queen. Tami must be her sister and that was why she was in Curacao. Tami had been a spy, then, at my party in Dakar, trying to find information about the dive boat for the Wrights, of course. The Americans wanted to find the same sunken treasure using the coordinates the weasel Stew sold them."

From the looks of the cannon-balls, he assumed that's probably all they found.

"A man can worship a queen who looks that alluring. I saw her eyes and recognize intelligence."

Juices in his body flowed and obsession overtook him. Feelings were rolling toward coveting this woman. She belonged to him. He felt ebullient. Mann felt like his old self. He felt like Santan, the super man. The rum drinks were taking their toll on his devious thought processes. He ate a third rum cake. He wondered if they could become friends. He could start with friendship.

Derek happened to touch Jess lovingly and that made Mann crazier. Derek pulled Jess closer. It was a very good thing that Mann missed the calypso dance, because he would have had his bodyguard kill Derek instantly.

The woman smiled at Derek and whispered something in his ear.

Mann started turning red. Maybe the woman didn't need him as a friend. For some minutes, he forgot his main objective in Curacao. All thoughts of Stew Avery were lost somewhere in his foggy brain.

"I should hire someone to take the husband out. It could be a *hit*. Then I can befriend the woman and feel unrestrained joy. His death might not be a loss to her. I will think about the hit. I mustn't rush into this project, but I want to do it. No, it was better to wait. I can wait."

He drifted back to his lost home in Africa. Mann remembered his house paintings. They were about the old calypso story. He would turn himself into the beloved Odysseus. He knew where to purchase or steal more elaborate diamonds. He saw Jess loved diamonds, because her hands caressed her necklace. If he asked her, she could give him immortality like in the story. He thought that he could be a person who stayed with one woman. He knew that he was fantasizing a little bit there. At least, he might try. If she liked him, he would make the effort.

The Greek temptress story of the daughter of Atlas tempered his brain. He had paid a fortune for the painting that he left behind. He could call the woman his calypso-diamond-queen. Mann was lost in the possibility of his dreams. He hadn't looked in the mirror lately to see his gray, thinning hair and yellowed teeth. His age was showing, and early demented thinking entered his orb.

His bodyguard motioned to Mann that Stew was moving again. The bodyguard looked toward the stage and saw what was spinning his boss into hallucinating ideas.

"It was always the blonde-haired women. The paranoia and blondes went together perfectly." The bodyguard looked at his boss in disgust. The woman on the stage was out of his boss's league. Enraptured by the woman's image, Mann needed to be shaken by his bodyguard that it was time to leave. He almost picked up a pufferfish toy to get his attention.

The video camera did a sweep and caught a faint side glimpse photo of Mann, or the former Santan, with his bodyguard. The two men missed the camera surveillance which was hidden in a tall palm tree.

Stew slinked back to the space party to await his girlfriend whom he thought would be off in ten minutes. She was bringing more food to the table. He couldn't understand why she was still working so hard. He was eating some dessert when he saw her and approached the table. Stew knew he would need to exit town shortly, but wanted to talk with her before he left. Maybe she would be useful to him later in Los Angeles.

Mann and his bodyguard were also back at the space party. They were close enough to Stew. Mann entered the crazy zone, remembering his objective. The objective was to destroy Stew. Mann nodded to his bodyguard. The bodyguard pulled out the gun as Stew bent toward his girlfriend. The bullet missed him and disappeared in the wall.

The second bullet hit the girlfriend in the arm who threw her tray of desserts into the air before she dropped to the flour. Stew left the girlfriend on the floor and ran. He exited the hotel permanently after he retrieved his money, airplane ticket, disguise, and new

190

identification card. The third bullet hit the red tribe leader who dropped. He was instantly dead. One of the weasels in the chicken coop or rather, another con artist lost.

Everyone in the space party ballroom panicked and ran out of the ballroom's double set of doors, causing a stampede. The Miami boys turned Stew-actor over to the police outside. When they heard the shots, they raced back toward the masquerade ballroom. They knew whom to protect.

Mann's crew exited the scene and disappeared as did the now leaderless red tribe group. The red tribe was running for their rented fishing boat. Mann and his bodyguard disappeared into the night deciding not to take the ferry exit route they previously planned. He kept his diamonds sewn in his black pant legs underneath the costume and they hopped a freighter ship that would take them to London, England.

Mann remembered all his bank account numbers in his head and the phone number of the real estate agent in London where he wanted to live. Mann saw Stew exit the hotel.

"My bodyguard did try. It was dumb luck Stew torqued his body at the last second. Stupid weasel escaped the trajectory and speed of a bullet. How did he do that move? Stew was never a normal criminal. He probably changed his name, too, or would shortly. Rats! The Knife guy was required in the future. I'm going to order a *hit*. This one will be on Stew Avery. The Knife guy can research and track him down. I'm done chasing vermin around."

Derek was notified of the gunfire and placed extra guards around Jess. She would stay for the finale, which was grand fireworks. He went to talk to any victims and witnesses at the space party.

The girlfriend regained consciousness on the floor and another waiter compressed napkins on her arm. He smiled at her and told her she would be all right. She smiled back and didn't care about Stew anymore. He left her wounded and bleeding. This waiter was nice and cute in her mind. She informed Derek that her old boyfriend was part of the disturbed bad men of the world. Her anger was kicking into the scene finally. She passed out again.

Derek would have to talk with her in the hospital. Derek ran back to the fireworks and Jess.

War Julio called Derek to let him know that he would take the air-boat and checkout this fishing boat his Curacao boys cornered. The police knew where Mann's diving ship was docked because someone phoned in a tip about stolen jewelry there. The police were heading to a company's private dock and had contacted the owner of the dock.

Mann's crew were caught on one of the ferry boats with the photographer's camera minus the memory card.

Derek remained with Jess for the fireworks display to start. "I don't want to leave you alone with anyone else. Let the others handle the rest of the gun show." He held Jess close and smelled her perfumed hair.

"Is that the fragrance you chose for the ladies in the gift bags? It reminds me of exotic mimosa and orange. I hope so, because the fragrance is driving me a little crazy."

She turned to him and said, "The flower combination works. It has been another strange night. We certainly can pick the location for danger. You tried to warn me about our trip. By the way, how crazy are you tonight?"

Derek laughed. His wife was her normal self. Danger was part of their life.

"You should know by now my feelings. I'm way crazy."

He could feel her warmth through the soft satin dress. Touching her always made him feel good.

"Can you please wait for later? Then we can properly go crazy, very soft and slow. I have a special piece of new music that I believe you will like." He kissed her sweetly in the night.

Her eyes twinkled with the first fireworks display. "For you, I will wait. What piece of music? The night is now filled with mystery and amore."

27 Almost Demise of the Red Tribe

THE CURACAO BOYS, who worked for War Julio, figured out the possible escape routes from the party. War Julio told them to read books on battles to learn strategy and to watch casino heist or spy movies. They knew there would be the noisy fireworks display and thought about the fish nets and scary toys. They couldn't use any padded trucks here because there was no rental place that owned them on the island. Most of the refrigerated trucks were out for deliveries.

They saw these foreigners who called themselves red tribe in secret when they thought no one was around. The Curacao boys knew the red tribe rented a small fishing boat and wondered about that. It was suspicious because there were no fishing rods on the boat. They put a watch person on the boat and were informed when the tribe loaded heavy suitcases and supplies. The boys moved some of their gear closer to the boat. They posted three more diver friends who would set everything up for them surrounding the small fishing boat. War Julio emphasized preplanning.

The red tribe group held the stolen wallets and cash with them from the space and pirate parties. Not too much was obtained at the masquerade because they noticed the security cameras. They transferred the wallets and cash from the suitcase into the boat locker along with the other stolen jewelry from previous hotel and house heists.

They believed they made it to safety. Unknown to them, the Curacao boys installed one of War Julio's remote-control nets that raised up and down around the boat. While they had done this job, they became acquainted with some seals that circled the dock and fed them some fish a few times. The boys used most of the plastic toys and placed them inside the net. They also added a banana or two into the engines and placed five extra anchors on the fishing boat and tied some of those around the dock under water for good measure.

The crew started the engines which coughed at first and one of the engines started so they could move the boat. The red tribe group believed the person who rented them the boat was cheap because only one engine worked. Untying the ropes, they saw the noisy fireworks display start in the distance.

The Curacao boys turned on the remotes to the plastic toys and raised the net at the same time to contain them. The plastic toy fish moved as did the large shark fins. The huge lighted Japanese crabs' movement scared the red tribe group in the boat who tried to gun the engine. There was no forward movement. The one engine strained. The smoke from the one engine surrounded the sitting-duck boat in the water, stinging the red tribe's crew nose and eyes.

Reaching for their guns, the Curacao boys appeared out of nowhere. One of the Curacao boys threw some fresh caught fish toward the back end of the fishing boat to get red tribe's full attention. War Julio's air-boat arrived around the corner with more artillery.

As the red tribe looked from the low water display and breathed in the smoke, two of the seals jumped out of the water to catch the fish and knocked two of the red tribe men into the murky moving water. The first seal caught the fish as it went overboard, chasing those two boys in the water to move farther away from the boat and mess. They swam toward the dock ladder.

The second seal mouthed his fish and landed in the boat with the remaining three other men who could not see very well. One of the Curacao boys shouted, "Shark."

Those three crew men touched the wiggly, slimy thing and jumped into the water. The second seal ate his fish and saw the moving objects and the other seal. The second seal jumped into the foray further scaring the men who were crawling over each other to reach the same dock ladder.

War Julio and his boys laughed so hard, it took a few minutes before War Julio could talk with Derek on the phone. Derek notified the police who picked up red tribe and hit them with a search warrant. The jewels, wallets, and money were found on the fishing boat. The red tribe went to jail for theft reasons and various assortments of other crimes like trespassing and movement of stolen goods.

The Curacao boys lowered the nets to let the two seals out forgetting the tide was moving outward. The plastic toys floated away. So entangled were they by the large Japanese spider crab legs, the mass formed a raft.

Next early morning all the plastic toys moved toward the canal and bridge. It took a while for War Julio's crew to get two of their boats for retrieval of the floating toys. A cruise liner filled with people was slowly moving into the mega large port to unload their passengers. The crew and passengers saw the plastic raft of strange-looking objects.

The two seals were still following the raft and would nudge one of the crab legs causing it to move. They were reminded of the rafts of the doomed *Aguamala* ship, the half-skeleton raft was out front of the cruise liner. The madness in the water was shown to their captain.

The captain said, "It is probably a loose crate from either one of the foreign cargo transports. Those ships lose things in the harbor that look odd all the time."

Then the passengers saw two fishing boats arrive alongside the raft. The fishing boat boys threw out fish to distract the seals. They maneuvered their nets, hooked onto the circle, and lifted the raft of toys. The cranes swung the hanging group of neatly netted toys off the back of the fishing boats. The boys were going to drop them in the hold.

But the passengers cheered, so they stopped their task. The cruise captain sounded his horn and decided to join the morning party by using his speakers to announce that the Portuguese ship, *H. Azores*, saved the day.

The passengers were smart. They, too, knew the story of the *Aguamala*. The passengers went wild. They clapped, waived, and whistled to the Curacao boys. The Curacao boys bowed. The passengers were delighted. The cruise ship captain knew the passengers would want to take another cruise soon aboard his company's ships.

The captain was told to look for opportunities to market their image.

"Perfect marketing tool. I want to hire those boys for another performance. The cruise ship could do a gourmet seafood with egg buffet on the front of the ship including espresso and latte coffee. Mimosas would work well. And, of course, chef-made sweet rolls and juice for the children. It could be a package deal where they did a movie the night before of creatures of the deep."

"I believe the captain is correct in his marketing ploy. The passengers were loving the play before them and enjoying the high entertainment value."

The captain's mate stepped out of the bridge and caught the boat names from the back of the two fishing vessels.

28   Fireworks Party End

THE FIREWORKS DISPLAY was awesome. Jess and Derek hired a special night video photographer to make a movie to show their children and anyone else who might have missed the display.

Derek held onto Jess who opened the very expensive, old bottle of scotch that Dean squirreled away in some of his refrigerated and frozen warehouses. The last two fireworks displays were two necklaces in silver and the final necklace light display was in gold with a burst of green. They decided to add one more just for Louisa. It was a large dolphin outline.

All the people slowly exited the party and the three hotel areas. The police were still at the space party.

Jess told Derek, "The masquerade party calypso dance performance was a good choice."

"Yes, you managed to do a great job with the entire party. The fireworks display is the best yet. The Miami father of War Julio's wife congratulated me. The man offered me some of his special hand-rolled expensive cigars."

Their hired limousine took them to their docked motorboat. He held her close on the deck and smiled.

"No, the party was better than great. Way, way better. He especially liked where she parked that glitter."

Jess glanced down. "I didn't know I wore glitter. Are you trying to persuade me for some reason?"

He loved the way she tempted him. "Absolutely do I want to persuade you and find all the glitter? I remember our dance tonight. Your dance moves drive me crazy. I love it when you look at me that way."

"How crazy? A small crazy, a medium or high. Or is it a super, one in a million crazy? Or maybe a crazy oblivion?"

Jess did the right left moves of the dance slow and smooth. The seduction was too much. The temptress did the moves one more time. Seduction was complete.

Derek needed an island. He couldn't wait any longer. Derek picked her up and carried her off to the master bedroom. More glitter fell from his shirt onto his beautiful wife. Bed was the closest thing he had handy as far as an island was concerned.

In the morning, he showed her the photos of the possible character, Stew Avery, the butler's son, which they found on the dead red tribe leader's phone. There was the glimpse photo image of Santan Chesin that Tami caught on the security tape at the masquerade party of two pirates. The police knew he was Mann Nisee.

Derek did tell War Julio and Jim about those photos. War Julio reminisced with Derek and Jim about the red tribe fishing boat incident. That brightened both men's day. War Julio shared with his wife, her father, and family all that transpired. Her father had the best time at their party.

Their children were brought back early. In two days, they cruised toward the Panama Canal and eventually home to Los Angeles enjoying the familiar journey from a prior boat trip with Dean. Jim's boat would be transported back home. They accomplished their masquerade party in remembrance of their friend, Dean Crain. The photos of Stew, and Santan, aka Mann were distributed to all the friends and family members and the police.

Later one of the Curacao boys sent out the image of the toy raft someone took from the cruise ship. It was an instant hit.

XXXXXX

About three months passed and War Julio received a package in Rio. His wife's father stayed around to check out the fishing business and horse estate that War Julio created. Her father would go home the next day with his crew. Her father thought War Julio should get a special scan machine because a person never knew what would arrive in delivery packages.

War Julio said, "The package is fine because it came from the Wrights in Los Angeles. It came on a special chartered airplane flight."

Opening the box, War Julio saw the top part of a beautiful peacock feather. He took it out and admired the colors. The aqua and blue reminded him of water and sky. The feather was soft and iridescent. He could imagine a chief wearing such an exotic flower or his woman. The object was from a living creature. The man believed the creature as something sacred like the water and sky.

"Montezuma. He loved peacocks more than gold. That is probably why he offered the Spaniards the lesser valued item, the hard and cold gold, a long time ago. The gold was nothing more than a rock. It was common like quartz or sandstone."

Then he removed more wrapping paper. War Julio took the items out of the box and sat down staring at the object.

His wife's father picked up the object and said, "It is real gold."

War Julio read the note from Jess and Derek, "A large picture will arrive later. Thank you, Love, The Wright Family."

"Derek and Jess sent me one of the four-pound ingots of gold from their amazing find of sunken treasure and a hundred silver coins from the very real second pirate ship."

War Julio dug further to the bottom of the package and pulled out the paper-wrapped sphere. It was a rusted cannon ball from the pirate ship.

"The Wright family sent the same packages to their friend, Jim."

War Julio talked to his wife about the amazing gifts from the Wright family.

"The Wrights' message is that things don't matter that much. It is friendship that counted in the world. If a person knows they are on their last journey, who does a person take with them?"

War Julio turned to his wife and told her that he would take only her and his children, and if there was room, her family. He said the correct answer because she held onto him all night long. He chose wisely becoming friends with Dean Crain, the Wrights, and the Michaels.

29   Diamond Smuggler

CHARLES MANN, AKA Mann Nisee, aka Santan Chesin lived in a comfortable flat in London, England. He thought it a joke that he held onto a part of his former name. He was still the man. No one would think about that twist. Charlie started getting careless. But he did change his appearance. There were reading glasses that he wore all the time and a bristly mustache. He picked beige plaid slacks for his wardrobe with a beige shirt and bright green tie. He wanted to blend in with the other old men in the neighborhood.

He was listed as a retired historian of diamonds and sunken ships. He talked to all kinds of people in the market, libraries, and neighbors. He wanted them to think of him with high importance. He signed up for online book clubs and received many of the pre-released book copies on his book reader. He missed the feel of a hardbound book in his hands and the feel of the paper.

The woman at the store showed him how to use the contraption. He found the little black machine easy to use and could buy books from his comfortable lounge chair. Consequently, the little reader went with him whenever he decided to visit hotels in England or to get out of the city.

Charles sat thinking. *My girlfriend is young, a little dish-water blonde, but still pretty. Except her dullness wears me out. She can't carry a conversation for very long.*

His depressed, sagging body showed age. Tired of her and bored with his new life, he called his bodyguard.

"You must find me new blonde women. I need high entertainment. Go find ones with a brain this time. This is crucial."

Perusing the book website, his eye caught a new pre-release of a book about dolphins and sunken treasure off Dakar, Senegal. He saw the two authors' names.

"It was the Americans." He sighed because he figured they wrote their silly book and here it was. It took them quite a while. His thoughts were that they probably paid a slew of editors, publicists, and press to get it noticed.

He set the reader aside and would pick it up later because some new potential ladies were coming to tea. He made an appointment first to get his nails trimmed and buffed. His toupee would also be washed and reset to fit his head shape.

A friend of the Miami family saw the photo one day that was distributed of the two pirates from the Curacao parties. He heard about this person through the grapevine. His mother lived in a flat in London who saw a strange neighbor with lots of blonde women.

Her strange neighbor was a diamond historian. His mother didn't think that was a viable title. What was a diamond historian? Diamonds came from mines. Everyone knew those facts. The strange neighbor talked of sunken ships in Africa and there weren't any sunken ships to find anymore. She believed the man was daft in the head. Therefore, he must be a criminal. The Miami friend wondered about the man. It was the sunken ships that bothered him. He went to his contact. The contact knew this person in Africa that was searching for a person with the same description, age, and similar job title. The Miami friend sold the photo to his contact to sell to the African.

Now the African happened to be the man named Sphinx. Sphinx sent his people to talk to the red tribe crew in jail in Curacao. The red tribe people knew nothing. They pointed him to another man from Africa that knew Santan. This man took a long shot. He put the blame on Ruse Blake. She always talked to Santan in Dakar. She was like his confidant.

Of course, Sphinx talked to Ruse. His boys picked her up one day at her beauty salon in Dakar, Africa. Ruse and Sphinx were hot for a while. She told him what information was told to the police. Santan loved London, England. She told Sphinx she didn't think the police believed her. Ruse read his London real estate brochures and remembered the names.

Sphinx believed her. He would send his hit man there. Later he changed his mind when the address was revealed. He decided to take care of the problem himself.

XXXXXX

Charles Mann poured himself a large drink and sat down to read the pre-release book he pulled up earlier on the book reader. He never looked at the pictures in a book until the very end. He read through their history of the boring migration of ever-dull dolphins and their first dive site, closed the book, and went to bed with his latest girl.

Charles dreamed that night of his queen. He talked in his sleep and kept repeating the queen's name. He kept saying, "Calypso."

The girl woke up and became worried. She heard him call the strange name. She figured Calypso might be a woman or an island. It didn't sound like any place near London. The parade of blonde women in the flat that day confused her. She was not jealous, but worried. This was a nice place to stay. The man didn't bother her too much. She remembered taking care of one of her previous boyfriends when she was much younger. But the money would stop if he replaced her. It wasn't the kind of replacement she had been thinking.

The old man became implacable and critical. Paranoia rolled in.

"Old Charlie is going to dump me in the river." She couldn't believe it. She hadn't done anything wrong, yet.

His bodyguard warned her. "The man's irascible nature became a huge problem lately and the boss was slipping from reality. Charles should see a doctor and get medicine for his condition of psychosis and dementia. I am done with him and will return to

Africa. He wants you gone and I won't harm you. The river won't carry your body on my account. I recommend you leave as well. I can give you some money, so you can live comfortable for a short time."

"I will need to think about my future."

Approached earlier that day by an African man who liked her, there was an offer of a lot of money if she did this one little favor. The girl went into the bathroom, turned the water on, and made the call. She would do the favor the next evening. The man informed her that he owned a huge estate in Africa and he would like to show it to her. It happened to be a diamond estate.

The next evening, Charles continued to read the book and read about the found sunken treasure that was smack dab in his front yard.

"I can't believe it. I need more rum because mine has run out. Call my bodyguard to get some."

His face and head became red, like a bloated pufferfish, as he continued reading. He threw the book reader at her on the sofa. Babbling and pacing, he glared at her in contempt, which scared the girl. He was raising his arms and striking the empty air. He moved toward her with a dark menacing look.

She sunk deeper into the white cushions of the sofa, trying her best to disappear. Her face registered no emotion. Only her actions were defensive. The girl in the gray sweat outfit hugged the yellow pillow as if it was her only shield. She wanted to tuck her feet up, but couldn't with her new flats. Her hair was pulled back from her face in a long braid which made her look younger. Charlie didn't like her to get the sofa dirty. He was very fussy.

"I've been cheated by the Americans who were the thieves? They are criminals. I curse them and their sub. I should have stopped the Wright couple, but I didn't know they were so crafty. Nobody cons me. It is all their fault I didn't find the sunken treasure first. How was I to know which one from the old paper was a *dead-on* coordinate? Dead on. Who talks that way? It should have read Cheerio bloke, right-on coordinates."

He took his shoes off because they hurt as well as his head. He glared at the woman in his place. He picked up the reader and shook it, gesticulating in the air with it.

"Then they found the second ship, a second ship with real silver. That makes me mad. It was a pirate ship. Who finds unknown pirate ships? In the book, they called the pirate ship a name close to my ship in Dakar and changed it to *Doomed Night*. It was the table of cannon-balls at their masquerade party in that stupid plastic case. The ice sculpture was there at the masquerade party as a distraction. I fell for it. They flaunted their find in my very nose."

He strode around his living space, not seeing any of his fine furnishings inside. He was overwrought.

"They found money in *my* Atlantic Ocean. It was my hallowed ground. They are laughing at me right now. I'm glad I hired a hit woman from London to take out Mr. Derek Wright from America. That will fix his clock permanent. They will feel my doom. Their fall is coming. The money I paid the hit woman was worth it. I can hardly wait for completion of that little project."

He hit his fist on the book reader cover.

"The money in sunken treasure I could have in my bank is extensive. It was mine to find. I had been looking first. It was my diving boat looking for a very long time for this specific sunken treasure. The ship was called *The Cathar*. How wonderful? They let those Italians have most of it. Gold and silver. Untraceable gold. I bet those Italians stole it in the first place. Vagabond criminals, they were. No, the Wrights and Italians are rogues who raked me. Dolphins helped find it. Stupid, stupid. Dolphins didn't know the coordinates. Humans did. I swear rich humans were more dangerous than any creatures of the deep. They wrote that the dolphins charged out of the water in a rise and fall motion. It was a glorious arc of perfection to draw their attention. Well, their rise isn't going to last long. The arc is going to break. I'm going to break it."

He glared at the small circle picture of a smiling dolphin on the back cover of the book. It reminded him of those emoji--smiling yellow faces. He wanted to change that smiling dolphin to an upside-down grin. Santan grimaced in an upside-down grin. He finally looked around for the ice bucket and filled his glass with the cold cubes. He saw the dolphin in one of the cubes jumping over a yellow raft. His mind was playing tricks. The dolphin was smirking at him.

"Their story was so fake. It showed their idiocy. Did you see the picture section? It was mostly the ocean creatures at the forefront. The millions they showed last. I had that coordinate in my hands, but that sleazy weasel, Stew, put it last on my list. He was the scammer person. The weasel handed a shiny, glittering fortune to them. Why? Wasn't I nice to him? My stories were only meant to scare people a little. He wasn't easily scared. Well, he will be now that he knows that I can find him."

"I would have found the beautiful treasure. I know how to do a dead reckoning in the ocean or at least my captain knows. I only hire the best. I am the best. I could learn to love playful dolphins. I would have noticed them. The dolphins and I could try to be friends. I carry fish on my boat with which to pay them back for their services. We would have found my millions together. I could have lived better than anyone. Yes, living a king's life on the snob green grass hill in England with massive servants. I might have installed dolphin statutes containing diamond dust near my front door. Well, just a little diamond dust."

Psycho level paranoia was rolling into the compartment of his mind. The dehydration and thirst were creating havoc with his mental faculties. He was moving back and forth like a demented person, opening every drawer in his house, trying to find something as if the gold would be there.

Charles slumped in the chair exhausted. The reader slid to the floor and bounced under the sofa.

"The treasure was right there. It was so close. I can touch it. I see it in front of me in the water. It was mine!"

He shook his head and drank the melted ice water. Charles's eyes grew dark, the deepest of dark, dark as an abyss. Blacker than black became his iris. His thoughts drove him into deeper anxiety and depression. He recognized the sadness and didn't want it in his brain. He reached for a calm-me down pill from an old stash that he kept hidden from his bodyguard. It didn't matter that the date had expired. Nor the fact that there was a random combination of pills in the jar. Charles popped a few more in his mouth, chewing them as if they were candy corn. He thought the calm-me down pill was working, except his pupils dilated.

He anxiously looked toward his bar. He felt the weights dragging him down again.

"Dolphins, huh."

He laughed or tried to make a sound that sounded strange in the air. It was more a moaning groan.

"It was that easy to obtain all those super, sublime, spectacular, sovereign, splendid, stellar pile of riches. So, so easy"

The girl worried about the pills. Charlie's words made no sense. The man looked funny and far gone. She saw him get up and stagger.

"Easy does it." She knew she shouldn't have said it.

His face grew more red. He tried to focus on the girl.

She thought he was going to explode.

Charles felt dizzy and terrible. His heart was hurting with a bar of weights stabbing the perimeter.

Maybe the pills weren't working. Santan needed to feel good again. He looked at the empty bar. He remembered that his name was now Charles. He forgot. He forgot a lot of things lately. He saw a dead forest. He wondered if he should see a doctor. There should be no forest. Then he saw the ocean. It was confusing. He rubbed his shark necklace. The gold felt supremely hot. He was super warm. Charles turned the heat down on the wall thermometer. Then he felt cold again. Charles turned the heat up to eighty degrees.

"I'm thirsty. Where is that lame bodyguard who recommended that I see a doctor? I don't need doctors."

The girl brought out a special bottle of rum she was given while she was at the market. She placed the bottle on the bar out of Charlie's reach. "The kind man at the market said that it was just a small bottle. It could be the good stuff or not. I don't know anything about the contents."

Charles's normal, careful precaution thrown to the wind, he stopped pacing. His vindictive attitude toward the American's and their wonderful luck at finding the fortune was out of control.

"Redeen, give me that bottle."

She didn't move from the sofa to give him the bottle. She shook her head.

"Redeen!"

She dared not move or breathe.

He yelled at her, "You are not worth anything. I will take care of you later because you are stupid, too. You don't know how to talk like intelligent women that

I require. There are other women more superior. I'm going to bring those other perfect women back to my place as soon as I get a drink of rum."

She still did not move. She couldn't move. It was as if she was frozen on the sofa. She said nothing, waiting for him to decide. She hoped he would and then she hoped he wouldn't drink it. Charlie appeared to be mad already. Perhaps he didn't need the poison after all. All she could think of was her freedom. Redeen would let fate decide. It was a waiting game.

She picked up the blue blanket and threw it on the floor. The room felt hot and stuffy. She kicked off her new gold and silver flats, which flipped to the center of the living room floor. Her feet were tucked under her on the white sofa.

Charles slowly approached the bar and looked again at his watch. He didn't understand the numbers on the watch nor why he was looking at the object. There was no movement. He tapped the watch. He held it up to the light. The hands were still. His expensive watch must have stopped. Charles thought the expensive watch picked a terrible time to quit. Bad karma or a bad jeweler who sold it to him, he couldn't decide.

"It's dead."

That did it for him. It would cost him a fair amount to fix the darned thing. There were some old shillings in his bank box. He could use them. Now the other problem. The rum was required.

Grabbing the small bottle from the bar, he raised it and saw the golden liquid. He tipped it toward his lips, suddenly remembering his bodyguard.

"I can't wait for my bodyguard to return."

Gulping down the rum, Charles looked at the floor. It seemed as if the apartment floor was giving way to an ocean below.

"How did the ocean get here in my place?"

He thought he saw gold and silver. He wondered if he should dive in and retrieve the valuable stuff.

Charles took a hurried step, stopped, gurgled, and fell face first into the blanket, landing on shoes. He was dead. The tainted liqueur snuffed him quicker than the wind tipped a raft. His body stretched out like the vile shark he was. His shriveled skin turned gray. His watch dropped and rolled on the floor landing in the bow of a shoe. The watch wasn't needed anymore. She didn't need the dead timepiece or her boss. The scales of justice began righting themselves. The Sphinx won in the end. He was the greater con artist.

XXXXXX

The police posted Charles Mann's bizarre-looking picture taken in the room. The article stated that the suspected persons were at large. They found diamonds sewn in his long pants in the closet and an expensive watch. They didn't know where the diamonds came from, but thought the stones were illegal. A few pounds of shillings were in a bank

215

drawer, but no other currency was found. They weren't sure why he kept the old coins. He paid his bills in cash. They wondered where his cash came from. The police were looking for an unknown girl due to the shoes and clothes found at the flat. Also, another man who evidently lived on the premises was missing.

Other people saw the photo of the deceased diamond smuggler man, read the article, and were relieved.

Derek's secretary handed him the folder in his office. The folder contained the photo and newspaper clipping of the story. Derek read the label on the folder and smiled. She was smiling as she walked away. Some days in this business were good days. The bad guys lost.

Derek reread everything and let Jess know, who let the crony's wives know, and distributed the knowledge further.

"Santan Chesin, aka Mann Nisee, aka Charles Mann, possibly a known diamond smuggler who once lived in Africa died. There appeared to be poison in a small bottle of gold rum and a heart condition that probably brought the man down in London. Some drugs were also noted to exist in his body and on the premises. There were no known relatives, friends, or business associates available nor did anyone appear at his funeral. The permanently terminated pirate was a pile of dust and shark teeth. He no longer contaminated this universe's oceans."

30   Book Signings

THE BOOK ABOUT their expedition was published and finally released for the authors, Derek and Jess Wright. They departed to one of their many book signings. There would be extra security for the tour, because the exhibit contained some rare objects from the dive site.

Included were one of the coins from the Renaliere collection and ten of the silver coins from the second pirate ship. They included some of the charred ship boards from both ships and cannon-balls. There also were beautiful pictures of the dolphins. Underwater videos of the dive site played on a television monitor. Both the exhibit and video were an instant hit with the young and old alike. The book was portrayed in an elegant cover filled with mystery.

Derek arrived at the book signing.

Jess kissed him. "I want to live with you forever."

He remembered that kiss on their first date.

"More of that please." Her eyes told him she wanted more.

"I want to buy you more diamonds."

"I would rather have a mist-colored sports car instead."

She would look magical driving that sports car, thought Derek. Derek leaned down and whispered in her ear, "We'll get you that car."

Jess smiled and would hold him to those words.

After their first book signing, he gave her the single violet-gray diamond necklace, which was set in platinum on a very strong platinum chain. It was a fifteen-carat rock that he felt he could afford. Their life was filled with new friends and activity, too.

The book sold out quickly and the electronic book's pre-sales were off the charts. They ran a fourth set of publication before the book tour was halfway over. Due to the high volume of pre-sales, the publisher agreed to run a sixth printing.

Jess did well to treat the narrative of the story, so it was cloaked in adventure to hold the reader in suspense. Her joy of the sea and the Renaliere story enhanced the book. Her history regarding dolphins and their playful nature at the dolphin run sucked the readers into the plot. A buried sunken ship and now-found treasure gilded the story even more. The surprise tale of a second pirate ship and the fiery descent of both ramped the reader's interest. Plus, they included the diver's thoughts and Skid's ideas into the book.

XXXXXX

It was during this time that Stew Avery, now known as Hamm Roe, stumbled upon the Wright book at a coffee shop in Los Angeles. They provided sandwiches and salads which weren't too bad. Hamm ate there most of the time to save money.

Some young pregnant hippie woman dropped the Wright book out of her diaper bag. The woman dropped the baby blanket twice now. He picked it up and put it back for her each time. She retrieved a bottle out of the bag for the whiny kid in the stroller with cookie mouth.

Hamm was glad he never married or had kids. He thought kids were the weirdest, nastiest things on the planet. Children were always a mess. He didn't put the book back in her bag. The two author names caught his attention. He quickly strolled out of the shop. The pregnant woman didn't even see him.

He read the whole book twice and looked at the pictures often. His beady evil eyes counted the money in his head.

"The idiot Santan Chesin couldn't find a hole in his own head, much less his creepy *Night Ship*. He never found the valuable sunken treasure nor the second unknown pirate ship. I gave the fool the coordinates and what did I get for that? Nothing. Absolutely nothing. I might as well have put the papyrus in a bottle and threw it in the ocean. I stole for that man."

Hamm was glad the man's bodyguard missed killing him in Curacao. He laughed. It hadn't been funny at the time. But he was still alive and had changed his appearance and name. Then he scowled.

"Two ships. Who finds two ships? Pirate silver in wood barrels. So much gold and silver on the first ship. Chesin was a moron. Then they found other valuable items. Two ships right in front of Chesin's nose. What an arrogant bloke? I hear he died. He should have died from acute stupidity, not poison or whatever. I'm glad Chesin is gone or I would have liked to kill him personally. Changing his name twice didn't help him. What a mug hammerhead!"

The rant and name calling would continue a little longer. Hamm was on a roll of selfless blame.

"I want something for all my efforts. The Wrights interfered with my plan. It was a perfectly simple plan. It should have worked. I put so much energy into every detail."

Hamm looked out the dirty window of his apartment. The landlord was too cheap to keep the windows clean. He didn't see the dirt this time. He needed to go for a walk. He put the book in his pocket and walked to the Venice Beach area. It was getting dark and the sun was slowly descending into the deep ocean. He wondered how far out in the ocean a person had to be to keep watching the globe turn into an oblique.

Hamm was drawn to some bag people who seemed to crawl out from wherever they lived during the day into the night to scavenge items left by the tourists. He watched them when suddenly, a garbage can had become alight with a five-foot-high fire. One of the bag men had thrown a piece of paper with a lit match into the filth that lay in the container.

Hamm looked around for any police and didn't see anyone near. No one paid any attention to the burning barrel. Hamm took the Wrights' book out of his pocket and threw it into the fire. He watched fascinated by how the edges curled inward. Then the book seemed to explode singing his eyebrows and lashes.

He turned away in disgust. It was probably from all that baby milk on the pages that caused the book to explode. Or else it was the numerous cracker crumbs wedged into the binding. Crackers were as bad as mayonnaise in his opinion. No, there probably was old mayonnaise and slimy lettuce in that filth. Maybe there was a carrot or two. Vegetables were explosive, right? The fire smelled like burnt banana peel. No, it was his cousin's ripped shorts in there. His cousin frequented this area. He thought he saw blue or was it gray? It was a little bit red, too. He squinted to make sure his eyes still worked. He wished he owned a handkerchief.

"Whatever! I should have thrown the book away somewhere else."

The mini-explosion should have served as a warning of more bad things to come. He was oblivious, because his mind was racing. He quickly forgot the barrel fire. Hamm was thinking of how to obtain money. He needed money. He walked back to his apartment. Hunger made him stop his mind from overload until he could fuel it from the ham sandwich he had purchased earlier. Swallowing the last bite, he felt better and more in control.

"I know of some fences who can sell silver coins. I need to make plans to steal the silver coin and other coins at the exhibit. I will attend the Wright's last book signing in Los Angeles. They owe me big time. I can do the robbery alone. I don't need anybody to screw things up again. I'm smart and know all about alarms, exits, and sprinkler systems. I've been in the building once before, and remember, there is a basement which contains lockers where a man can hide."

Hamm purchased some tools for the locker to remove the upper shelf and jimmy-rig the lock. He planted some water and food in the locker in case he needed to stay longer. He also bought some clothes so that he could change. The pants and shirt looked like the maintenance workers he had seen enter the book signing building earlier. He was going to be prepared this time.

31 Chesin's Hired Set Up

STEW AVERY, NOW Hamm Roe, made mistakes the same as the original Mr. Chesin. He really wasn't that smart, but just thought so. He told someone where he would run, and it was to a woman. Women remembered every little detail no matter how insignificant at the time. They also loved to talk, not nervous at all, revealing important information. The word *incommunicado* was not in their vocabulary.

His girlfriend in Curacao talked to Derek, to the police, to her new waiter boyfriend, to her employers, and to the maids at the hotel. The communication flowed like a million bottles with notes in them crossing all the oceans. The message went adrift in the many oceans' great currents, moving in all directions.

Mr. Chesin met this man on a trip to China and became fascinated by his knife skills. Chesin wrote his name down in code in his head under If All Else Fails.

"The knife man could afford to hire thugs and thieves to track prey down."

A special group known as The Blade contacted the Knife and wanted the job of finding this person, Stew Avery, aka Hamm Roe. A deal was made.

The Blade followed Hamm to the coffee shop. It was easy to find this guy because his habits repeated over and over each day like clockwork. They stopped the nice pregnant lady.

"What book are you reading? We saw the ugly person who stole it from your diaper bag. We didn't like the person who took advantage of you."

The woman became distraught because she only read half the book. She just read in the book the part about the second ship. "I want to know what happens next in the story."

She looked around and didn't know which ugly person ran off with her favorite book.

"How did the story finally end? I hate guessing."

Wanting to know how the story ended, she knew she must buy another book. Her husband would be upset she lost something again. Last week it was a bag of diapers and before that the baby's juice bottles. Then there were her car keys lost in her old jacket pocket that her husband found for her.

"I forgot to make his lunch one day, too, and my husband had to pay for an expensive sandwich. He never understood how I could run out of gas on the freeway. He didn't understand all the distractions I face every day with a small child. I won't tell my husband about the missing book. What harm can that cause? I absolutely must replace the book."

The pregnant lady told them how wonderful the book was to read and who the authors were that participated in the adventure. She mentioned that she must buy another book. She would attend the Wrights' last book signing in Los Angeles. She gave the friendly group the time and date.

The Blade group checked out the book, the rich authors, and Hamm's activities. They figured out what he was planning and took their findings to the Knife.

The Knife readied his distraction crews and he began sharpening each knife very carefully. Experts were hired for the distraction piece. He readied his special jacket. This was going to be an easy kill. His people checked the book signing and saw little security detail. Only an act from some place other than hell was going to help the Stew, Hamm guy. He would be slices of inedible pork shortly. If Hamm even knew what was coming, he would have crawled under a rock and never came out.

Fortunately, Hamm's thoughts were fixated on the silver valuable coin and pirate coins which were his temporary ticket to somewhere better than where he existed.

He could feel all those party women catering to his every whim with the money he would obtain from the sale of the silver coins in the underground world. That was the lifestyle that shark-creep Chesin took from him. He won't be eating sandwiches any more at the self-serve coffee shop. His dinner will be a two-inch porterhouse steak in a grand restaurant with expensive wine. He could even take a trip to Mexico. Hamm had heard Puerto Vallarta was a fun place with great restaurants. No fifty item menus or fried cheese jalapenos. Maybe he would move there permanently.

His mind wandered to sunny sand beaches and tourist women he could potentially meet in the Mexican hotels. He knew how to work the hotel circuit with waitresses and kitchen cooks. His last job as a pool attendant worked fine. There was no more Mr. Chesin to spoil his fun. Hamm picked up some brochures regarding Mexico and checked airline flights. Yes, he was on his way to a richer life in his mind. There was no room for errors at the book signing.

32   Last Book Signing

THERE WAS ALWAYS a protection crew around the Wright family. Derek insisted upon protection for his wife. She had bodyguards around her and their children. Or ones that could reach them in less than five minutes. Derek wouldn't take anything less than that for their security. Their circle of extended family and friends also were available. They could afford it.

Jess was at the last book signing having a great time talking to everyone. She was relieved the day was moving quietly forward. It was a noisy quiet of excited fans. Derek arrived later in the day. The book tour would be over, and life could settle down. She had some dress designs she wanted to try selling.

As he arrived at the old building, there was still a line of people out the doors. He saw the pregnant woman with her own ink pen in hand with her look of anticipation toward meeting Jess. There was a young man next to her that Derek thought might be her husband. He picked up the pregnant woman's sweater twice now. His physical traits looked familiar, but this person wore a mustache, long hair, beard, and dark-lensed glasses.

The two were getting close to the front of the line. There were quite a few people admiring the artifacts and paintings. Derek wasn't required at this location, so it would be a nice surprise for everyone. Today, they could meet both authors.

The delivery truck arrived with more books and Derek decided to help them unload.

Jess looked up and gave him their sign "Save for later. We will be done this afternoon."

The opened book boxes stacked beside Jess, and the unopened additional boxes were placed on her side and under the table. The books formed a barrier around her, so people couldn't get too close.

The building was an old one that the owners recently upgraded with sprinklers. There was a basement and actual tunnel that went under the street to another building. The delivery truck parked over the tunnel. Under the tunnel ran some city sewer lines.

Derek looked at the author table and Jess was signing the pregnant woman's book.

The Knife person decided that he would throw three knives first. Then he would throw three more. The woman dropped her sweater again, so Hamm bent down. The woman stepped back catching a knife in the back of her arm and Hamm also received a knife in his arm. The third knife hit the wall and clanked.

Derek shouted, "Knife!"

His men drew their guns and immediately zeroed in on the Knife guy who saw all the guns. He was surprised at the protection squad's numbers. Stew ducked under an entry table, ran for the door, and basement. The pregnant woman stumbled and fell toward Jess. She landed on the table of books.

Jess ducked, and several men helped remove Jess from the building toward a different door.

Suddenly, the sprinkler system turned on as Derek's men fired at an arm full of three more blades. Hamm reached the door and had not yet turned the corner.

The bullets took the knifeman down and Derek called the emergency number requesting the ambulance and police.

Jess was driven to a safe location. One of Derek's men helped the pregnant woman up. She grabbed the book Jess just signed, wiping the wet cover with her sweater, and put it in her purse. She dug her car keys out. Derek's man told her to wait and he would find her help.

The delivery boy standing in the book line looked at the company truck. His delivery truck was empty when it blew up and landed hard in the middle of the street. He was truly impressed and wondered how that happened. Everyone moving out and away from the building panicked more. They ran to their cars.

The pregnant woman heard the explosion and ran. She reached her car and sat inside. Deciding she accomplished her objective in getting the famous book, she drove toward home on the busy freeway. Traffic moved slower than normal. Her right arm hurt, and she didn't know why.

She looked at all the blood on the right side of her dress and passed out. Her car hit three cars before it came to a stop perpendicular to a high cement freeway wall. The three cars hit other cars. The entire freeway traffic came to a screeching, tire grinding halt on all three lanes and the side lanes.

No one could move because of the high cement wall and barriers on the road. Several trunk lids popped open and wouldn't close again. The explosives guys' trunk was one that wouldn't close.

A cop was involved in the mess and saw the explosives in the trunk. He couldn't believe it. He called for backup, ambulance, and fire trucks. He walked up to the car with his buddy and they pointed their guns at the Blade group and some Chinese women. The Blade group hijacked their car. They were in deep doo. Kidnapping would be added to the charges.

Back at the old building, the knifeman was dead. The sprinklers were on for a short period and stopped. Derek talked with the police.

"I know the man next to the pregnant woman wasn't her husband, because he hadn't tried to help her. He ran instead."

When the police arrived, they followed the small trail of blood down to the basement and tunnel.

"The wounded pregnant woman has disappeared," said Derek.

The police sent a notice out about her.

While they were in the basement, they heard the explosion and ran back upstairs. The debris surrounding the truck was tight, except the impact on top of the truck was more. Having blown a hole in the inside of the truck throwing its rooftop made what happened next logical. The bomber, after all, was an expert in his industry.

Next, the ground under the delivery truck gave way and the truck vanished. The truck fell into the large sewer pipe hole into the sewer water. The police went back down the basement again to find the truck. They followed the same blood trail in the tunnel to the hole and another set of police checked the other side of the tunnel. There were no blood trails on the other side. The wounded guy must have disappeared in the sewer.

The sewers checked, not one body was ever found. The wounded man also escaped. The pregnant woman was located and taken to the hospital. She was all right and received a case of signed books and a personal visit from Derek and Jess, the authors, while in the hospital.

Jess told her she was extremely brave and strong. She bet her baby would be the same. They left a large bouquet of flowers and a card containing a five-thousand-dollar check for the woman to go crazy in a baby store, plus a little extra to buy skinny clothes later. Her friends would hear about the story for years.

About a month later, Louisa told the Wrights that Stew Avery disappeared. He always called his father, the butler, once a week, and there were no calls. The cousin in Los Angeles hadn't seen him either since he attended a book signing.

"The young man with the beard was more than likely Stew Avery. He was the person that the knife thrower wanted to kill. It was Stew Avery which the next set of three knives were aimed at and not you or me. You were taken through a different door."

"Yes, I was, thanks to the quick thinking by our security detail," commented Jess.

The Knife man wore under his jacket a total of twelve very sharp knives at the time of the attack. Derek felt it was a professional hit probably hired by the now deceased, Mr. Chesin. Chesin probably was upset his diving expedition didn't discover the sunken treasure and possibly blamed Stew.

The police needed to check where the young man had been living. The apartment showed a couple receipts for trips to Dakar, Senegal, in Africa, stuck as bookmarks in some books. There were also rental car receipts with mileage that matched a direct route from the airport to Chesin's house and back.

Derek wondered at the time about the fact that Santan Chesin's boat was exactly sitting dead on center to their third set of coordinates. Hamm or Stew sold the coordinates to Chesin, because the old ship scope was found in his apartment. The papyrus was missing. Derek knew Jess would be glad to know the discovery and want the scope back to donate to the museum with the other items. He was fortunate to have made a copy of the papyrus and the museum kept the copy on display in the exhibit. He knew the original papyrus was lost.

33 Louisa's Dream of a Killer

LOUISA CALLED JESS one day and told her to tell Derek to be careful. That other diving boat captain hired a killer in her dream. Derek knew to listen to any visions or dreams.

They put extra security around Derek and the rest of the family. They purchased a padded van with a quick releasable ramp and special designed air vents that Jess or Derek could hide their vehicles if needed. They practiced loading and unloading the van.

There were two motorbikes with helmets that also easily released from the insides. They bought a large vehicle that could traverse a lot of difficult terrain with high heavy wheels that would always follow the truck. They installed bulletproof glass and doors on the all-terrain vehicle.

The killer, hired to take out Derek, was chosen for her expert gun skills, driving ability, and cunning. She knew him as Mr. Chesin. Mr. Chesin paid the hired gun in small installments which was her preference. She received the last payment and called him. Another job was taking longer. Some more time was required before the hired gun could arrive in Los Angeles. Mr. Chesin told her there was no problem with the arrangement. He had all the time in the world.

The killer read about the dead man in the newspaper and knew it was her contact, Mr. Chesin.

"Who murdered him? I know Mr. Chesin was maybe poisoned and I really don't need to do this job. But like all hired assassins, I use my location for vacation which for now is in Los Angeles. There are fabulous beaches along the coast. While there, I can check out the Wrights. Then I will make my decision," thought Stace Keats.

The only problem was the Wrights were in Rome attending to Louisa's funeral. She passed away peacefully in the night. Her doctor was with her when her heart stopped. She felt poorly, but thought it was indigestion from getting old. Her heart slowed down.

The funeral was a quiet affair with a white coffin and old family burial plot. Her tea party friends and many other friends attended the outdoor garden party at her favorite old hotel. Bouquets and bouquets of flowers were everywhere. There was good food and red wine per her handwritten notes.

Jess found her notebook with the key for the bookcase. She began reading about the great-great-grandmother Renaliere. An auction house took away the furniture and other items. The butler reluctantly left the premises. Louisa left him a small amount of severance pay. The apartment was now empty. They were surprised to learn that she owned the apartment and they hired the place cleaned.

A real estate company quickly found buyers for the now upscale, older, desirable neighborhood location. The apartment sold and closed quickly to be inhabited by a new family. They went back again to her lawyer for the final reading of the will and settlement of the estate.

The gold diamond and emerald necklace, diamond pin, and diadem were given to Jess and Derek. The diamond platinum necklace that matched Jess's necklace was given to their daughter Sami. Two of the silver coins were given to Sami and their son, Justin, would receive four.

Four coins would be given to Skid. He could buy his dream surf shop in San Diego. Skid had visited her many more times in Italy and wrote Louisa wonderful letters always with a story before she passed on. They found his letters. He was a good friend. Then two coins would be given to two of Louisa's closest friends.

The last three coins were donated to the same museum in Los Angeles that Derek donated the relics from the sunken ship. Those were the same part of the items that were shown at the book signings. The money from her apartment was given to Derek and Jess minus any costs for any funeral expenses, church donation, and legal fees. She left them a private note.

"There is no need for a new marker, just an additional date and inscription on the stone. I want a pretty dolphin put there," was the last written request from Louisa Renaliere to the Wrights.

It took over a month to get everything completed and then the Wright family flew a private chartered plane home, grateful for Louisa's friendship and impressive kindness.

34   Stace, Friend or Foe

WHILE STACE KEATS waited for the Wrights to return, she went surfing the Southern California beaches and enjoyed herself immensely.

"There is enough money in my bank and I can retire if I want. My mind keeps returning to the subject while I'm surfing. I like the Los Angeles beaches, but think I will drive farther south around Laguna. Then later I can embark upon the San Diego area while I'm waiting. No sense wasting blue skies and good surf."

Stace dropped her nose cream some place in the sandy beach so stopped at this small surf shack. She saw the cute shop on her walk down to the beach. The guy out front was repainting the sign. There was a soda machine outside. The painting done, the guy disappeared inside.

She read the sign, Skid's Surf Shop. She bought a soda and opened the glass door.

Skid said, "Hello, welcome to sunny California. Was there anything I can help you with today, tomorrow, next week, or next year? You must have a pretty name. Hi, let me introduce myself. My name is great surfer dude and expert diver, Skid Peters. I could give you my resume, but I think it now is about twenty pages long. I've tried to eliminate some of the dive sites, but it's hard because each one was so much fun. I left off most of the pirate ship finds or it would be thirty-five pages long. Am I boring you?"

Stace laughed. "No, you are very entertaining, but I do need to purchase some nose cream."

"Right, let me ring this up for you."

"My name is Stace Keats from London here on vacation for a little while in California. I've been doing the surfer stroll, moving south from Los Angeles. For some reason, my nose always gets overly burnt, peels, and looks messy. Hence, that is why I stopped at your shop."

He was fun. Stace was a little Asian, a little, Japanese, Chinese, and a lot of other unknown nationalities. Her skin was medium toned and very tanned, her hair long and shiny black, and her face beautiful. She modeled for a while and walked with grace and ease. She worked at a little bit of everything from a high wire act in a circus to race car driving. She knew karate and various other skills. She was a sharpshooter and a knife thrower.

Stace was once the girl in a disappearing underwater magic act. She knew all about diving for sunken treasures. The two young-aged people hit it off. He couldn't believe his luck.

"I purchased the shop only a week or so ago because a friend of mine found investors for me. I sold my silver coins. A grand old lady from Italy bequeathed me the coins as a gift. She left the coins to me in her will. I'm totally blown away and surprised by her kindness toward me. There was another rare coin I received from a diving expedition in Dakar, Senegal, Africa. It was a bonus from a wonderful sunken ship dive site. It was the highlight of my diving career. But I retired to a safer vocation which is this shop. No sharks here, just a few on occasion. By the way, I don't put you in the shark category."

Telling her old sunken ship stories to scare her, he learned she wasn't afraid. Then they made love one evening after dinner and wine. Skid made her an Italian dish he had eaten in Italy. He understood the ingredients and replicated the dish. He ate the dish at this old hotel in Rome with his elderly lady friend and her tea party girls.

"I recognize the dish as I ate at the same old hotel in Rome. You created the dish perfectly. It is a strange coincidence."

"I don't think it is strange at all. I think it is karma. Because you and I ate at the same hotel, you visited Los Angeles and San Diego. Visiting those places effectively threw you across my path. Thereby, pushing you into my handsome, capable tanned arms. Tranquility taken to the maximum. I'm the person who put you in that special state of mind called calm, because I am very good. Even the fish are calm when I'm diving. See the great cause and effect that happened, crazy karma. You must feel it because I am very much seeing smooth water today, blue skies, and hot beach which is a good part of a calm spell. We can make our own waves."

Skid grinned at his new girl staring at him in his shop.

She liked Skid very much, especially when he said nonsensical things. He was correct about calm. She was in a lull period of her life. She had time to play. She chose to play with the person in the shop.

They made love when Skid asked her to stay over. Skid was good, very good. He held her like she was some jewel or pearl that he found at a dive site. He wrapped her mind up with his love of life and the ocean. He told her about all the sea creatures and their names. Skid was a smart, funny guy. Stace enjoyed the interlude and tranquility.

He introduced her to all his friends. They went horseback riding with some friends on a horse estate. Wonderful bonfires were enchanting entertainment at a private beach house. Pizza was bought and plenty of beer drank. They ate crab at the wonderful restaurants around the wharf.

They danced and partied when Skid was not working. Sometimes she helped him in the shop. Afterward, they made more crazy love. It was the most contentment Stace felt in a long time. It was the closest she allowed anyone for long time. She thought she would never feel this way.

Stace's thoughts were beginning to churn, and she was getting anxious. "I know no one would recognize me. Whenever I do my hits, I wear black tight-fitting clothes, gloves, and mask. I buried the mask on the beach a distance where children wouldn't find it. It is time to get the mask and do my assigned task. Tranquility always ends."

Heading to the beach, there were police cars everywhere. A blind woman and her dog were sitting near the spot. It was the place she put the mask. There was a huge hole. The blind woman's dog dug her mask out and laid it on top of the police car. Stace backed away from the beach area.

"I need another mask or can create one. The task must be postponed for a little while. I will move the date out on the chop-shop illegal car rental place. It is all right because they will have another car when I am ready. They guaranteed me a vehicle to my exact specifications when I require it."

35   The Mask

DEREK HUNG UP the phone after his call with the London police. They sent him the information and the only photograph of the masked woman assassin. It was one of those times she hadn't done the real crime, but was captured by a security camera on the premises. She had missed the one hidden in a worn child's bear toy. Her deductions were that the employer either ordered two assassins or there were multiple people who wanted the victim dead. The person was a stiff body before she arrived.

The mask she wore was unusual, like some antique item. The buried mask in Laguna Beach was identical to the assassin's photo from London. The Los Angeles police put an article in the paper regarding the mask. Their hope was someone saw the person who buried it on the beach. The mask generated a lot of excitement, but no leads.

Stace went to antique stores and looked for another mask. She found one in a larger store that owned two security cameras and possibly another one in the buffalo head.

"I need to leave you for a week or more to meet an old girlfriend."

"Okay, there is no problem about your time away. I'm easy," said Skid.

Stace lied to him because she must obtain the antique mask and attempt her task. She realized she shouldn't have moved in with him and needed to be more careful. She told him she must visit an old girlfriend who was currently visiting mutual friends in London.

He dropped her off at the airport and kissed her goodbye.

"Do not lose my address or phone number."

He gave her a stack of his business cards rubber banded together.

Stace smiled. "I won't. See you soon." She took one of his cards and gave the stack back to him.

She stole the antique mask and a few other items from the large antique store, disabling the alarm easily. She picked up the car and started her next task.

XXXXXX

Jess drove Derek's priceless sports car because hers was in the shop. His windows were tinted, and it was hard to see inside his vehicle at night. Jess noticed the sports car following her on the freeway after her late-night yoga class. She stepped on the gas and the vehicle kept on her tail. She contacted the two security trucks and Derek.

"There is a dark sports car tailing me. The driver seems erratic. The car approaches and drops back. To be on the caution side, I need the special van right away. Here are my coordinates."

Derek was busy on another incident at an antique store break-in some miles away. The only reason Derek was there was because an antique mask was part of the stolen items. He believed Jess could handle herself with his security detail.

The strange vehicle came up close beside Jess on the freeway. She saw a dark figure in a mask with a gun. Her reaction was swift. Jess swerved into the other sports car, whose driver was skilled at moving out of her way. The other vehicle was on the right side of her, then the left, back and forth. Jess was reminded of their calypso dance. She let her body and mind relax and feel the dance moves.

It took several tactics of Jess driving straight into the rogue sports car, which swerved with their rims touching and blowing sparks before the sports car swerved out of her way. The rogue did it repeatedly, right side and left side. Jess did the dance controlling Derek's classic, specially designed, vehicle on the long freeway.

The truck notified her of their position. Jess knew her hands were gripping the wheel too tightly. She needed to get out of there. Jess saw the designated exit. She stomped on her brakes as the other sports car went ahead of her on the left. She exited the ramp. Driving into the awaiting truck, the vehicle was whisked off in the opposite direction.

Jess jumped in the all-terrain vehicle. Their vehicle went after the sports car which somehow disappeared.

The hired killer sat at the next off ramp on the other downside ramp. The car was in the ditch with her at the wheel scanning the area with night binoculars. She saw the all-terrain dark vehicle go past. In the distance, she saw the van truck moving the opposite direction up the hill.

Stace said, "Very clever. I must prepare a different plan. Derek, the investigator, hired his security team extremely well. The van has hidden his sports car."

Turning her rented sports car around, she took side streets back to the return location. She hopped an airplane to London. Her small rented flat was a hideaway to think about things. She did contact Skid so that he wouldn't worry.

"This is a risky business. I could have been caught. There was always the possibility of prison or death. I didn't care until I met someone. I entered this business after another someone broke my heart. I honed my skills to be able to kill my former lover and his new girlfriend. Every time I killed someone, I shot that cheating ex-lover and his sorry girlfriend. The only problem is that I can't bring myself to kill him. There must be something wrong with me."

She thought about her past. "My killings were jobs to do bad guys in for some other bad guy. It is a game of a con artist killing another one or I call the murder zero plus zero equals infinite zero. The kills were nothing that bothered her. I feel nothing when the job is over. The police should be happy about it. I know that Mr. Chesin was a bad guy. He hired me to kill a rich American who pissed him off. I'm not sure I want to kill the good guy with the pretty family. Perhaps there is a conscience buried inside everyone. The Wrights can afford the very best protection because I saw a fine example of his skills and machines. It would be difficult the next time if I decide that route. Besides, I am bored with killing people."

Derek arrived home and held a relieved Jess in his arms.

"This was not supposed to happen. I'm glad we practiced the escape with the sports car and trucks. You knew exactly what to do. You are always deadly calm in strange situations with the living bad people. You freak out only when there is a surprise dead body."

Derek didn't want to let go of her. "I am so sorry I wasn't there. The killer was after me and didn't know you were in my car. I won't let you drive my car until the killer has been caught. I need to buy new rims on all the tires. I'm not sure how they are so damaged. The assassin must have wider tires. The police will check around for other vehicles with similar damage."

He showed her the mask picture from the robbed antique store.

Jess confirmed, "It is the same mask I saw in the dark. I can't tell you anything about the person's face or hair. The car inside must have been black and her inside dash lights were dimmed off, but not the outside lights. The car is also dark and flat like what an underpaint color would be. The person maintained major control of their vehicle. I wish I could be more concise, but everything happened so fast."

"Honey, that's okay. At least, you aren't hurt. Now the police and I know that the assassin killer has reached the Los Angeles area."

Derek called War Julio in Rio and Jim in Los Angeles for additional protection support. The craziness started again.

Finding a race car video of the moves the assassin drove that night, Jess showed Derek the fast car moves. He became angry with the killer.

"I wouldn't have known how to recover from those extremely expert driving skills. The assassin toyed with you before a final ploy to run you off the road or worst, into a brick wall. You are fortunate our trucks were close."

"Yes, I am very glad we have good people on board. This was too close, even for me. The person has super skills. I'm not sure you are seeing this correctly about the woman toying with the car. I think there was some of that at first, but there may have been a slight hesitation toward the end in completely obliterating me. Perhaps she realized I was a woman or there was some other reason. The woman was in perfect control until I exited the ramp into the awaiting truck. Then I was in control until she disappeared from the scene."

He told Jess that they both needed some race car driving lessons. He would set them up immediately. No wonder his rims and tires needed to be replaced.

"I am so mad at that person. She put you in harm's way. I put you there, too, due to your association with me. You are always placed in danger because of my job or who I am."

He remembered her cottage and the poisoner creep. Jess was found by the poisoner, because of Derek. His job was important, but never more than Jess or their family. If the situation occurred again, he would move heaven and earth to keep them safe.

"Nothing is going to touch my family ever. In the future, I will be wiser and faster to remove them from harm. You will see a scary husband matching the bad guy at crazy."

Jess touched Derek's hands. "We both will do it together, okay?"

"Yes, we certainly will."

Derek put another search out for the vehicle including the snapshot their truck had taken of the back of the rogue sports car before it vanished. Someone knew something about that vehicle. A police report came in later about a stolen sports car matching their description.

The sports car was missing for three months when the owners were in Europe. They knew about the theft, but didn't report it right away, because their daughter sometimes used the vehicle. They finally talked with their daughter at the drug rehab center. She never thought about using their la-di-dah car.

The stolen sports car already was disassembled at the chop shop. Nothing would come of the search. The assassin was a pro. She was the hired best in the business. She was familiar with the unknown illegal chop shops around LA. If one disappeared, another one always popped up. They were easy to find. She only needed to go to the nearest country club where elegant cars were valet-parked.

After a week, Stace made her decision to return to Los Angeles. She joined a gym and put her mask in a rented, locked locker along with her other dark clothes for now. It was time for serious thinking. Then she bussed it back to the airport.

36 Friends of Friends

SKID PETERS TALKED with Derek who told him about Jess's high-speed chase incident and about the mask. Skid was relieved they were both unharmed. Derek told him to keep a look out because a person never knew who they would run into. Derek informed him there was a woman assassin loose in Los Angeles. Skid was glad his new girlfriend was in London at the time. He locked the shop and drove to the airport to pick her up.

Skid lifted her high in the air and twirled her around when he saw her at the airport.

"I was anxious to see you and get you back to our room. I prepared a special dish sitting on the counter ready to cook, after we make love first."

It was a blissful next week. Skid shared with her information when he was younger.

"I was not a very smart boy. I hooked up with this gang one weekend. In a drunken state, I married this girl. Amy was a huge mistake. I manipulated a quickie divorce from her, but she didn't want a divorce and was angry. Fortunately for me, she married the gang leader, Minnow Surf, and they robbed a bank. Amy went to prison along with Minnow and moved out of my life. I went into the diving business right after our divorce. It was so she would have a hard time tracking me down. It is the thrill of the deep that kept me in the diving business for a long time and helped me successfully avoid marriage."

Stace was glad he disengaged from the Amy person. "Who in the world would marry someone with bait for a name?"

That made Skid grab her and carry her off to the bedroom.

Then she received news her ex-lover died in a car racing accident in France. She told him about her race car experience and her race car ex-lover with a new girlfriend. Flying to Paris, France, Stace would pay her respects and later fly back to Los Angeles. She was solemn upon her arrival back from Paris. Skid gave her space. While Skid was working, she sat on the bench with the elderly blind woman and her dog. Feeling guilty about involving them somehow in the buried mask, she bought the elderly woman and her dog some hot dogs and soda. The dog was her friend for life.

"What do you, dog, know?" She reached down to pet the animal and waved to the woman as she left the bench.

She pondered about her prior life. "I feel empty, empty of all the rage against my ex-lover. He was gone and there was no more need to kill. I'm not sure I can change. Why did I let go of my small apartment base in London? I let it go, because I'm tired of the whole business. It's time to get out."

"Ever since I met you, I slowly changed. You enveloped me into your life."

"I'm glad you feel things have changed between us. I feel the same way," remarked Skid. "But I must open the shop and will see you this evening."

After he left, Stace picked out a book from his bookshelf. The authors were Jess and Derek Wright. She read the book cover to cover and waited for Skid to come home.

She touched the rusted, corroded cannon ball he kept on his desk under a large wooden stand with a brass plate, *Unknown Pirate Ship*. He told her about picking the cannon-balls up when he was at the dive site in the submersible.

When he returned that evening, she asked him to tell her the story about his relationship with Louisa Renaliere. Skid Peters told her everything that he knew. Then she asked about the Wrights.

"They own a state of the art motorboat and sub. I participated in the find of the sunken treasure in Dakar. You want to know about the Wright family? There is pretty Sami and smart Justin. They go snorkeling together. The family invite me on cruises and share their friends. I attend some of their great parties. The parties are extravagant, out-of-this-world affairs to honor their old friend, Dean Crain. The Wright family is absolutely the best friends ever. They are one of the super best things that ever happened to me. Both Jess and Derek were kind and smart. They donated most of the artifacts to a museum in Los Angeles. Oh, and Derek put Amy and Minnow away. He's good at catching bad people."

Skid stopped talking and looked at Stace. "You are also the beyond wonderful best thing that happened to me. Whenever you are around, I feel like soaring."

He told Stace how much he loved her and how he would like to have a family someday. The love in his eyes shone. It was love for the Wrights and love for her.

They went to bed and made more heated love. Stace was lost in thought the next day. Louisa gave Skid coins from a diving expedition paid for by the Wrights. The generosity of the coins provided Skid a new life and his shop which she accidentally stumbled upon. The coincidences of everything were impossible.

She was also pregnant. How did that happen? I never become pregnant ever. Skid was her friend and lover. "I can't kill friends of friends. Leaving is the only logical choice."

Skid talked about karma which could also be called fate or destiny.

"This baby is my fate. Finally, I can do something good."

Skid changed everything in her life. Meeting him brought sanity to her mind. She needed to try harder and be responsible. This baby required a beautiful future. Her time would be devoted to doing that very thing.

Stace left Skid a short sweet note.

"Je t'aime, je t'adore."

Those were the French words he whispered to her before they fell asleep.

"I love you and adore you, also, but I need to move on."

Stace needed her freedom to live her life and didn't want to be locked down to anyone. It was just the way she was built inside. Where she went shouldn't matter to him. She wanted him to remain who he was, a wonderful person inside.

She let him know in her note that she would be safe and didn't want him to follow her. Stace took multiple flights to confuse anyone who tried to track her. She disappeared and landed finally in Willemstad, Curacao, having been there before a long time ago.

"Derek will be safe from me, the hired killer assassin. I can't stay because of my crimes. Someone might recognize me and turn me over to the police. I can't allow prison to happen, especially now. Staying in America would be destruction."

The killing task she took on as an assignment was tossed in the garbage. The gym locker items emptied in the garbage at the airport, never to be used again.

Her lawyer was called and given her new address. She included Skid Peters in her will as the father of her child. He would be the inheritor of her worldly possessions if anything happened to her.

37   Maggie Keats

SKID WENT CRAZY for a while trying to find Stace Keats. He couldn't understand her note at all. His friends watched the shop for him. She was nowhere to be found.

Jess talked with him about women and they might have hidden agendas on occasion and real fears. Perhaps something happened that changed things. Something was there that Stace couldn't tell him. They didn't know much about her history. It was hard to know her true world. Sometimes, life was difficult. For Skid, the days were long without her.

Soon he started dating again and everyone was glad that he would be all right. Worried, Jess and Derek invited him often when they went out on the motorboat. The threat from the killer seemed to have also dissipated. War Julio went home as did Jim.

One day, War Julio's wife met this pregnant girl in a beauty shop. Every now and then they would see each other. The pregnant girl was happy and beautiful awaiting the birth of her daughter whom she planned on calling, Maggie.

She told War Julio's wife that her name was Stace Keats. The two women went baby shopping one day on a spur of the moment to a baby shop nearby.

War Julio's wife bought her a small baby carrier for the car, an outfit, and dolphin toy. The women shared a fun time.

She told War Julio's wife where she lived and which building was her apartment complex. War Julio's wife said they lived in a condo in Curacao, but owned a horse estate in Rio de Janeiro. Stace asked if she could use her as an emergency contact at the hospital. The woman agreed, and they exchanged phone numbers and addresses. Stace gave her a card of her lawyer in London just in case she ever needed a good one. War Julio's wife gave her a card of a good lawyer in Curacao.

War Julio found out about the pregnant woman from his wife who promptly gave War Julio her name and number. War Julio checked her out and there wasn't a lot of information out there about her. Stace was raised by a single parent and went to school and college in London. The parent died. She dated a race car driver and did some racing herself. She worked in a circus. There were some acts in Las Vegas. The girl went surfing all over the world and modeled a short gig. There existed sufficient funds. She really didn't need to work.

War Julio asked about the father of the baby. His wife told him women never talked about men.

Eight months passed and Stace took her maternity leave from her job as receptionist at one of the smaller hotels. Not feeling well lately, her doctor assured her everything was fine, just some anemia.

Stace worried that her health might be a problem. She felt exhausted most of the time.

While she was doing laundry, she fainted and fell. Her labor pains started. Her water broke, and she started bleeding in the laundry room. Her phone was in her room and she was unable to get up the five stairs. Another woman found her and called the ambulance. She lost a lot of blood. The baby girl was born. Stace hemorrhaged some more and died.

War Julio and his wife were in Curacao and rushed to the hospital. War Julio's wife wept for her beautiful new friend. They contacted her lawyer who told them the name of the baby's father.

War Julio received the address and phone number from the lawyer. He immediately recognized the father's name. It was the person who was with the Wright's motorboat and helped find the sunken treasure. Derek was informed. They went to see the beautiful, dark haired child with a very pretty mouth. War Julio's wife told him the baby girl looked pretty like her mother.

Derek drove down to Skid's home. The door was partially open, and Skid was sitting on the sofa with his cell phone. He was staring into space remembering her. The lawyer contacted Skid as well. Derek went to the bar and poured two drinks.

Derek said, "Stace is gone."

Skid nodded.

"War Julio's wife was her friend for a while and didn't know who she was. She hadn't known you or anyone else was looking for her. Stace trusted her. They met at a beauty shop in a nice hotel in Curacao. Stace felt comfortable enough to use her as an emergency contact."

After talking to the doctor, War Julio and his wife called Derek back. The baby was just fine at a healthy six pounds, five ounces.

"Did the lawyer tell you what name your child is called?" asked Derek.

Skid smiled, "It is Maggie after my mother. Stace thought it was a nice name."

Skid would be all right. Derek and Jess would fly down with him to help with the funeral and bring little Maggie back. Maggie would have a wonderful, loving group of women to raise her just like Sami.

Derek checked Stace Keats's background. He wondered a little bit about the race car driving. Derek knew the five million dollars would be a huge surprise and help Skid in raising the child.

Pulling up the picture on his cell phone that War Julio sent, he handed his phone to Skid.

Skid smiled wider and said, "Maggie is real, and I am a dad. How did she know a child would make me want to soar?"

"I have been there. A whole new adventure awaits you. Women just knew things. That is the magical part."

38   Sphinx Overthrow

SPHINX REEKER GAVE Chesin's girl, Redeen Pyra, the small rum bottle filled with poison. She told herself that she was only the delivery girl who had no clue what was in the bottle. She made sure not to ask him.

"Anyway, that would be my defense if caught. The poor Charlie greedily drank the bottle half down stopping his heart instantly. It would be a good time for me to leave London to check out Sphinx's diamond estate."

Redeen made her second phone call to the man named, Sphinx.

"I can travel to Africa with you, but want to change my name to Queenie Pyra. My parents did put a Q in front of my name for some reason. I figured Queenie would be a good name instead of a letter. Would that be a problem for you?"

"No, my lawyer can handle it. A name change is a small detail compared to the rest of my business. I'm glad you will be going with me. That name pleases me," said Sphinx. He wondered why she didn't want to change her last name as well. He decided that she was a young, inexperienced person.

The Pyra last name could be from the word *pyramid*, but her last name should have been spelled Pira for *piranha*. She was a young piranha and didn't belong. Perhaps it was the country that was her problem. She had a hard time connecting. There was always the dust. It settled everywhere. Then there were the riches. Queenie saw how rich people lived. She wanted. A restlessness grew within her soul. Her mind was always thinking. She needed a plan.

"Later, my decision changed about living with the man in Africa. I wanted to leave and see the world."

Perusing flyers around the Venezuelan coast, the plan began to formulate.

She read books and learned all about the African tiger fish who lived in her world.

"I must figure out a way to catch the Sphinx when he is unaware. How does a person get rid of someone without being involved? Think, think, and do it quickly."

She stopped and frowned at the stormy sky. The weather matched her mood. Dark thoughts roamed inside her brain. She wanted to put him on another planet, but didn't quite know how to accomplish that aspect of distance. She frowned. Queenie thought of a black hole. She knew a river could be a dark place. Old Charlie had wanted to put her there.

"I should have the man dumped into the Congo River to be eaten by the other big tiger fish. My idea is excellent. It was where he belonged. No one will miss him, except a few of his other women. I don't care anymore."

Queenie built her own crew of piranhas. Armed and more dangerous, anyone who entered too close to her would be eaten alive.

She contemplated her short time in Africa. "The man lied to me. He didn't have a diamond estate, but occasionally ran into some diamond deals. He really was a drug trafficker. I don't do drugs. He lied about the women. They make me even madder. He told me that he owned me. I'm not owned by anyone. I wanted to leave, and he laughed at me. Condescension is what he gives me."

Queenie knew she should have taken the money from Chesin's bodyguard and run away. Her thoughts turned to regret. She wouldn't be in another fix like her previous one had she made better choices. It was time to grow up.

"I can't ever leave. He told me I belong to him. He bought and paid for my life. He reminded me again about the tainted bottle of rum in London."

She twirled her ink pen in her hands. The pad of paper was still blank in front of her.

"He told me all his women brought their problems with them to his house, but eventually settled down. I won't settle down and come around to his way of thinking. No one could leave unless he allowed it. Sphinx controlled everyone."

She pried open the locked drawer where he kept his business accounts. She wrote down in her shorthand formula the name and location of the banks and the account numbers. She also wrote down the id and passwords. She ripped the paper off the pad and closed the file drawer. She made sure it was locked tight.

"I haven't forgotten the tainted bottle either." She strolled outside and sat in a patio lounge chair.

Queenie was an intelligent woman, but didn't know it yet. She was young, but knew human entrapment was wrong. She studied the ants moving on the ground. The ants scurried back and forth looking for their next meal. She moved her foot out of their way. The ants had more freedom than she did. Having maneuvered escape before, she knew that she could do it again. It must be locked and strong to hold him. She decided her life was more valuable to her than it was to him.

Queenie plotted her revenge and escape route. She learned about his business and hid the stolen bank account information. She set up her own new bank accounts because she knew he wouldn't set her free nor give her any of his precious money.

"My game is survival of the smartest."

The storm brewing in Sphinx's house would first strip him of his money and business in those accounts. Then he would lose his extra women and his muscular-hunk body. Queenie thought she was part of the checks and balances on the scale of life. The scales would tip in her favor for some time.

There was no way she was ever going to feel trapped again. She flung her weight against the scales. Her youth and love of life pushed her out of Africa toward freedom. She made another last attempt to talk with him about her release.

"I don't want to be controlled by you, changed, or your toy. I want to be me. No more being your object to display at your important parties. That is total idiocy. I want to live my life."

Sphinx listened and tried to barter with this strange creature from London. He knew at the time that she would be a challenge.

"I can give you riding lessons as an interim to make you happy until you change your mind, but that is it for now. You need to not push me," exclaimed Sphinx.

Queenie knew to lay low for a while. She took the riding lessons so that he would believe that she came around to his way of thinking. She hummed to herself. Waiting was not wasted time. There was plenty to do.

She set up her fake vacation for her cover and next made her real plans to the Venezuelan coast. When everything was set in place, she moved forward with her plan, the red-bellied, sharp-toothed piranha plan. She kissed Sphinx goodbye, only he didn't know she meant the kiss to be her last with him.

Queenie came back with her crew. They waited for Sphinx's party to wind down and waited until he went off to bed. She transferred all his money to her accounts. Her crew waited until the women were leaving. They didn't kill the women. They let them go. The women were smart, chose to hide, and not ever talk.

Next, they trussed up the Sphinx and placed him in a locked crate. Her crew would deliver the crate to a client who would drop it in the Congo River.

Queenie and her crew disappeared to their destination.

"I won everything. He should have run from me in London while he could. My resilience to a bad situation has improved. The tremendous suspense was over. Life is looking good. I'm going to play from now on. It's celebration time. I will surround myself with guards to keep unwanted people out of my life."

She glanced into her new compact mirror.

"I know that I am beautiful because I see the girl in the mirror who bloomed into a woman. The other prostitutes he kept weren't as pretty. I am going to have fun."

She put her lipstick on and looked in her gold compact one more time while touching her hair.

She told herself, "Go get them rich boys or, perhaps, men." She wasn't going to exist in anyone's shadow, except there was an advantage to dating the rich. "Men might be more interesting."

The beautiful young golden tigress had arrived. The tigress didn't need the drug lord anymore. The police in London called her, young evil woman. Their assumption was that the woman may have been involved in Chesin's murder. The police would later change their files to Queen and then Queenie.

The Queenie girl didn't know the con artist game very well. She was playing her own game of piranha, so she could escape this way of life. It was the only way she thought she could disappear.

Queenie knew she must develop her image and change everything. Every action she took would make her stronger. She would become strong and would be loved by a real live tiger.

What she did was release the true evil tiger man who was an excellent tracker. The reason he would hunt her down was because she hadn't understood the levels. She didn't know the tiger man wouldn't stop.

The suspenseful drama theatre of her life continued and moved upon a new stage. The game moved her into the highest level of danger zone. She grabbed herself the newbie con artists, blissfully unaware. The experienced-loyal ones were left behind. Following the crate, they found their boss in the Congo area.

39   The Congo

WHEN THE SPHINX woke up in the crate, he said, "I know that I'm in trouble. There are no clothes, just underwear, and the only thing in this cage is a loaf of bread and a bottle of water."

He searched his cage and called out. There was no sound other than an engine.

He was on some ship going somewhere. He ate the bread and water and wondered why they fed him. They wanted to keep him alive for some reason. They shouldn't have. He supposed he should be glad she didn't drop him in the deep crater lake Nyos near Cameroon. The volcano there sometimes degassed into the ground and the lethal gas killed people. A poisonous cloud formed and killed the village people in the late eighties. He had mentioned the story to Queenie. After he ate the dry meal, he chuckled.

"Sulphur and carbon dioxide. Boom! No more Sphinx. Guess she felt the conditions weren't just right in the lake. Or it may have not been haunted enough. No, she read about the pipes they put in to defuse the gas buildup. She was always reading. Then where could these men want to take me? What were the places we talked about? The Congo, it must be the place. I told her about the Congo River on the Atlantic side. She will get rid of me then. It is a far more dangerous place, but I am used to danger. That's how I make my money."

Then his voice turned into a higher evil sound. The face grew solemn.

"I kept only a few of my accounts in my file drawer. The major portion of my wealth is safe for now. The accounts were hidden in my special room behind a panel. I need to worry that my group of loyal men might not find me in time. All my money will be for naught. No, I can't give up. They will wait until we are on land. They know the roads. They've been to the Congo before. I never told her those pieces of information."

Sphinx thought of his current predicament.
"If I make it, I will honor my men for their efforts with money. It will ensure their silence. Then I should change my name to Tiger, but Tiger what? The plan must include total breakage from my past. I will need to trick her. She tricked me."

He would have to think about the name. "What payback did Queenie deserve? First, he wanted to scare her or maybe not. A killing was exactly what she deserved. Anger fueled his thoughts. Could he kill her? Sphinx was vacillating. He wasn't sure."

The next morning, he awoke. There was more bottled water and bread. He peed in the empty bottles and saved them. He found some soft boards in the crate. This was where he did his business hoping the excrement would further rot the crate. Days passed, and the same ritual was done. Then the boat stopped.

The crate was moved to a truck, and he could smell the changed air. They were leaving the ocean and heading inland. It occurred to him where they were taking him. He was correct in his assessment. They were taking him to the Congo River. They would eventually put him on another boat and dump his crate in the deep part of the river.

The truck finally stopped. The men driving the truck must have gone inside a building because it was quiet. He went over to the loose-soft boards. He could move one of the boards free.

Peering into the woods, he encountered nasty bugs. They came into his cage, and he quickly put the board back. He tried to remove another board and another board, putting them back in place. He pried six boards loose, enough for a man to climb out. All the boards were placed in their original position. He would wait. He spent the night killing the bugs that flew inside his cage. In the morning, he saw the men come out of the house.

"I do not know any of them, so they were hired kidnapers. They did not give me anymore bread or water. I will remember their faces."

They were close to another hand-off. A different team relieved the men, and they drove one more day, stopping on the outskirts of a city. These men threw him some water and jerky, which he greedily ate. The men left for town.

He removed the boards and escaped into the night. He washed in a small stream and stole some clothes from a house. The bugs didn't bother him as much as before. He would live. Heading toward lights, he needed transportation fast to leave the area.

He saw some of his old men in town and followed them to their hotel room. Sneaking into the room, it was a leader he had trusted. He kept two of the bottles filled with pee, his only weapons. He didn't need it because his friend hugged him. His men had followed the truck and lost it. So, they had been unsure where to look for Sphinx. His old friend brought him food and wine.

Awaking the rest of the boys, they snuck him in their truck and escaped the area. They pushed onward and continued until they could hop a freighter travelling north along the coast of Africa.

The Sphinx went to Dakar, Senegal, and purchased Mr. Chesin's old house. An investor bought it and wanted to dump it. The Sphinx bought the property under his new name, Tiger Black, and moved his men and operation there. His lawyer also moved there. Judge Daken heard about the new resident and decided to give up and retire.

Tiger's revenge plan was aimed at Queenie. It wasn't so much the fact that she had bilked him, because now he knew she was smart. He must outsmart her. The boys set fire to his old home because he did not want any reminder of it. His lawyer helped sell the land to a construction business. It would be sold under a different business entity and difficult to trace the real owner. The tiger fish would rise as Lazarus had done.

It would take Tiger Black some time to find Queenie Pyra because she moved from Venezuela. She decided she didn't want to be there anymore and bought a building in one of the Americas. She moved to the

Magic City and liked the original French name, *miamioua*. She thought the city would be a wonderful place to live.

Queenie didn't realize that scales sometimes tipped a different direction. His money was taken which he would have allowed her.

Tiger contemplated what to do. "I should have let her go to begin with. I could let her run free. Money comes easily for me. But she walked away with two objects which I greatly treasure. That was unforgiveable. I want the objects back."

He knew she wouldn't win the next round. Queenie wanted to party and be a part of the young, beautiful people she saw in the recent travel brochures. She touched their glossy pages and smiled. She desired play time with the rich. Queenie missed so much. She wanted the glamour of the night.

Her life had been dull before, but it was worse in Venezuela. She was unhappy again. She needed to find a different crew. She knew she made poor choices once more. On the lookout for more experienced con artists to join her group, she realized then she would be strong.

Queenie's contacts in the art world also saw the released art drawings from the Wrights. They gave her the information. An idea hit her brain about auctioning the two objects she held. Then she placed the two items in her private warehouse for safekeeping.

Looking at the two rare objects, she touched the gold crown and matching gold clasp with an eagle design. The Wrights' drawings were a match. The

Wright's mentioned to the auction house that the objects were very old. They had verification that original owners were royalty. She decided to place them up for sale through her auction house contact.

That move would be her doom. The auction clerk once went to *miamioua* and knew the cruise ship's last call for boarding. The agent told his African investor client who now knew an approximate location of the owner. The valuable knowledge would help track the woman down.

"Did the Lazarus fish have enough time for someone who rose from the dead to kill the enemy? I will find the time," said Tiger.

The burning began in Tiger's heart over the golden objects. He went to his doctor because the pain became worse. He felt the raw tear and skip in beat to his heart were caused by her. He would need to slow his pace. It was a loss he hadn't expected.

40   Robots and Things that Move

WHILE AT THE masquerade party in Curacao, Derek talked with the owners who sponsored the Space Party. Their knowledge of rockets, drones, and robotics were extensive. Derek went alone to the Space vendor company's headquarters. They discussed some designs he and Jess talked about recently.

While there, he saw some newer concepts and made another appointment to bring Jess.

They were given access to one of their technical designers to finalize their plan before building their various projects. Some of the projects would be built by other companies that this vendor owned. The money from the sale of their book would be used to purchase some of their new toys.

The first was four drones of varying degrees of design, size, speed, lift, and landing capabilities. The other piece was the sophisticated cameras and remote control, distance, and trajectory capabilities. The other part was the weight of such items and if it could carry cargo. They worked on the weight distribution of various things.

The second was small rockets with a special design. One of the capabilities was that the rocket would float in the water when they came down with a transponder, so their crew could retrieve them for reuse.

Derek was thinking they would be fun to use for one of their annual parties or possibly something else, because the rockets also contained the special cargo areas. He ordered sixteen of these items. His plans were to send some to War Julio. When War Julio saw the drones, he would order two of them.

The last was the robot structures. There was a company making ones that looked like humans that moved and had a few speech commands. They ordered one that looked like Derek. They called him Junior.

Derek teased Jess, "I don't want you to run away with the mechanical brainless robot."

"I'm already married to a sweet man who was clueless on occasion, and I don't need one full-time."

Derek and the children laughed. "I will dump the robot unless you order one, too. Then there would be two brainless robots in the house with their idiot children."

Sami and Justin performed a mime of the idiot robot children.

Jess threw a pillow and the pillow fight party started.

Extra mechanicals were installed on their vehicles because the killer had gotten too close to Jess in the sports car chase. War Julio did the same. The three took driving lessons at a special track from a retired race car expert and stuntman. War Julio also bought the special truck with ramp and motor bikes. The Miami group liked the cars, but skipped the truck as Florida was too crowded to pull off such a stunt. There were never that many empty freeways to stop a truck. Shooting tires worked better.

The robot wasn't done yet so at the next annual party, they used the small rockets for their games.

The party was held in Los Angeles. They hired a barge boat for the day. A small rocket tech launched the rockets from the barge. They loaded the rockets with real and fake plastic numbered gambling chips. Then they divided into teams and each team selected their number rocket. Derek special ordered numbers to be painted on the sides of the rockets at the factory. Whichever rocket went the farthest won the chips in that rocket. That team dropped out and the rest of the teams played.

The money ended up being evenly divided, and everyone enjoyed a good time. The crew and protection squads raced each other to retrieve the floating rockets. The food theme was Mexican with various enchilada and taco bars with tequila drinks. The children's rocket piñatas were filled with plastic chips of their own they could exchange for prizes.

The little girl, Maggie, was fascinated by the rocket launch and later the fireworks when they woke her up. She was a quiet, pretty, little girl and didn't cry much. She never got a chance around the Wright's because someone was always picking her up. She didn't seem to be afraid of anything and wanted to play with Justin's shiny race cars the most.

The robots would be completed before their next year's party, but would be saved for the year after that. She found a jeweler who could create small gold scepter pins for the women that would attend the party. They were a one-of-a-kind original Jess Wright copyrighted design. She saw the idea in the drawing book Louisa had left them. She found a cologne house that made her a fragrance. She personally selected the smell as a signature blend for the event. The cologne house made a scepter bottle, which the ladies would receive at their next party. She developed an eagle-wing money clip, a new copyrighted design for the men guests.

Jess picked up her drawing board and looked at Louisa's notebook. It was time to let her energy flow. She drew a woman's pantsuit with a semi-sheer design of the eagle wings down each leg. The bodice of the pantsuit contained a gold-thread eagle head design.

Derek saw the design and loved it. She drew Derek a special tie with the eagle-wing design for a surprise for his birthday. She wondered where their plans would take them for the next party.

41 Louisa's Notebook

RESEARCHING LOUISA'S NOTEBOOK story about the great-great-grandmother Renaliere earlier, Jess decided the story would make a good second book. Derek agreed.

Work as an investigator continued for Derek and their children were busy with their school projects. Sometimes, they tagged along to the library or their air-conditioned warehouse large room where they stored Louisa's old valuable books. Jess planned to donate the books, but first wanted to read them for any background history.

Her children liked to read the pirate stories, so they could try to scare War Julio the next time he visited. They also liked the diving stories and used them for book reports. Their teachers were impressed with the historical nature of their reports and gave them a high grade on every report. Louisa had given them an educational gift and love of old books.

Their world was currently at peace, giving everyone a needed break. There were no more problems with any other super bad con artists or murderers. The Wright family were together. Their children left the library to make their sandwiches in the small kitchen and then head to the bunk room to watch television. Jess and Derek were alone.

"No bad guys this evening?" asked Derek.

Jess said, "They were either lying low, moved to another part of the world, or were waiting for the scales to slide in their favor again."

"You are correct. Tell me what you found out so far. It looks like you are almost through with the notebook."

"I've had to put it down frequently to check on some other things. It truly is mysterious."

Derek chuckled, "Why do I feel there is more coming?"

Jess read, "The notebook was about a wonderful love story between two families that were not exactly friendly toward each other, but set up the arranged marriage to combine their strength. It was a common concept in those perilous times. Alliances were built. The two people fell instantly in love to the delight of both families per Louisa. Their children were born. The man's side of the family were the richer, more powerful one. The man's father owned a gold crown and gold scepter. It did not appear to have been passed down to the son who was the great-great-grandfather Renaliere. Later, it talks about the scepter being sold. When the Renaliere mother died with no heir living other than her son, the gold, diamond, and emerald necklace passed to him. He instantly gave it to his beautiful wife along with the stick pin and diadem. He could have placed it under lock and key or fashioned himself something spectacular. But he didn't because everything he owned was hers. That collection was our wonderful sunken treasure find."

Derek nodded.

"There seems to have existed four valuable objects that they once owned. Louisa had drawn a picture of the gold crown which showed an eagle carved into the gold with the wings wrapping around the head. There were no jewels in the crown in the drawing. The design of the eagle was very clever. I remember her talking with Sami about the crown when we were in Italy. She was proud of her heritage."

Jess looked at the old book again. Louisa did not list any engraver's name on the drawing pages.

"The scepter looks large. It may possibly be three and a half feet long with a large eagle head on the top. The artist again cleverly engraved the eagle wings and feathers to wrap around the scepter to the very bottom. Under the head were two rows of small diamonds. The eagle's eyes were emeralds and it carried a gold branch in its beak with what looks to be a large ruby on the very end. I'll have to try to determine the carat size of the gems, but then she may not have known precisely how to draw them to my specifications."

Jess showed Derek the drawings. "The way she drew the scepter, it came apart in the middle of the staff and then the head. There is a compartment within the head with a lock mechanism that an experienced jeweler would look for. It seems like they enjoyed puzzles and locks to keep things hidden. They obviously didn't trust their safes back then either. The compartment is large enough for storing the stones and makes perfect sense. There was another more easily accessible compartment in the upper part of the scepter and head which might be there to confuse people. The lock mechanism again is a different one. It's almost as if the head lock was added later and by someone more experienced."

Jess flipped through a couple pages.

"The story told about the sale of the scepter which was completed to help pay for their hired mercenaries. Evidently, the war lords fighting continued for a long time. Money was required. The scepter was sold to an investor-type person and the family thought they could eventually buy the precious object back. It doesn't mention the crown again."

Derek said, "The eagle was part of the Renaliere's family crest or emblem. The scepter and crown were specially carved for the family from their riches they acquired. It would make sense if they sold the crown to the same investor, but at different times."

Jess and Derek saw some figures at the Louvre Museum in Paris. The staff or scepter at the museum showed figures with a smaller staff.

"Were the stones secured within the head before it was sold?"

Jess said, "I don't know as Louisa didn't talk too much further about the scepter in the notebook. Perhaps that part of the story was kept from her. Or perhaps Louisa knew and was afraid to reveal too much in her writings."

"Then why write down the information about the head with the hidden clasp?"

"Louisa might have wanted to confuse anyone who gained access to her notebook. It's always that confusion thing to throw people off. You remember how reclusive and the length of time it took them to reveal the sunken ship location?"

Derek threw up his hands. "Yes, he remembered." He sometimes didn't get where Jess and her female logic was taking him, much less Louisa's. He did better dealing with the criminal mind. They loved to reveal their secrets at the most inopportune time, like right before they figured out they were really going to jail or die. But maybe the criminals just liked to brag about their jobs. Then he remembered the bad guys used secrets as weapons. Derek decided he had better let Jess continue.

Jess told Derek that she was given the secret and promised the old woman that she would not reveal it.

"More secrets? Oh, I believe I figured it out. There was another unknown compartment in the lower part of the staff. This family was into strange connections and weird locks. I would imagine it was really difficult to open and you're thinking the gems are still inside the scepter."

He had remembered Louisa pointing lower.

"Smart husband."

"The investor man who held the scepter vanished. That piece of information was in her story. Oh, here is a page that was folded back that I didn't see before. Let me read it."

Jess looked at Derek and frowned. "The family also sold the gold crown in a final attempt to hire more men to help fight their cause. The money gained, however, wasn't enough to fend off the other war lords.

The families fled for their lives, taking only easily carried items which would have been their jewelry. That was when they lost their small castles and moved on with their lives."

Derek said, "We should check museums for the items."

"I already did that."

"Of course, you checked. The items could be in someone's private collection or lost forever. Sometimes, people melted the gold down for some other use."

"I hope the beauty of the valuable art objects kept them alive and they exist in some private collections. When those collectors pass on, the next generation usually does sell the collection, so they could go on vacation or buy new furniture."

Derek commented, "Why don't you create some drawings to give to our major auction house in case the objects come up for sale? You could request to be notified before the auction took place. It should be a simple way to reach the high-end investors."

Jess agreed, "It is definitely worth a shot and can add credibility and further salability to our second book."

Jess turned the pages of Louisa's notebook toward the end. "Louisa forgot to mention something. It was that something word again."

"What? Not dolphins?"

Jess laughed and showed him the last set of Louisa's drawings.

"Unbelievable designs," said Derek.

The drawing was of a man in a beautiful cape or cloak that showed a gold clasp holding the fur part of the garment together at the top. Then Louisa drew the clasp in two pieces. The eagle head was on the left clasp with the left wing and the right clasp was the other wing. The clasp was in gold with the same carving as the crown and scepter.

She showed him the ring drawing with the same eagle design, the family's crest. The ring contained diamonds.

"The family or grandmother tracked down the clasp to a Jewish jeweler in Germany. They hadn't sent the money yet to re-purchase them when the jeweler closed shop and disappeared. The jeweler hadn't owned the clasp, but some other family did. The name of the shop was Goldstein Jewelers, and no one knows who those owners were."

Derek said, "This is sort of like the name Smith in America, very common."

"It was a start because if the clasp exists, the possibility is that the other items may have survived. It could also be possible an investor-collector owned some or all of the wonderful art collection."

Derek and Jess moved forward with their graphic design person to achieve drawings close to Louisa's in design. They weren't sure the correct proportions so guessed at the dimensions.

42 Underworld and Two Objects

DEREK AND JESS talked about the release of the drawings. It could bring forth all the unsavory people into their world again. They waited until Derek wrapped up his other cases and they felt capable of dealing with any new threats. Derek was trying to help Jess find the objects. He was curious about them. He knew there existed the underworld investors. Some walked the line where illegal dealings rolled in. He hoped they wouldn't run into those people.

They received most of their robotic toys. They told their friends about the Louisa antiquities story and let them have a pre-release of the drawings. War Julio and his wife were fascinated. Another Wright adventure was about to unfold. All the Miami people were being alerted plus the rest of their crony world.

Derek came home with an expensive bottle of champagne, flowers, chocolates, oysters, and caviar for Jess. Her husband was ready to release the drawings. It was a very good evening as they crept out to the bow of the motorboat in their bathrobes on a starry night far away from the Los Angeles city lights.

They filled their glasses with the last of the champagne. They toasted, "To Dean, let the magical adventure start."

"Was he in?"

Derek knew Jess's radar was always finely tuned. Derek couldn't help, but laugh. His enjoyment with his wife and life showing. It was going to be another strange ride.

"Absolutely, all the way, every time. Me, your handsome knight husband, was in."

Jess was pleased.

XXXXXX

An auction house person was helping review newly submitted pictures when he saw the Wright's drawings.

Wondering how these people knew about the objects, he contacted his African investor collector who owned two of them. The African investor was pleased that there existed a third and fourth piece. The person sent the investor collector the copy of the drawings. They could begin looking for the third and fourth extremely valuable objects, the scepter and ring. The person smiled because the commission would be high. The person contacted his black-market friends to begin their search once he received word to proceed.

The underworld would enter the game. The con artists would gather again for there existed those two words *diamonds and gold.*

The investor collector friend received the drawings. Tiger Black, aka Sphinx, walked out to his negative edge pool and looked toward the ocean. He motioned his trusted man to authorize the search and funds for the extraordinarily valuable scepter and ring.

"The beloved eagle design became my obsession many years ago, much like I feel about a lot of things."

He watched the gold fleck in his pool tile catch the sunlight, turning it into a gold blur in one spot.

"I can afford to be obsessive for I am very rich. Sometimes my obsessiveness gets me in trouble. My last obsession was a disaster. I almost lost my life. I shared information with someone whom I trusted."

Tiger thought Queenie was special, and in a weak moment, he showed her the secret treasure room. He shared with her two of his most revered objects in the room. Tiger would never go there again, other than to kill her. He stayed there by the end of his pool looking westward for a long time, remembering. Then he walked toward his empty house. His heart was betrayed and empty.

He called his new house empty, but it was filled by his designer with the most modern, chic pieces of furniture, rugs, and art. He looked at everything and thought it displayed a good cover for himself. She removed anything navy blue and filled his world with gemstone colors plus a little black and lots of gold. The room contained many shiny things. Even his ashtray was shiny. The blue pool tile remained to remind him that some things should not be changed.

The designer became his new girlfriend. He knew man needed woman, but this time he was prepared. He kept five men tailing his new girlfriend.

He installed two generators in case of electrical failure, heightened security all around the premises. A second set of brick walls were built higher than the first with a four-foot moat surrounding the house. His home was a fortress.

The tiger fish began to alter his business image. He let all future drug and diamond sales pass him by. He invested his money in honest businesses, restructuring most all areas. He became a respected businessman in his part of the world. He married the designer girlfriend and had children. His life was good, temporarily.

He was getting older and wiser. He rid the earth of the worst of the worst scum. He stayed out of the local new judge's court. He expected his men to do the same. There were no active prostitutes allowed on his property.

43   Miami Dead Girl

THE POLICE ENTERED the apartment of the young blond and very dead, beautiful girl. It appeared to be a suicide from the looks of the body, a hanging. There was no note at all. There was no booze or drugs found. She was one of the hotel's cleaning crew. They talked to some of the other women who only knew that she was from Venezuela.

They checked her fingerprints and her name was Carmela Dubarde from Maracaibo, Venezuela. She owned several high-powered guns in her apartment, some clothes and that was it. There were no photos and no other items to show that there might be a boyfriend or girlfriend.

The police wondered if Carmela was more than the cleaning crew. She might have been part of the hotel's security. Protection was a common occurrence in Miami.

They contacted the owner of the building about the dead woman. She was listed for an emergency contact. The owner was Queenie Pyra and currently was out of the country on an African safari vacation. The manager of the building told them the dead woman had no relatives. The coroner came to pick up the body.

When Miss Pyra was back in town, they wanted to talk with her. They checked out the Pyra lady and found it odd that the two women looked very much alike. A small article about the woman's death and her photo were put in the newspaper in the hope they would receive more information.

Queenie was in Guinea-Bissau, looking for Sphinx. She knew the hanging of her employee was a case of mistaken identity by his hit man. She was the supposed target. That made her mad. Somehow, information leaked about her whereabouts.

On the way to his house, she dropped her gold compact and instantly picked the favorite item up. "We can't lose you or else I'd have to buy another one in Africa" Her compact was one of the few items that she was never without.

Upon arrival. Queenie found that Sphinx's house burned, and there were three dead bodies inside burnt beyond recognition. The bodies were some of the Congo guys who had come back to this town. Sphinx recognized them as the drivers taking him in the crate to dump him with no food or water on the journey inland to the Congo River. Somehow, they ended up in a cage in his house when the fire broke out. The police assumed the body was the owner and a couple of his bodyguards in the burnt ashes.

In the house location now stood a construction building. No one there ever heard of anyone named Sphinx. Consequently, Queenie was at a dead end and assumed that Sphinx no longer existed. The drug trafficker people knew the drug lords and he was no longer around. She asked the diamond people and was told the same thing. He could have hired the hit on her before he died.

She flew back to her wonderful building in Miami and felt safe. Queenie told the police that she knew very little information on the girl. She then cleaned the apartment and found another girl to take her place. She outwardly showed no emotion or grief for the death of the lost girl.

Tiger Black read the article about the dead cleaning lady at a Miami hotel. He knew Queenie was in Guinea-Bissau asking about him or the other version that she knew. His contact thought Queenie believed the Sphinx was dead because she returned to Miami. His hit man messed up.

Tiger waited until Queenie would feel safe and then he would find a way to kill her. Otherwise, she could come after his family. He knew she couldn't change. Alive and out of his control, she was a problem.

The two precious items that Queenie kept in her warehouse were removed from the auction house sale because the seller didn't want to part with them yet. She told them she was sentimental about them. That's what the auction house was told to tell any further inquiries.

The problem was she thought she could make more money on the internal investor market. That was one of the reasons for the withdrawal. Currently, she was flush with the dead Sphinx's money. She felt safe because she installed two separate security systems.

Unknown to her, Tiger's men followed her home, watched, and waited until she went to the warehouse. Now Tiger knew the address where two valuable items from his collection may be stored.

44 Objects from Auction House

CONTACTED BY ONE of their auction friends, there was a possibility two of the golden items may come up for sale. Derek told her what the auction clerk gave him for the estimated sale price. It was for the two items, a gold crown and gold clasp with a very unusual eagle design and very old. The woman who owned the objects wouldn't allow a photograph of any kind for verification of their value.

Jess talked with Derek and agreed the price was high, and they would pay an upfront fee if they could preview the items first. Jess contacted her auction friend to set up the preview deal.

About a week later, her auction friend let Jess know the woman withdrew the items from the sale due to her inability to relinquish the sentimental objects.

Jess and Derek still wanted to see the valuable objects and asked if they could contact the woman. Normally auction houses do not share private information, but their friend helped them find investors before. He had been paid a huge commission from the deal. He also knew they were trustworthy people. He only knew her name and she lived in Miami. Her name was Queenie Pyra.

Derek ran a check on Queenie.

"Her original name was possibly, Q. Redeen Pyra. The person lived in London in foster homes. She was in a hospital for a week due to a beating by a boy at fourteen years old, and she disappeared. Sometime later she reappeared as a person named Queenie Pyra in Guinea Bissau, Africa. She went to Venezuela before arriving in Miami. She currently owned a building in Miami. There was no indication about where she obtained money to purchase the apartment building. She told them her money came from a dead friend. The police thought it was possibly from a rich lover."

Derek saw her current apartments' income. There was a strange suicide of a female cleaning girl who worked for Queenie that the police marked as suspicious. The dead person looked very much like Queenie.

He told Jess his findings.

"Trouble, most definitely. The girl sounded like someone who knew a challenged life. Destruct at age fourteen must have hurt. I am still very interested if you think we should proceed."

Derek couldn't get past the report.

"High probability trouble existed here. I knew you would pick up on the young woman's prior problems. That was why I hated bringing them up. Your sympathy toward women was high. I am troubled about the lack of asset existence. Where did she get her original money? She didn't really explain that to our satisfaction. As far as owning the valuable antiquities, where did she get them?"

Jess stood up and walked over to where Derek was sitting on the sofa. She sat down and talked.

"Either the person owns fakes, or the objects are stolen, or the gold objects are real. If they are fakes, we were dealing with a scam artist. If they were stolen, the original owner could be looking for them in which case there is a thief involved. Where there exist thieves, anything followed. If they were real, then other investors would be our competitors in any future auction."

Derek took her hand and recommended, "Let's hire a couple of the Miami friends to follow Queenie for a month. It is the best way to go for now. I will let you know their report."

Jess agreed that she would wait for the report. "This situation can become complicated. I feel something is wrong, but I can't pinpoint my fear. There was an edgy feeling surrounding the woman. Something is hidden."

"I hate to hear you say the something word and hidden. That meant way more."

Derek looked at his wife and she nodded.

He knew this whole situation could explode. Derek knew if it ever did, he wouldn't be surprised at all. He knew his wife. Her insight was super real.

The reports came into Derek's office. He reluctantly went home and informed Jess.

The first report: "They found out she secured a warehouse which she frequently visited, and we have the address. She parties extensively and attends all the high-society fashion shows, spending a fortune on new clothes. She went to hotel spas and bought all manner of beauty treatments. She ate in only the finest of restaurants and her female drivers take her around the area in a black new limousine. Her female drivers look like Queenie."

Jess handed Derek a cup of coffee and a plate of chocolate chip cookies.

"Our Miami men saw two African-looking men also tailing her. The Miami men knew the two security companies that Queenie has hired. They play dart games with them because the security men joined their dart league out of boredom. The Miami men learned about the seven security cameras and the access codes to get into the warehouse. The information was obtained via a female Miami family member who learned the codes when she temporarily worked at the security company. I've asked them to wait on entering the warehouse."

45   Miami Party Plans

DEREK KNEW JESS wanted to see the items, but they both thought it was too risky to ask the Queenie person. Everything about this situation was ringing loud and clear, *very wrong*. Whatever the two objects, they believed they had been stolen from someone in Africa. However, there was no proof because no one reported them stolen.

They informed the Miami people, War Julio, and Jim about their findings on the Queenie girl. All the Miami wives had been told to secretly avoid her. The Miami women knew what secret meant and followed protocol. Secret meant extremely bat-crazy person, possible murderer.

Jess was happy at the thought that there may still exist the two items. The high probability of the other items existence was good. Derek saw the wistful look in her eyes. Jess wanted to at least, see, feel, and touch all four items.

Derek sat down with Jess and took both her hands. If he took her hands, she knew he was serious.

"Honey, we cannot hire this one out to anyone. The situation was too dangerous. We can't approach Queenie now. Let the Miami police do their job and we'll see where that leads."

She moved away from Derek because the *power of gold* was strong. Jess looked at Derek, because he knew her too well.

Jess thought about their dilemma. She wanted to hire an intermediary, but knew it was a bad idea. She already rejected the idea from something Dean Crain, her friend, told her. Dean showed Jess the good and the bad side of the world. It was something Dean failed to show his beloved, dead daughter. Dean taught her everything he knew.

Jess could easily float between the worlds that existed on this earth. But then Dean knew she went to a place beyond the earth. Dean knew that was the *magical* that would always protect Jess. Dean was glad.

Dean told her, "The eagles fly in pairs because the two of them work together and that they are a wonderful king and queen in their territory. The eagles knew to stay in their own safety zone and to guard each other. If the eagles had to move, they went together."

Her mind was turning things over and over. She wanted to do just that, fly out on her own, out of her safety zone. She knew Derek protected her. She would always do the same. They had all the wonderful families and friends that Dean invited into his and their world for additional protection.

Jess would have to wait until the time was right.

"I will move when you tell me and our protection team that we can. My heart and mind know which direction to take."

"I am glad, because I thought for a minute that I lost you." He was relieved.

Jess told Derek she would have to tell him some of the astounding stories Dean told her about his Miami days. The stories were out of this world.

Derek smiled, "I want to hear the stories. I, too, loved Dean. I know your bond with Dean Crain was an exceptional one. Our relationship with Dean was way beyond normal when he was alive."

Jess laid the brakes on her desire for the capture of the gold eagle objects until they could work the scene together. Jess waited for everyone else to catch up.

He knew Jess, even in the face of imminent danger, she would not be afraid, but would be at a deadly calm. He saw that look before. When that look appeared, Derek knew to duck and remain hidden for a second. She would set up the scene for the bad guy's downfall. Derek collected the bad guy. She only left a scene as a cautionary measure to come back for the kill if needed. Derek would arrive to help arrest the final, true villains.

Jess picked up the lingo of languages in the area like she would pick up a box of cereal at the grocery store. Within minutes, she could converse with the local natives. Jess was unstoppable. She could be a formidable foe. At times, he didn't know the person that would arrive. Jess would pick up the fallen sword and lead the charge with an army of eagles and angels behind her. He watched her totally amazed. It was a difficult thing to protect her.

Yet Derek was always glad to stand by her side. He would bring his army. Their combined fired-up, heavily armed, knowledgeable army of other friends would join them. Derek laughed because alongside would be Tami and her academy friend with their invisible bazookas. He forgot to tell Jess about that part of the Dakar story.

Derek remembered that he owned visible, mini-style bazookas. The rockets would be reserved for the possible, invisible need. For once the rockets fired off, they seemed to disappear until they hit their mark. Then Derek thought of the drones and the possibilities that existed there. Their enemy should have run.

Jess came over to Derek and held him close. Derek stroked her hair and kissed her gently.

"We'll find the precious objects. I know we are close. We will help anyone who needs it."

"I thought we were close. I'm glad you want to help. I think things may come down to helping the young woman. What about having our next party in Miami? It could be perfect cover for us to do our own research."

Derek knew she hadn't for one minute given up on finding the antiquities. He wondered what awaited them in the future.

46　Golden Obsession

SHE TALKED WITH Derek the next day about the annual Miami party and a tentative plan to lure Queenie into their den. Derek was ahead of her this time. It was the only path to take. He talked with his men in Miami. As soon as they knew some of the details, he would bring Jess into the plan.

They were currently finding a warehouse very close to Queenie's to possibly lease. They leased an apartment across from Queenie's and installed men and equipment. Even though the party was nine months away, they wanted to have all bases covered. The men would blend in the neighborhood and find any set patterns of behavior.

Derek told her the projected plans.

Jess said, "We should find a warehouse large enough to accommodate the party in case that might provide better cover. We don't have to lease it right away. I think the hotel will still want to cater our party because they checked with the Curacao hotel. I believe the Curacao hotel wanted us and our extended family to come back to their hotel. Their business doubled after our masquerade party and now it is 90 percent booked. It is good to know our options and keep things open for our next party."

"Your ideas are good ones. I'm delighted the hotel in Curacao liked our business. It was a great party despite the gun fireworks."

Derek let everyone important know what to look for as far as a future location regarding the annual party in Miami. The plans were moving forward. He told the crony groups that Jess said the plans were tentative. All the wives knew something major was up.

Jess and Derek's code name for their next project was *Wild Golden Obsession*, due to her fragrance's scepter bottle design. The real scepter would be difficult to find and keep. It may be in pieces and parts. Perhaps the object was a mere illusion. Or it could be *something*.